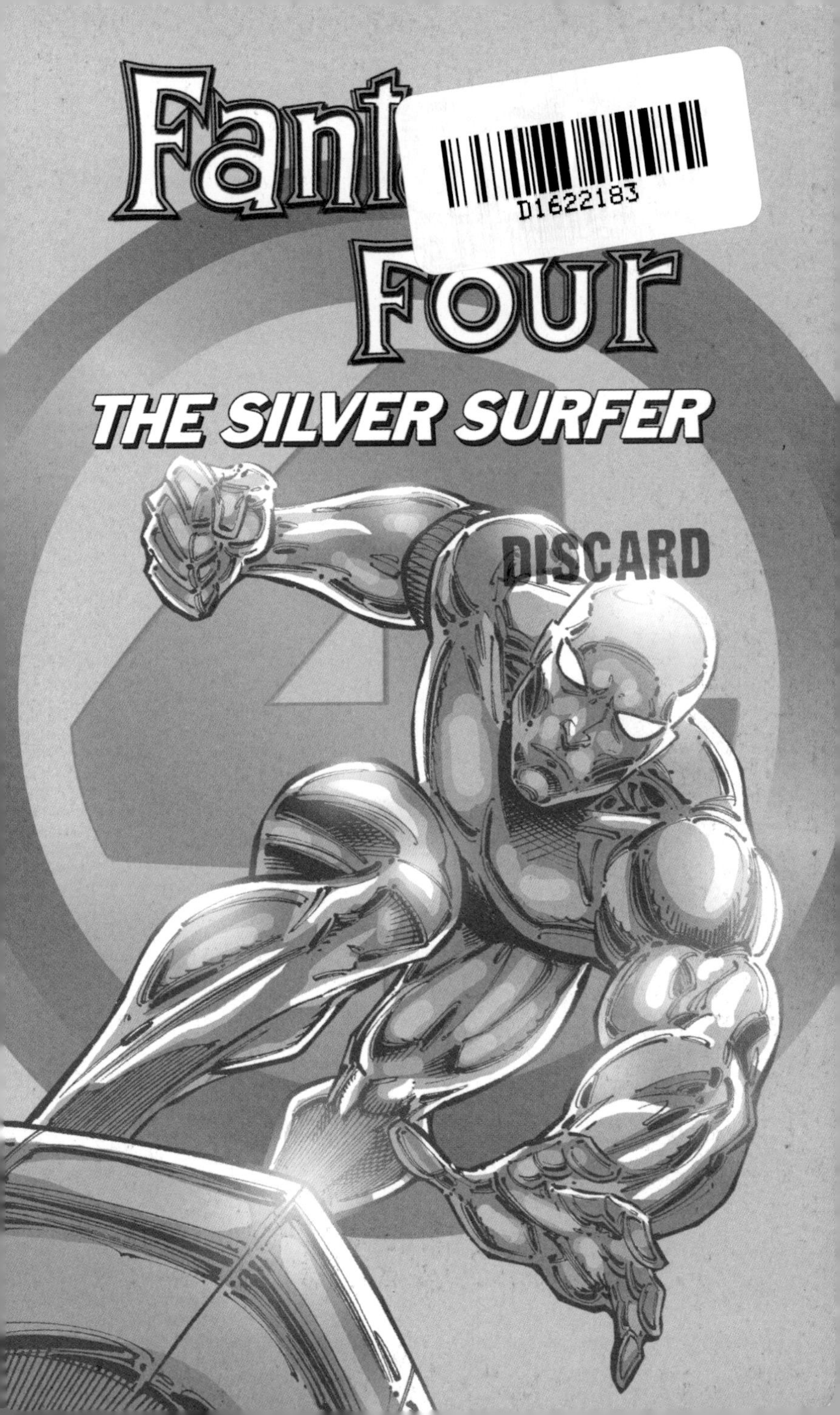
Fant
Four
THE SILVER SURFER

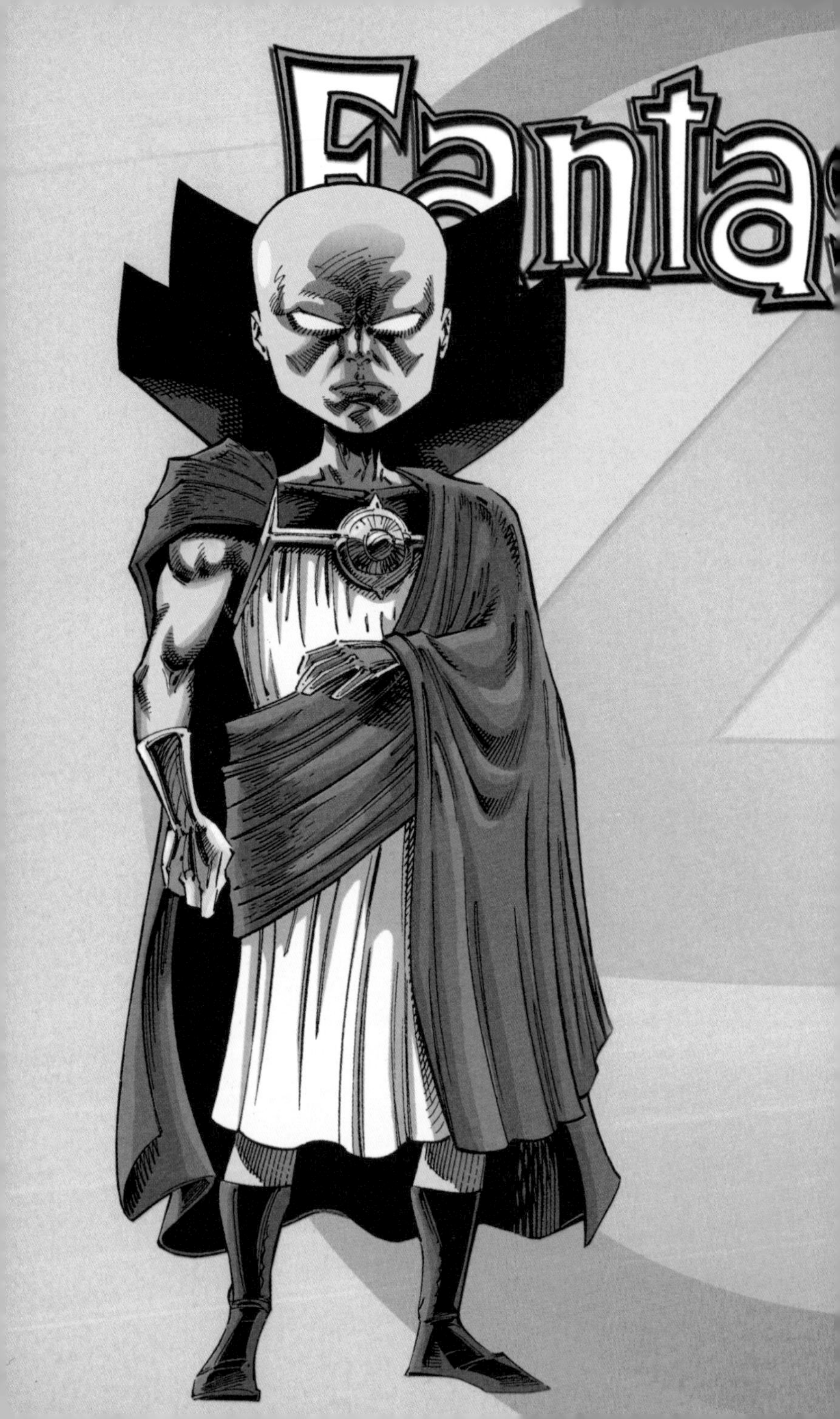
Fantas

tic Four

THE SILVER SURFER

Writer:
Fred Van Lente
Art:
Cory Hamscher

Colorist: **Lee Loughridge**
Letterer: **Dave Sharpe**
Cover Art: **Paul Smith with**
Christina Strain & Lee Loughridge
Consulting Editor: **Mark Paniccia**
Editor: **Nathan Cosby**
Special Thanks to Crystal Skillman and Margot Blankier

Collection Editor: **Jennifer Grünwald**
Assistant Editors: **Cory Levine & John Denning**
Associate Editor: **Mark D. Beazley**
Senior Editor, Special Projects: **Jeff Youngquist**
Senior Vice President of Sales: **David Gabriel**
Vice President of Creative: **Tom Marvelli**

Editor in Chief: **Joe Quesada**
Publisher: **Dan Buckley**

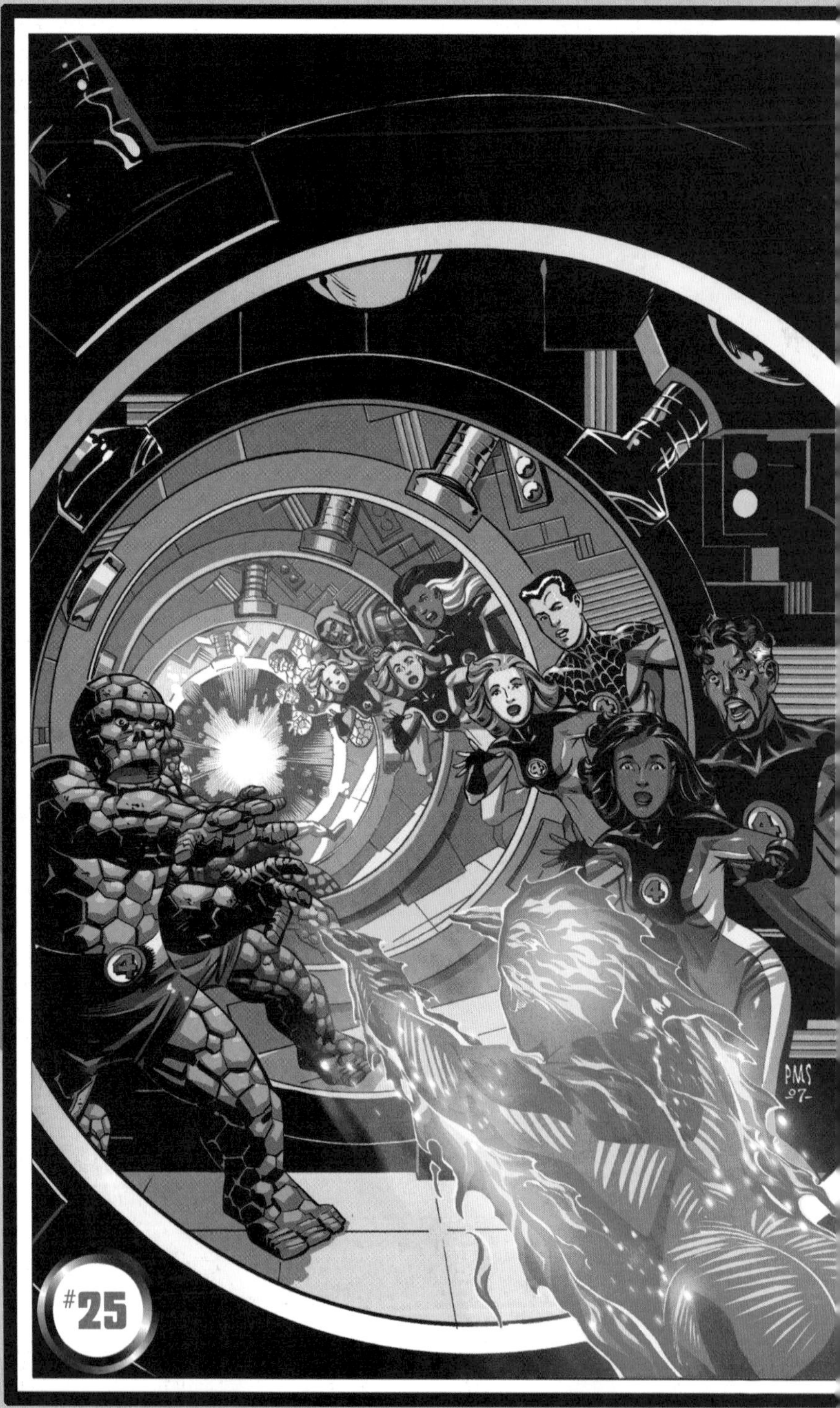
#25
PMS
07

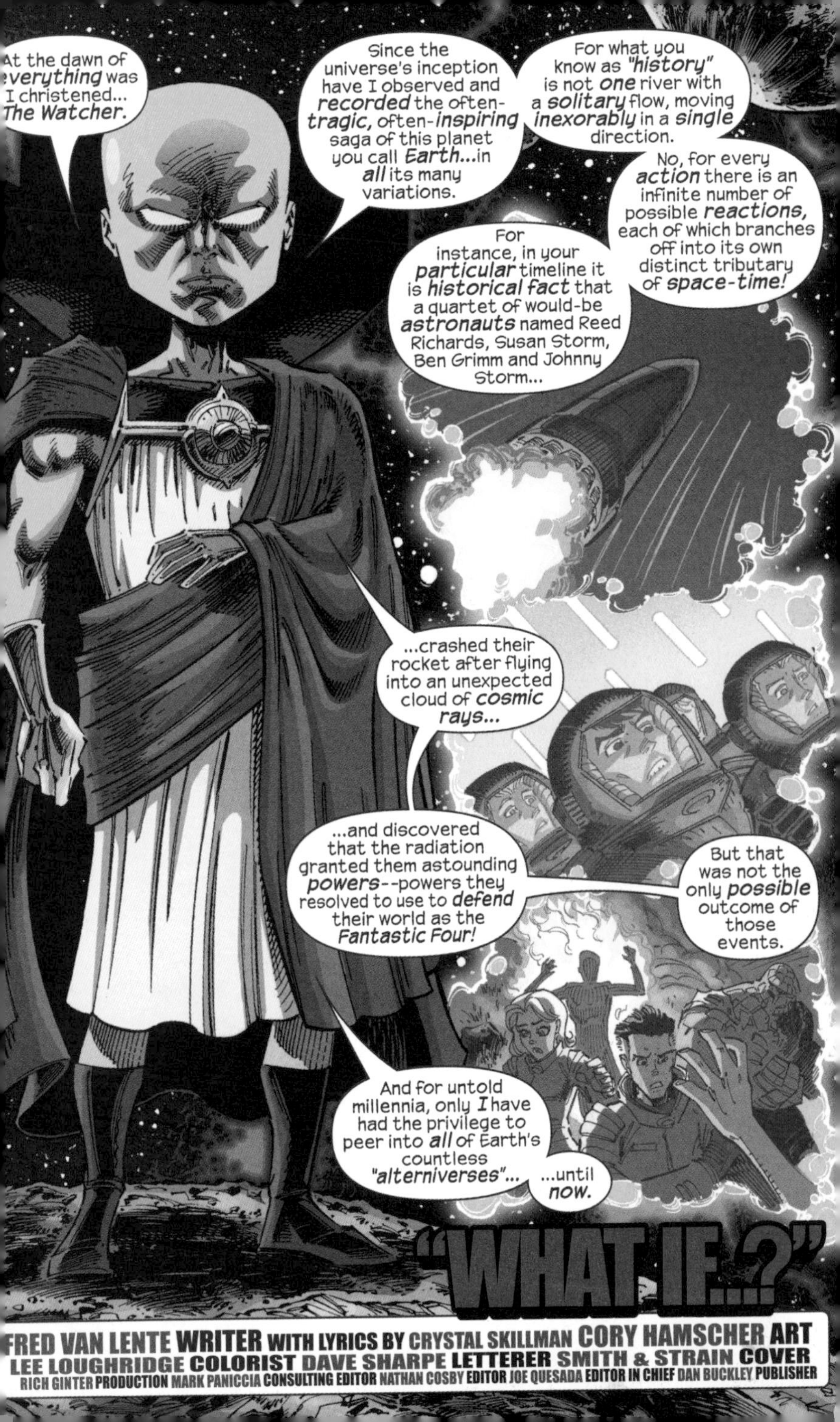
At the dawn of everything was I christened... The Watcher.
Since the universe's inception have I observed and recorded the often-tragic, often-inspiring saga of this planet you call Earth...in all its many variations.
For what you know as "history" is not one river with a solitary flow, moving inexorably in a single direction.
No, for every action there is an infinite number of possible reactions, each of which branches off into its own distinct tributary of space-time!
For instance, in your particular timeline it is historical fact that a quartet of would-be astronauts named Reed Richards, Susan Storm, Ben Grimm and Johnny Storm...
...crashed their rocket after flying into an unexpected cloud of cosmic rays...
...and discovered that the radiation granted them astounding powers--powers they resolved to use to defend their world as the Fantastic Four!
But that was not the only possible outcome of those events.
And for untold millennia, only I have had the privilege to peer into all of Earth's countless "alterniverses"...
...until now.
"WHAT IF...?"
FRED VAN LENTE WRITER WITH LYRICS BY CRYSTAL SKILLMAN CORY HAMSCHER ART
LEE LOUGHRIDGE COLORIST DAVE SHARPE LETTERER SMITH & STRAIN COVER
RICH GINTER PRODUCTION MARK PANICCIA CONSULTING EDITOR NATHAN COSBY EDITOR JOE QUESADA EDITOR IN CHIEF DAN BUCKLEY PUBLISHER

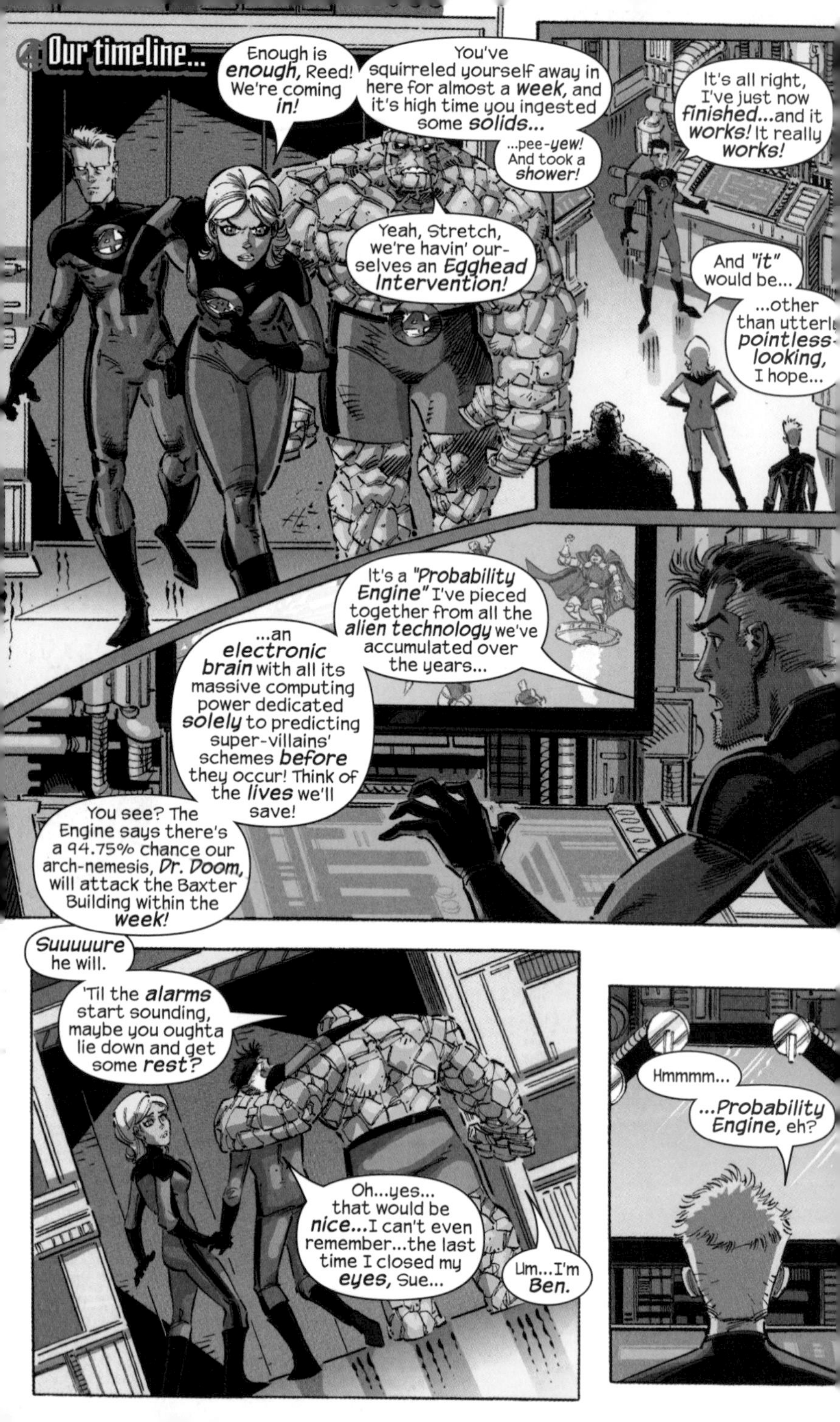
Our timeline...
Enough is enough, Reed! We're coming in!
You've squirreled yourself away in here for almost a week, and it's high time you ingested some solids...
...pee-yew! And took a shower!
Yeah, Stretch, we're havin' our-selves an Egghead Intervention!
It's all right, I've just now finished...and it works! It really works!
And "it" would be...
...other than utterl pointless-looking, I hope...
It's a "Probability Engine" I've pieced together from all the alien technology we've accumulated over the years...
...an electronic brain with all its massive computing power dedicated solely to predicting super-villains' schemes before they occur! Think of the lives we'll save!
You see? The Engine says there's a 94.75% chance our arch-nemesis, Dr. Doom, will attack the Baxter Building within the week!
Suuuuure he will.
'Til the alarms start sounding, maybe you oughta lie down and get some rest?
Oh...yes... that would be nice...I can't even remember...the last time I closed my eyes, Sue...
Um...I'm Ben.
Hmmmm...
...Probability Engine, eh?

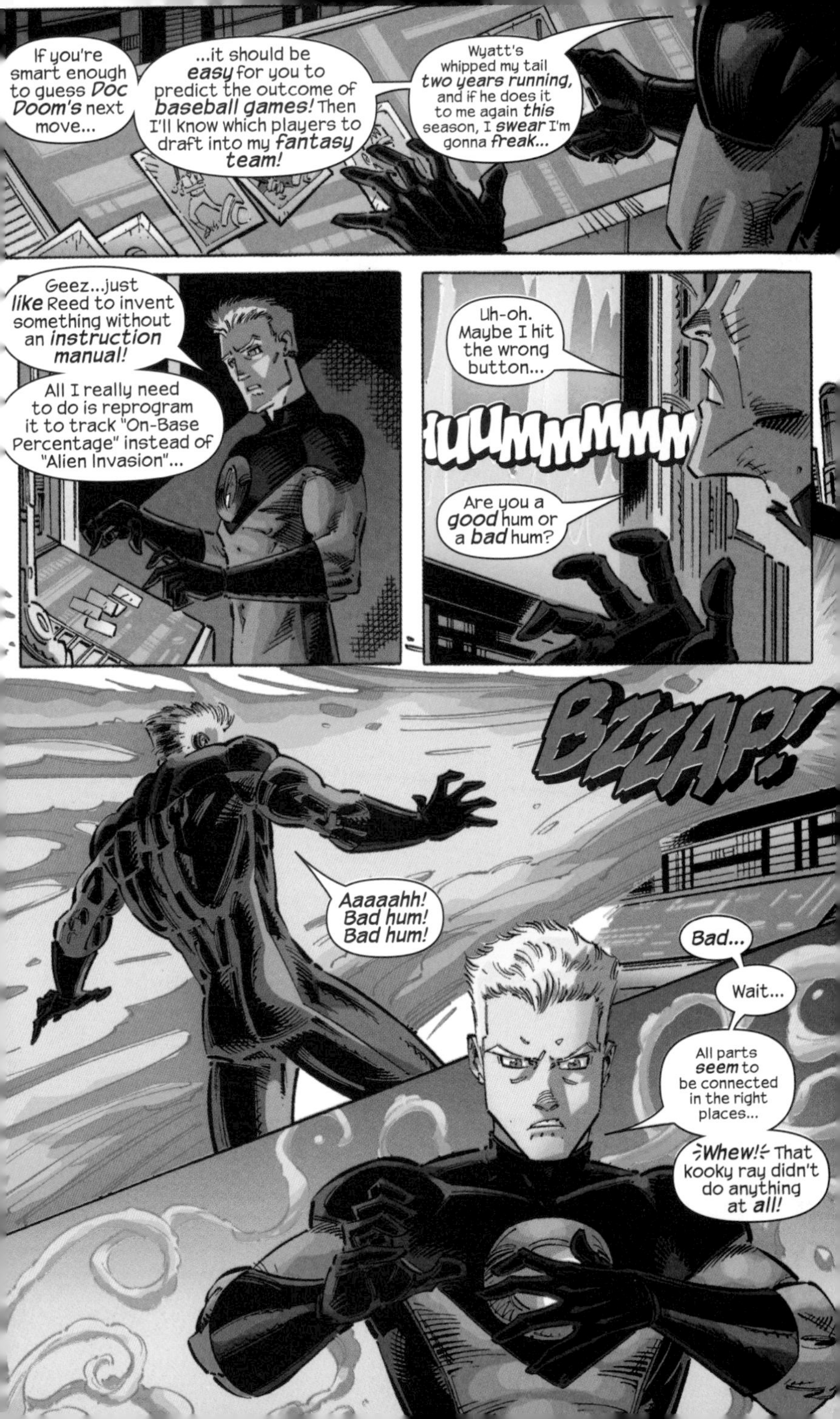
If you're smart enough to guess Doc Doom's next move...
...it should be easy for you to predict the outcome of baseball games! Then I'll know which players to draft into my fantasy team!
Wyatt's whipped my tail two years running, and if he does it to me again this season, I swear I'm gonna freak...
Geez...just like Reed to invent something without an instruction manual!
All I really need to do is reprogram it to track "On-Base Percentage" instead of "Alien Invasion"...
Uh-oh. Maybe I hit the wrong button...
HUUMMMMMM
Are you a good hum or a bad hum?
BZZAP!
Aaaaahh! Bad hum! Bad hum!
Bad...
Wait...
All parts seem to be connected in the right places...
Whew! That kooky ray didn't do anything at all!

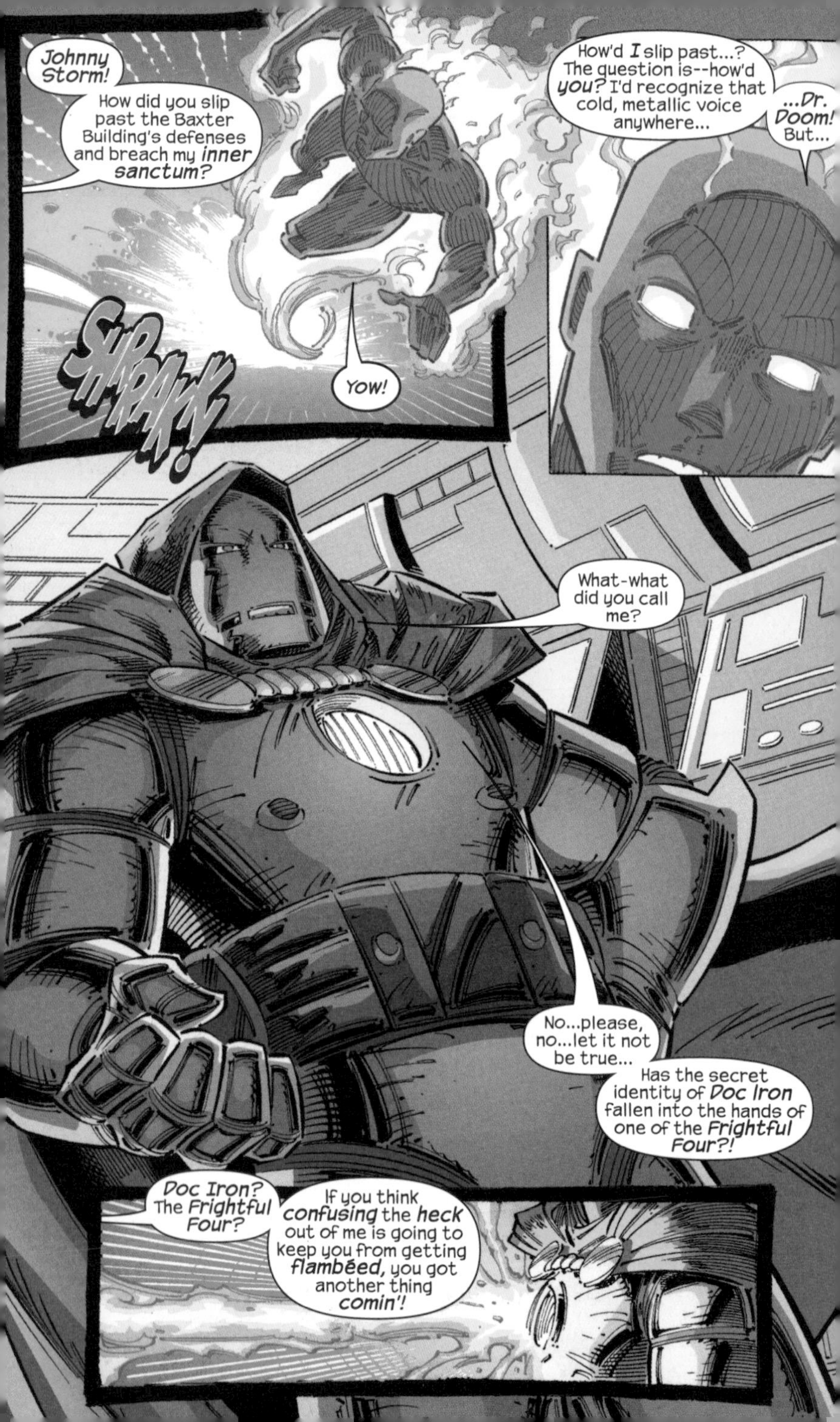

Johnny Storm!
How did you slip past the Baxter Building's defenses and breach my *inner sanctum*?
SHRAKK!
YOW!
How'd *I* slip past...? The question is--how'd *you?* I'd recognize that cold, metallic voice anywhere...
...Dr. Doom! But...
What-what did you call me?
No...please, no...let it not be true...
Has the secret identity of *Doc Iron* fallen into the hands of one of the *Frightful Four?!*
Doc Iron? The *Frightful Four?*
If you think *confusing* the *heck* out of me is going to keep you from getting *flambéed,* you got another thing *comin'!*

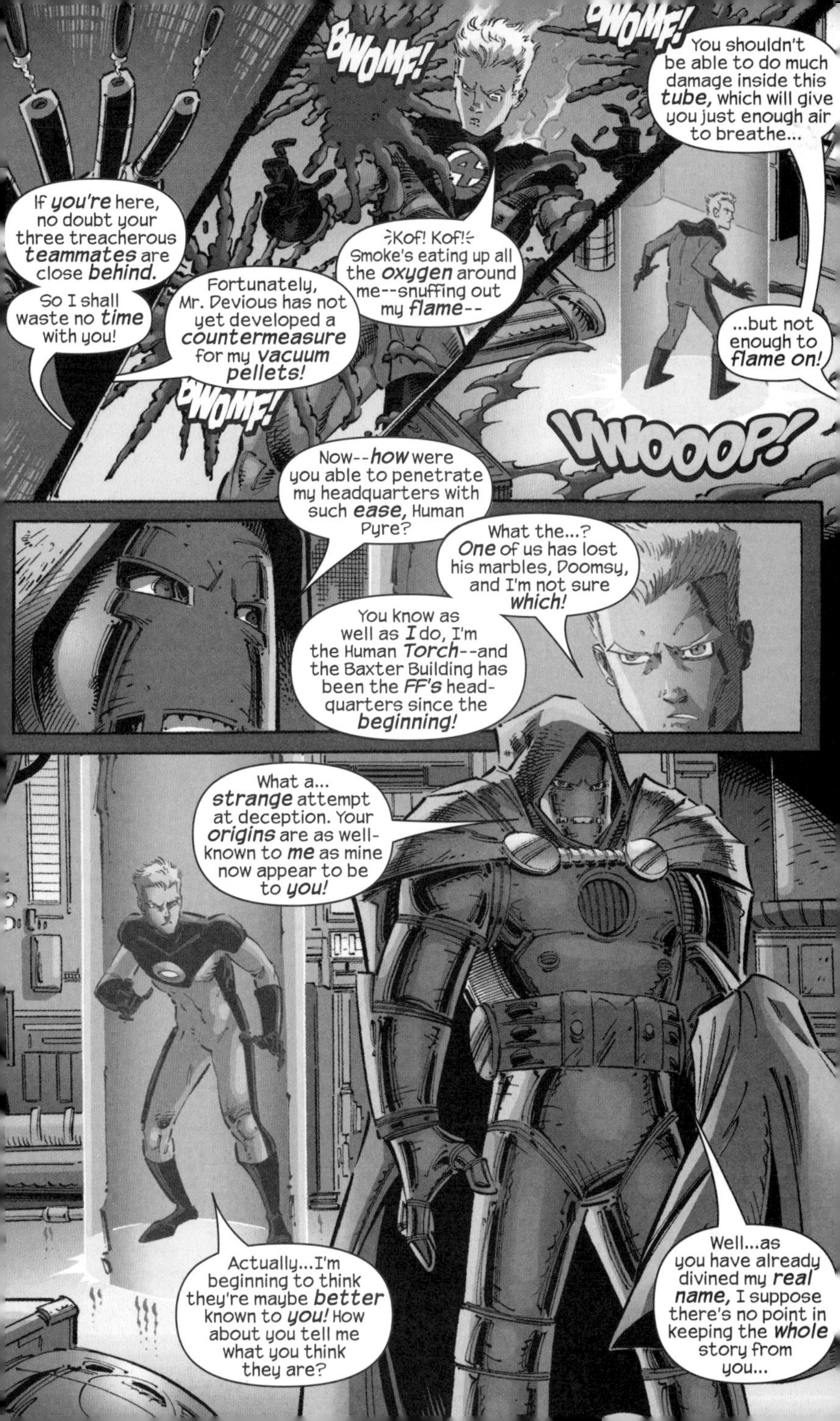
BWOMF!
BWOMF!
You shouldn't be able to do much damage inside this tube, which will give you just enough air to breathe...
If you're here, no doubt your three treacherous teammates are close behind.
So I shall waste no time with you!
Fortunately, Mr. Devious has not yet developed a countermeasure for my vacuum pellets!
BWOMF!
Kof! Kof! Smoke's eating up all the oxygen around me--snuffing out my flame--
...but not enough to flame on!
VWOOOP!
Now--how were you able to penetrate my headquarters with such ease, Human Pyre?
What the...? One of us has lost his marbles, Doomsy, and I'm not sure which!
You know as well as I do, I'm the Human Torch--and the Baxter Building has been the FF's head-quarters since the beginning!
What a... strange attempt at deception. Your origins are as well-known to me as mine now appear to be to you!
Actually...I'm beginning to think they're maybe better known to you! How about you tell me what you think they are?
Well...as you have already divined my real name, I suppose there's no point in keeping the whole story from you...

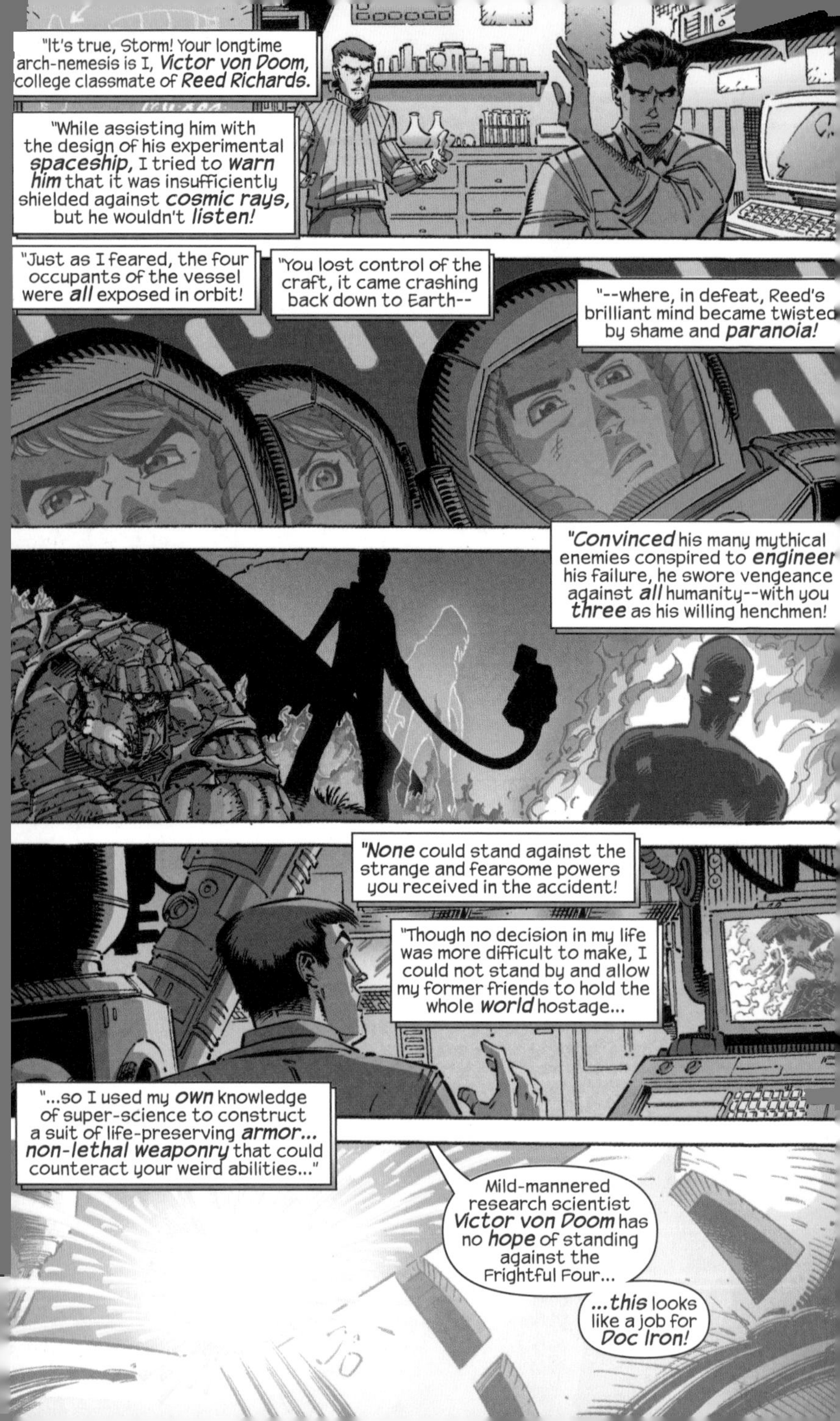

"It's true, Storm! Your longtime arch-nemesis is I, Victor von Doom, college classmate of Reed Richards.
"While assisting him with the design of his experimental spaceship, I tried to warn him that it was insufficiently shielded against cosmic rays, but he wouldn't listen!
"Just as I feared, the four occupants of the vessel were all exposed in orbit!
"You lost control of the craft, it came crashing back down to Earth--
"--where, in defeat, Reed's brilliant mind became twisted by shame and paranoia!
"Convinced his many mythical enemies conspired to engineer his failure, he swore vengeance against all humanity--with you three as his willing henchmen!
"None could stand against the strange and fearsome powers you received in the accident!
"Though no decision in my life was more difficult to make, I could not stand by and allow my former friends to hold the whole world hostage...
"...so I used my own knowledge of super-science to construct a suit of life-preserving armor... non-lethal weaponry that could counteract your weird abilities..."
Mild-mannered research scientist Victor von Doom has no hope of standing against the Frightful Four...
...this looks like a job for Doc Iron!

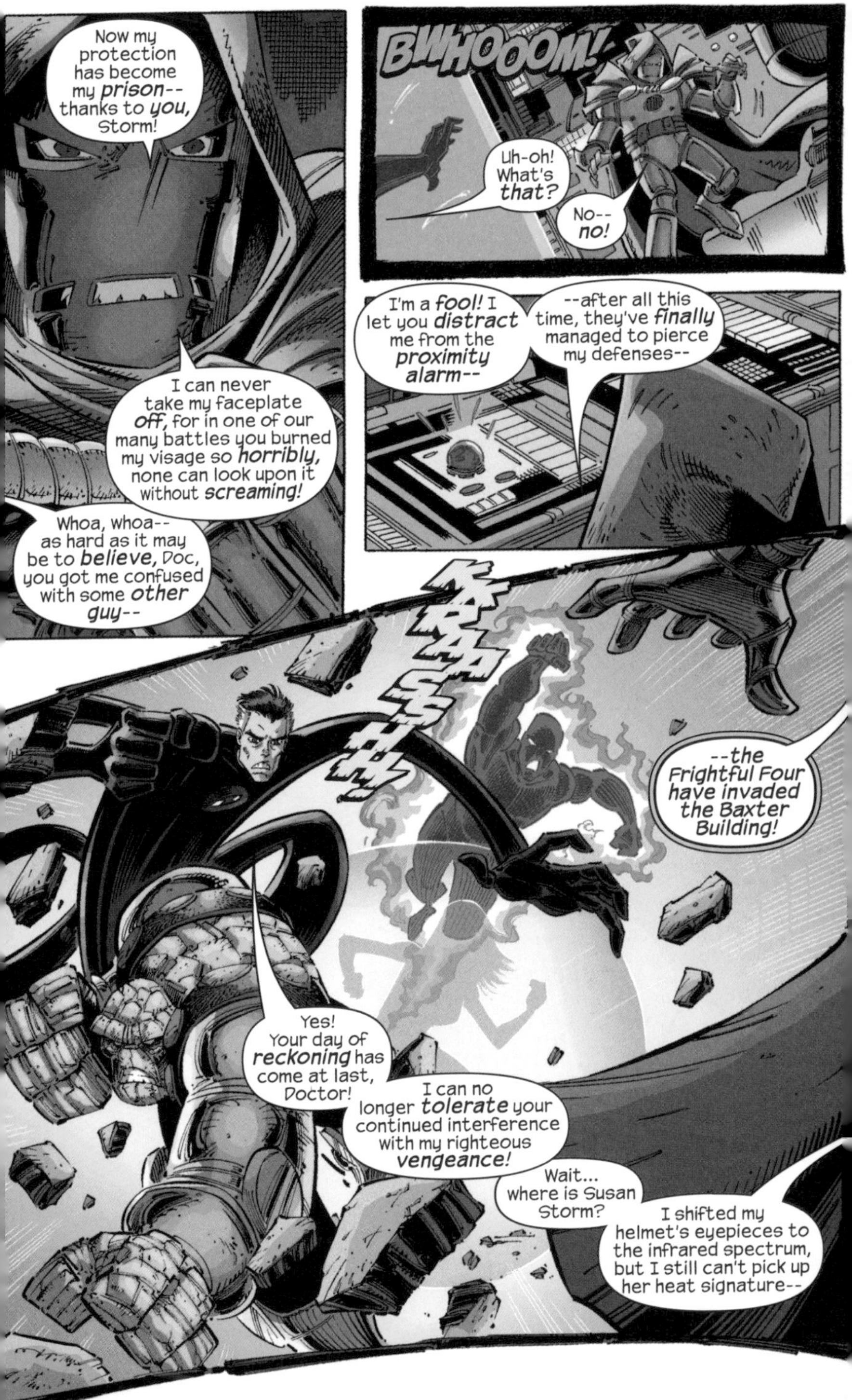
Now my protection has become my prison--thanks to you, Storm!
I can never take my faceplate off, for in one of our many battles you burned my visage so horribly, none can look upon it without screaming!
Whoa, whoa--as hard as it may be to believe, Doc, you got me confused with some other guy--
BWHOOOOM!
Uh-oh! What's that?
No--no!
I'm a fool! I let you distract me from the proximity alarm--
--after all this time, they've finally managed to pierce my defenses--
KRAASSHH
--the Frightful Four have invaded the Baxter Building!
Yes! Your day of reckoning has come at last, Doctor!
I can no longer tolerate your continued interference with my righteous vengeance!
Wait... where is Susan Storm?
I shifted my helmet's eyepieces to the infrared spectrum, but I still can't pick up her heat signature--

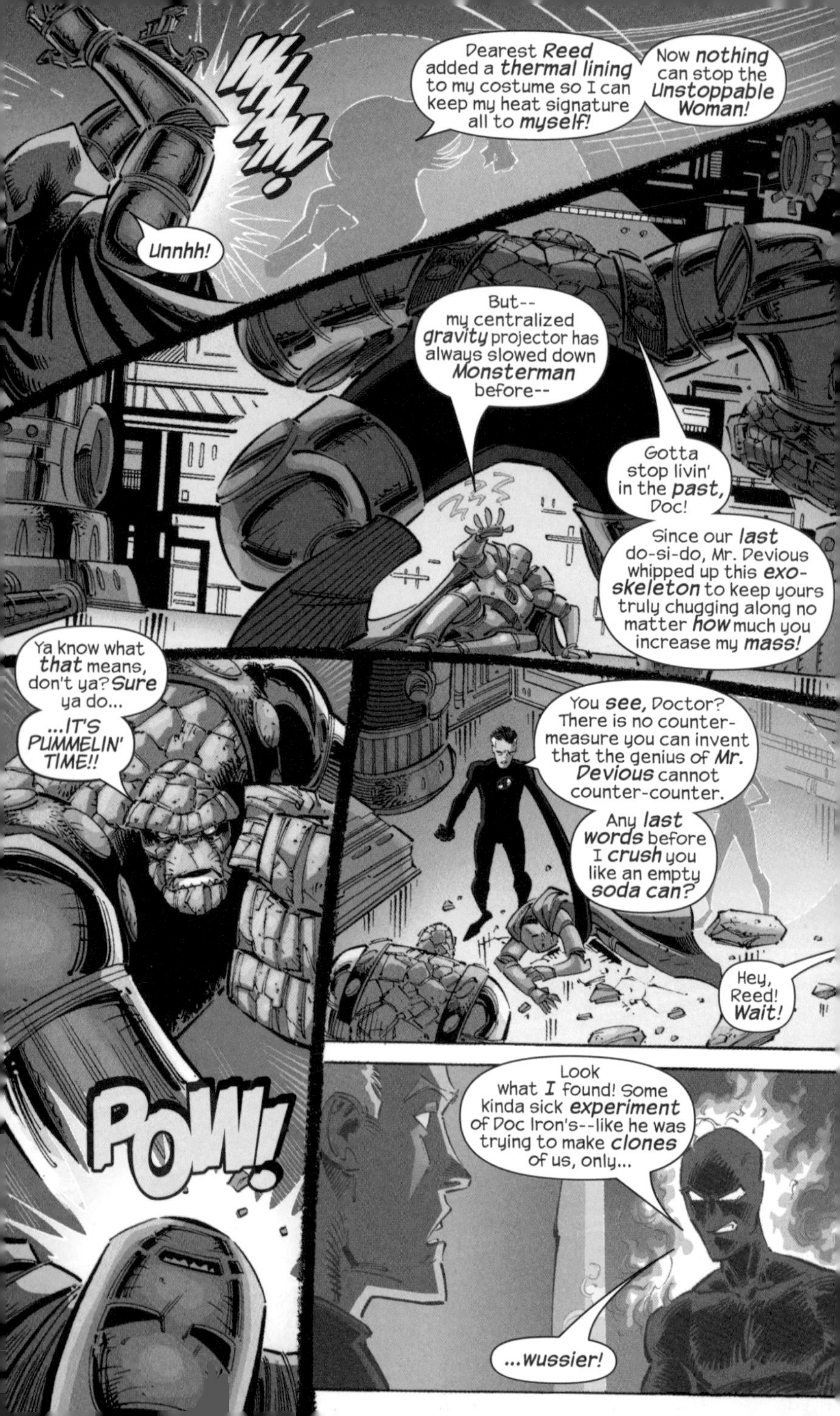WHAM!
Dearest Reed added a thermal lining to my costume so I can keep my heat signature all to myself!
Now nothing can stop the Unstoppable Woman!
Unnhh!
But-- my centralized gravity projector has always slowed down Monsterman before--
Gotta stop livin' in the past, Doc!
Since our last do-si-do, Mr. Devious whipped up this exo-skeleton to keep yours truly chugging along no matter how much you increase my mass!
Ya know what that means, don't ya? Sure ya do...
...IT'S PUMMELIN' TIME!!
POW!
You see, Doctor? There is no counter-measure you can invent that the genius of Mr. Devious cannot counter-counter.
Any last words before I crush you like an empty soda can?
Hey, Reed! Wait!
Look what I found! Some kinda sick experiment of Doc Iron's--like he was trying to make clones of us, only...
...wussier!

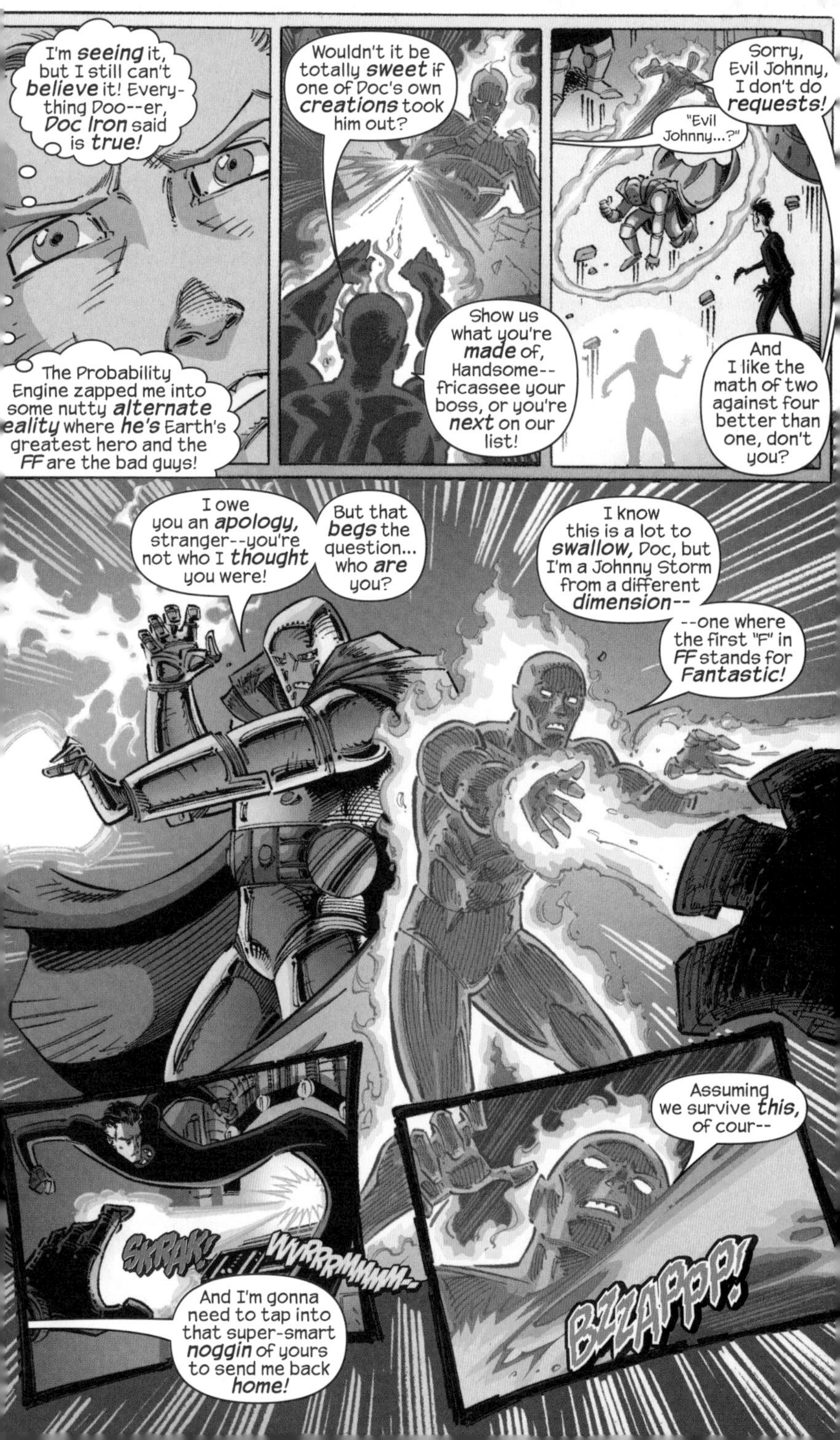
I'm seeing it, but I still can't believe it! Every-thing Doo--er, Doc Iron said is true!
The Probability Engine zapped me into some nutty alternate eality where he's Earth's greatest hero and the FF are the bad guys!
Wouldn't it be totally sweet if one of Doc's own creations took him out?
Show us what you're made of, Handsome--fricassee your boss, or you're next on our list!
Sorry, Evil Johnny, I don't do requests!
"Evil Johnny...?"
And I like the math of two against four better than one, don't you?
I owe you an apology, stranger--you're not who I thought you were!
But that begs the question... who are you?
I know this is a lot to swallow, Doc, but I'm a Johnny Storm from a different dimension--
--one where the first "F" in FF stands for Fantastic!
SKRAK!
WVRRRMMMM-
And I'm gonna need to tap into that super-smart noggin of yours to send me back home!
Assuming we survive this, of cour--
BZZAPPP!

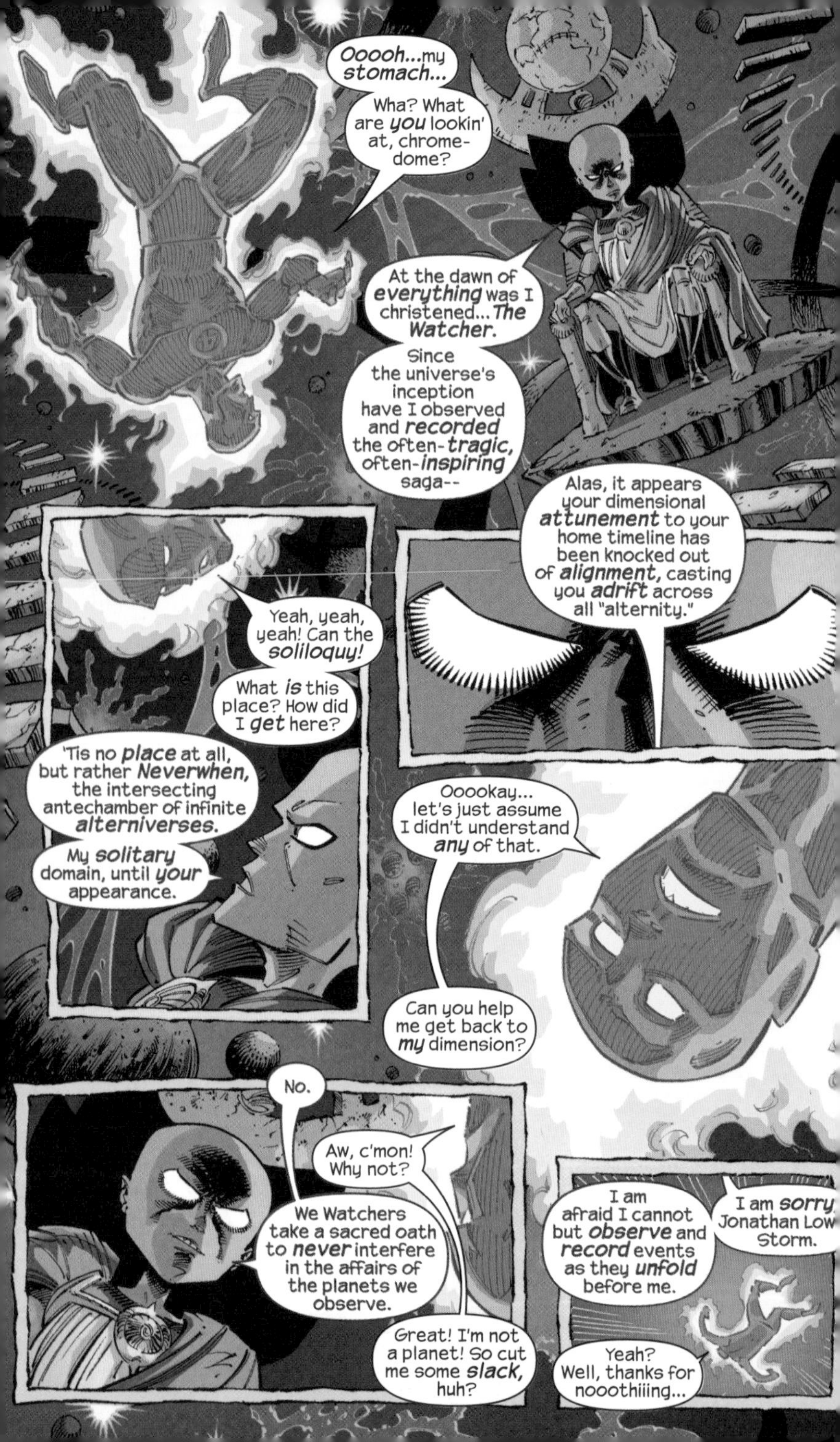

Ooooh...my stomach...
Wha? What are you lookin' at, chrome-dome?
At the dawn of everything was I christened...The Watcher.
Since the universe's inception have I observed and recorded the often-tragic, often-inspiring saga--
Yeah, yeah, yeah! Can the soliloquy!
What is this place? How did I get here?
Alas, it appears your dimensional attunement to your home timeline has been knocked out of alignment, casting you adrift across all "alternity."
'Tis no place at all, but rather Neverwhen, the intersecting antechamber of infinite alterniverses.
My solitary domain, until your appearance.
Ooookay... let's just assume I didn't understand any of that.
Can you help me get back to my dimension?
No.
Aw, c'mon! Why not?
We Watchers take a sacred oath to never interfere in the affairs of the planets we observe.
Great! I'm not a planet! So cut me some slack, huh?
I am sorry, Jonathan Lowe Storm.
I am afraid I cannot but observe and record events as they unfold before me.
Yeah? Well, thanks for nooothiiing...

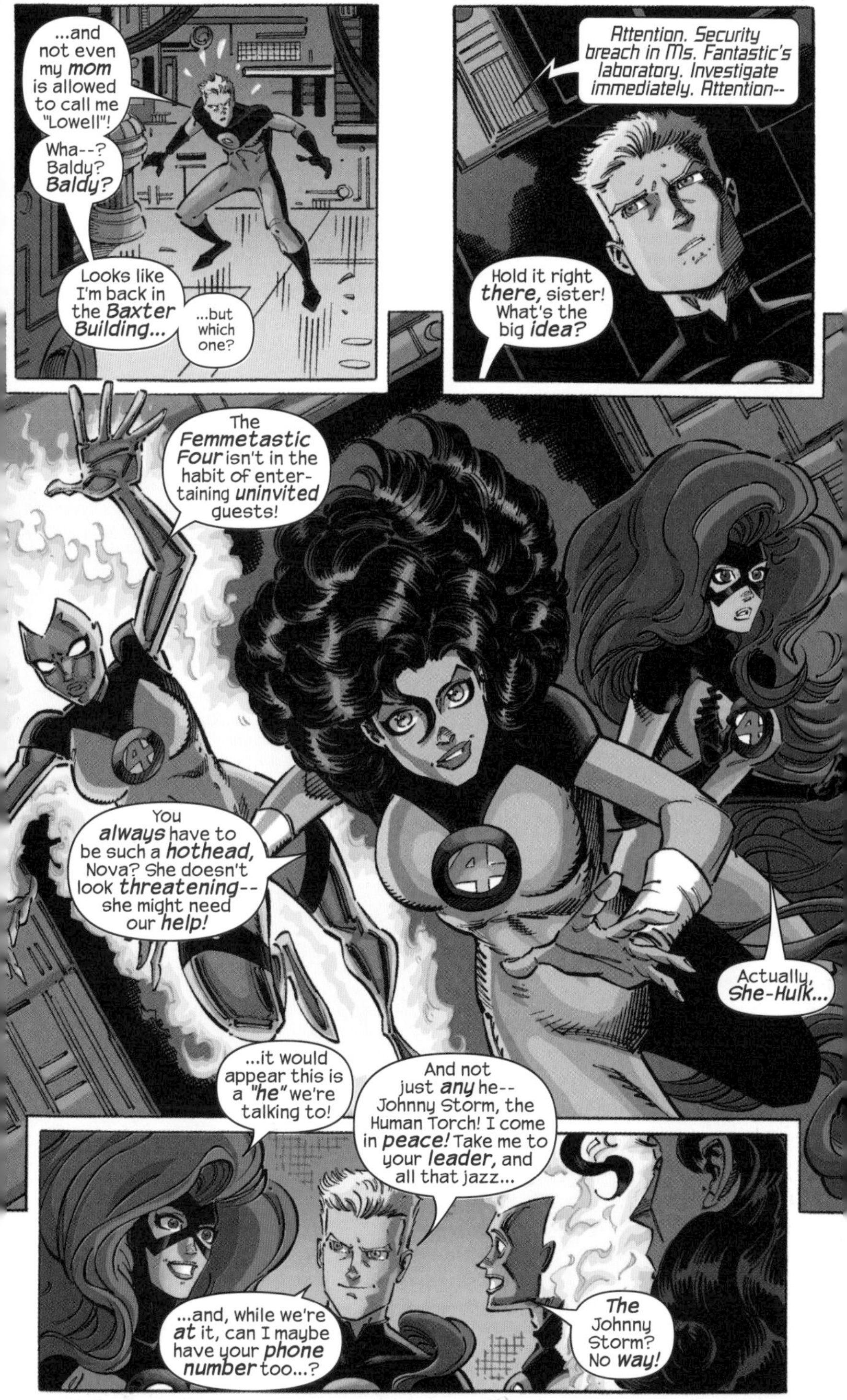
...and not even my mom is allowed to call me "Lowell"!
Wha--? Baldy? Baldy?
Looks like I'm back in the Baxter Building...
...but which one?
Attention. Security breach in Ms. Fantastic's laboratory. Investigate immediately. Attention--
Hold it right there, sister! What's the big idea?
The Femmetastic Four isn't in the habit of entertaining uninvited guests!
You always have to be such a hothead, Nova? She doesn't look threatening-- she might need our help!
Actually, She-Hulk...
...it would appear this is a "he" we're talking to!
And not just any he-- Johnny Storm, the Human Torch! I come in peace! Take me to your leader, and all that jazz...
...and, while we're at it, can I maybe have your phone number too...?
The Johnny Storm? No way!

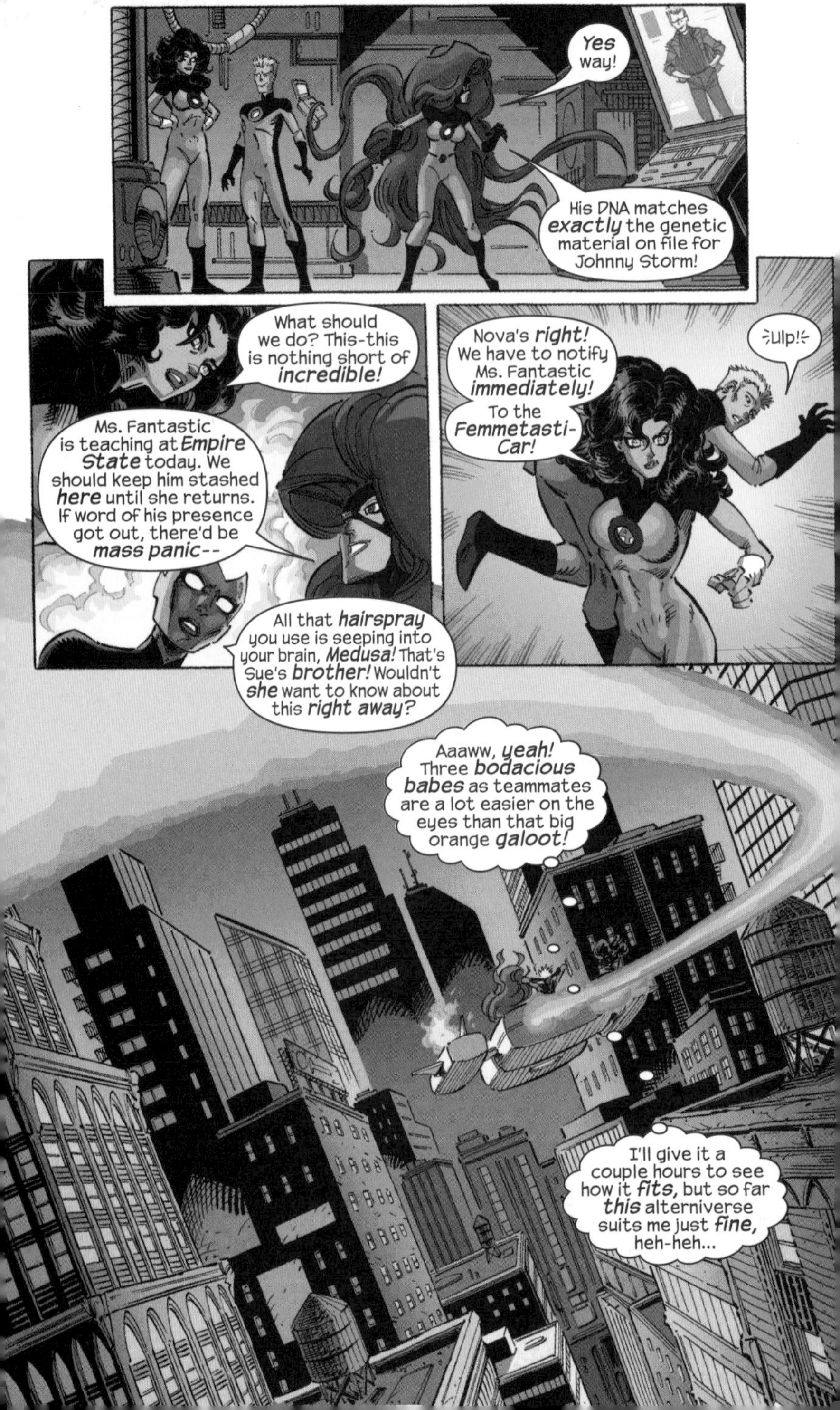

Yes way!
His DNA matches exactly the genetic material on file for Johnny Storm!
What should we do? This-this is nothing short of incredible!
Ms. Fantastic is teaching at Empire State today. We should keep him stashed here until she returns. If word of his presence got out, there'd be mass panic--
All that hairspray you use is seeping into your brain, Medusa! That's Sue's brother! Wouldn't she want to know about this right away?
Nova's right! We have to notify Ms. Fantastic immediately!
To the Femmetasti-Car!
Ulp!
Aaaww, yeah! Three bodacious babes as teammates are a lot easier on the eyes than that big orange galoot!
I'll give it a couple hours to see how it fits, but so far this alterniverse suits me just fine, heh-heh...

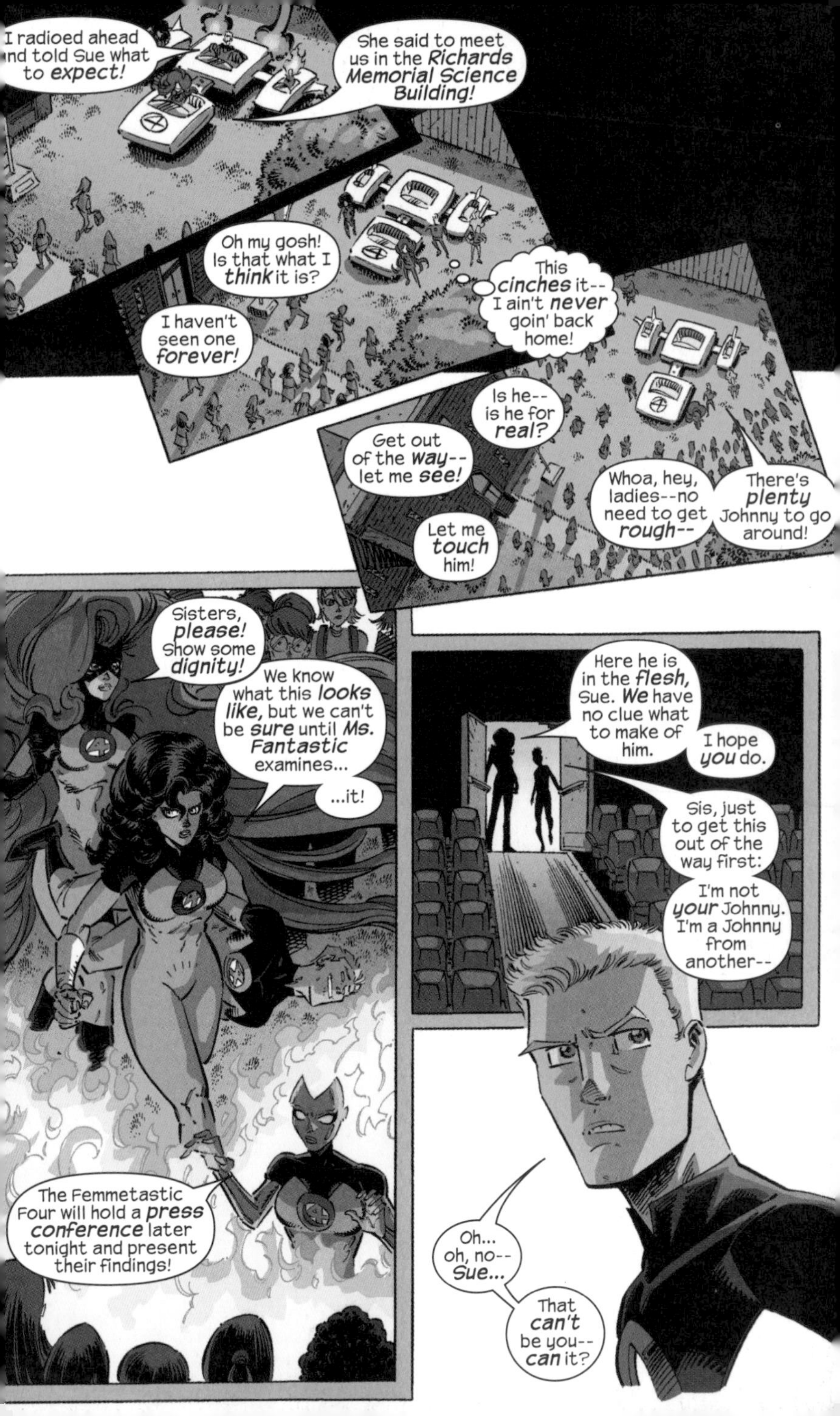
I radioed ahead and told Sue what to expect!
She said to meet us in the Richards Memorial Science Building!
Oh my gosh! Is that what I think it is?
I haven't seen one forever!
This cinches it-- I ain't never goin' back home!
Is he-- is he for real?
Get out of the way-- let me see!
Let me touch him!
Whoa, hey, ladies--no need to get rough--
There's plenty Johnny to go around!
Sisters, please! Show some dignity!
We know what this looks like, but we can't be sure until Ms. Fantastic examines...
...it!
The Femmetastic Four will hold a press conference later tonight and present their findings!
Here he is in the flesh, Sue. We have no clue what to make of him.
I hope you do.
Sis, just to get this out of the way first:
I'm not your Johnny. I'm a Johnny from another--
Oh... oh, no-- Sue...
That can't be you-- can it?

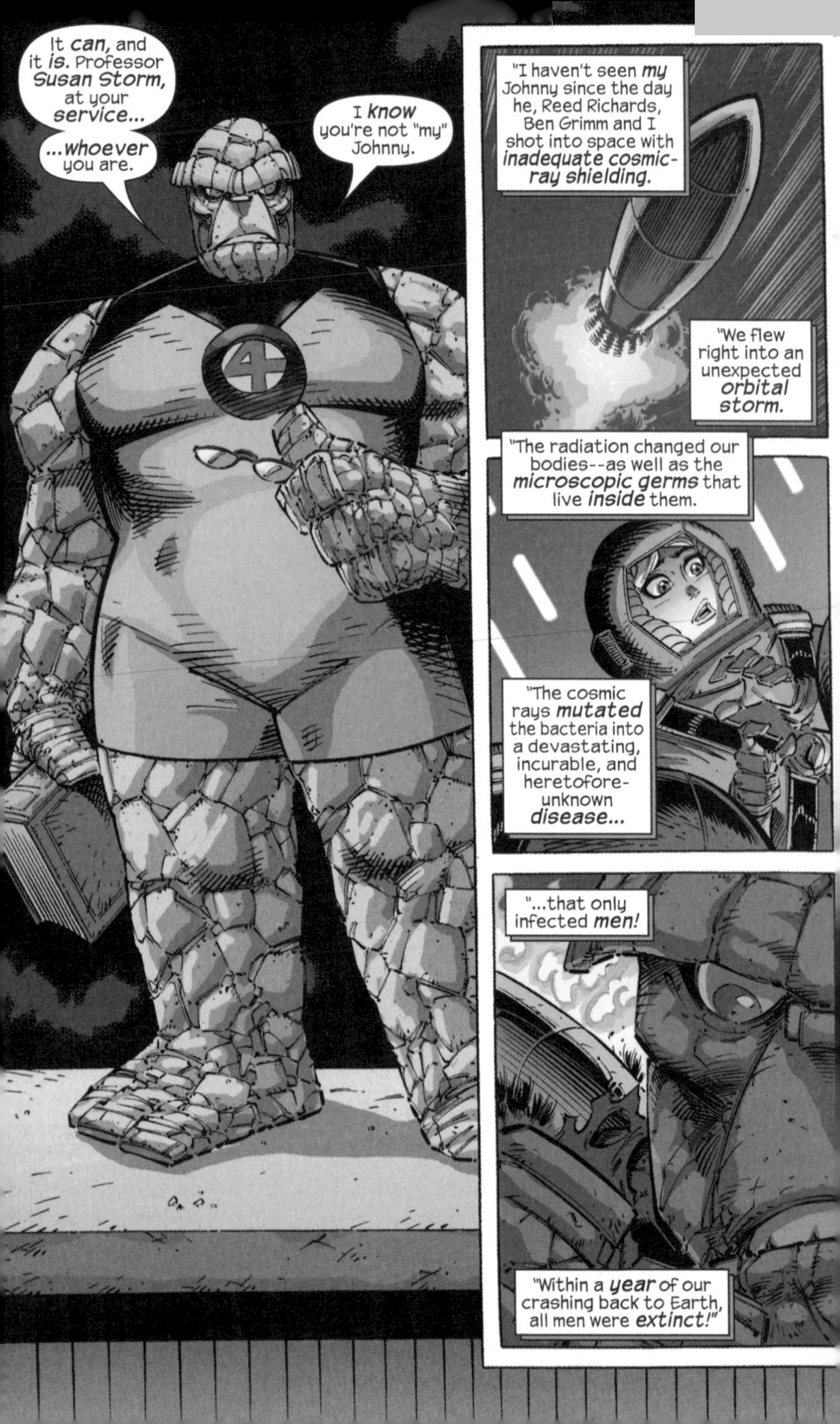
It can, and it is. Professor Susan Storm, at your service...
...whoever you are.
I know you're not "my" Johnny.
"I haven't seen my Johnny since the day he, Reed Richards, Ben Grimm and I shot into space with inadequate cosmic-ray shielding.
"We flew right into an unexpected orbital storm.
"The radiation changed our bodies--as well as the microscopic germs that live inside them.
"The cosmic rays mutated the bacteria into a devastating, incurable, and heretofore-unknown disease...
"...that only infected men!
"Within a year of our crashing back to Earth, all men were extinct!"

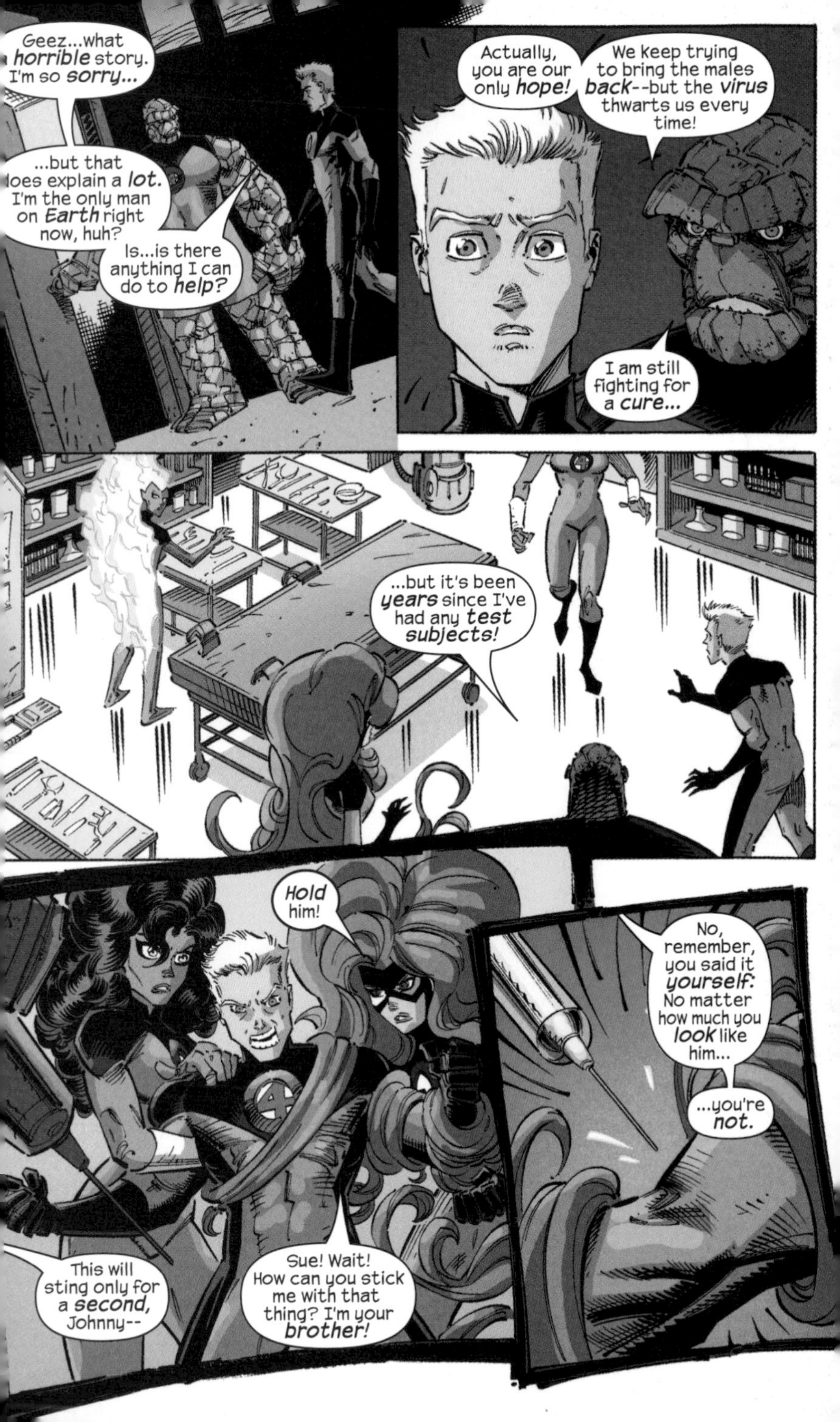
Geez...what horrible story. I'm so sorry...
...but that does explain a lot. I'm the only man on Earth right now, huh?
Is...is there anything I can do to help?
Actually, you are our only hope!
We keep trying to bring the males back--but the virus thwarts us every time!
I am still fighting for a cure...
...but it's been years since I've had any test subjects!
Hold him!
This will sting only for a second, Johnny--
Sue! Wait! How can you stick me with that thing? I'm your brother!
No, remember, you said it yourself: No matter how much you look like him...
...you're not.

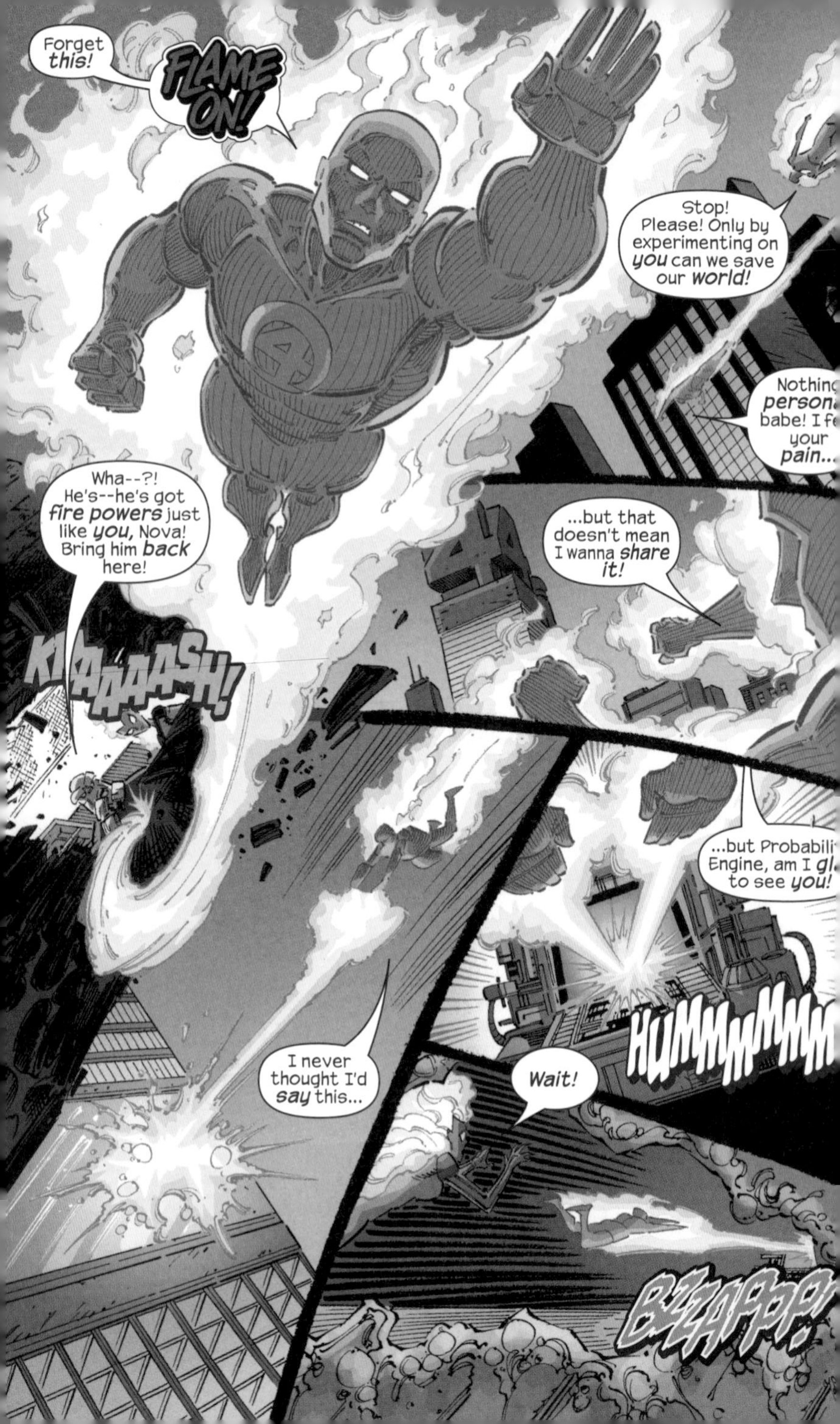
Forget this!
FLAME ON!
Stop! Please! Only by experimenting on you can we save our world!
Nothing person babe! I f your pain...
Wha--?! He's--he's got fire powers just like you, Nova! Bring him back here!
...but that doesn't mean I wanna share it!
KRAAAASH!
...but Probabili Engine, am I gl to see you!
HUMMMMMM
I never thought I'd say this...
Wait!
BZZAPPP!

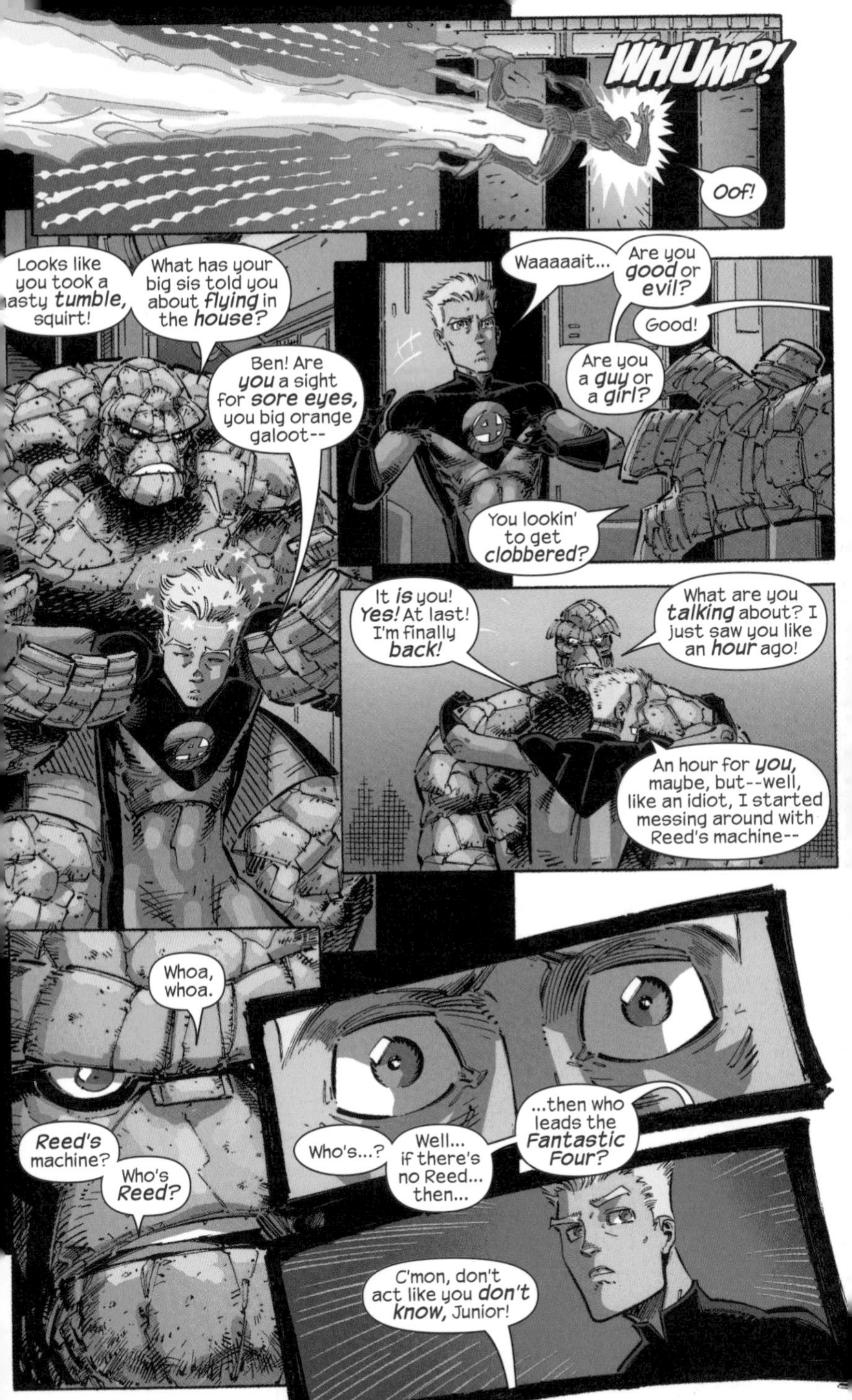
WHUMP!
Oof!
Looks like you took a nasty tumble, squirt!
What has your big sis told you about flying in the house?
Ben! Are you a sight for sore eyes, you big orange galoot--
Waaaaait...
Are you good or evil?
Good!
Are you a guy or a girl?
You lookin' to get clobbered?
It is you! Yes! At last! I'm finally back!
What are you talking about? I just saw you like an hour ago!
An hour for you, maybe, but--well, like an idiot, I started messing around with Reed's machine--
Whoa, whoa.
Reed's machine?
Who's Reed?
Who's...?
Well... if there's no Reed... then...
...then who leads the Fantastic Four?
C'mon, don't act like you don't know, Junior!

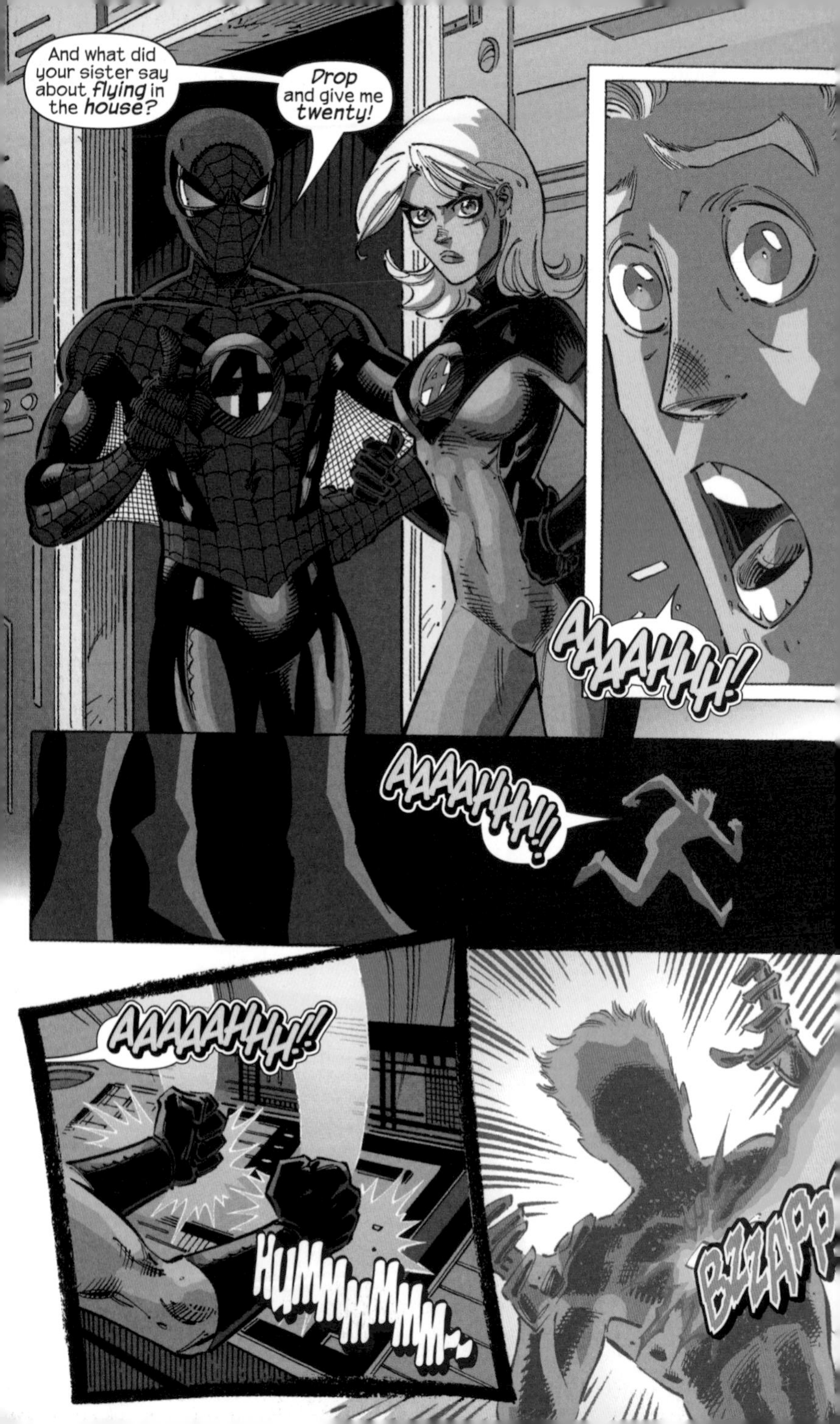
And what did your sister say about *flying* in the *house*?
Drop and give me *twenty!*
AAAAHHHH!
AAAAHHHH!!
AAAAHHHH!!
HUMMMMMMMM--
BZZAPP

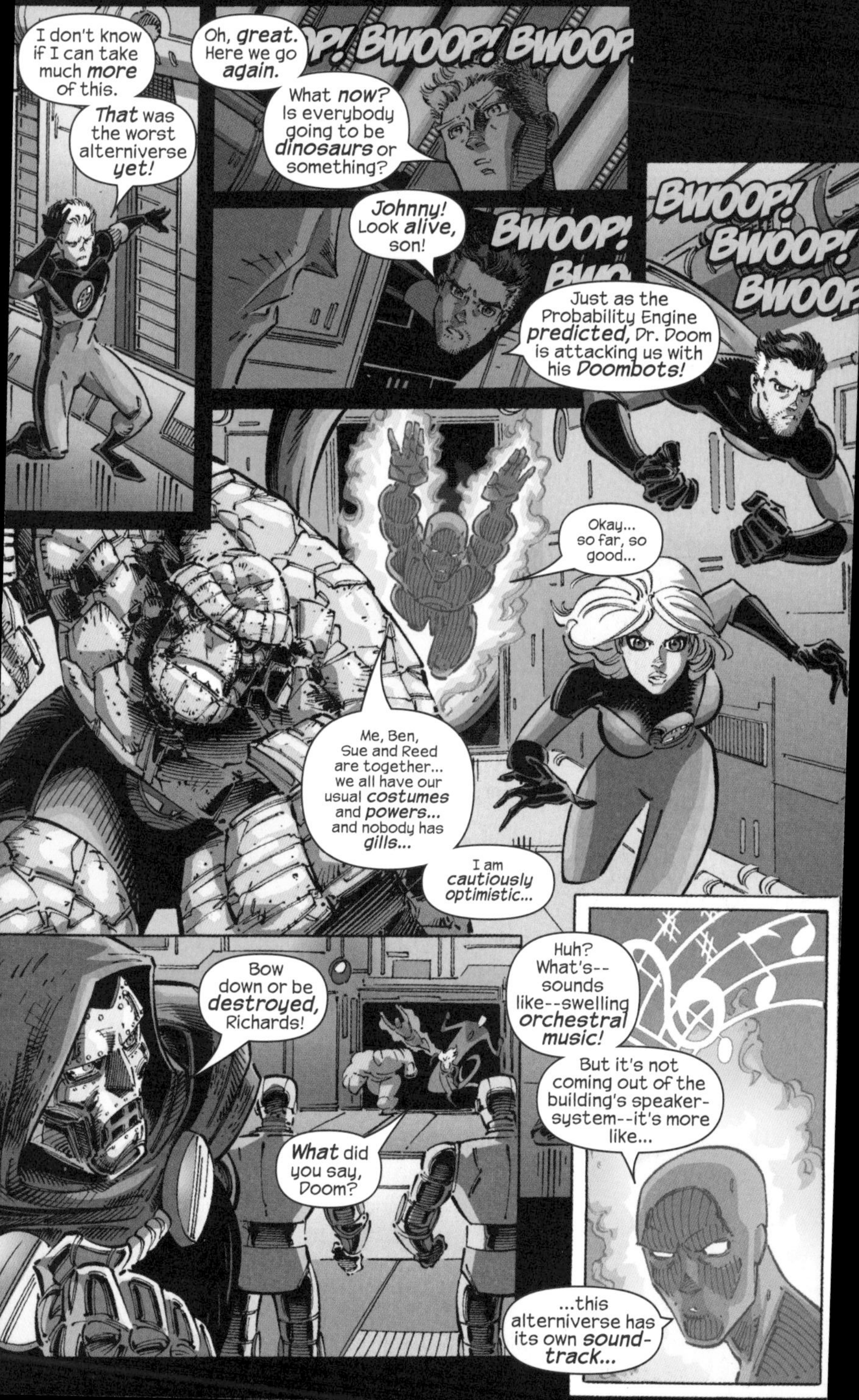
I don't know if I can take much more of this.
That was the worst alterniverse yet!
Oh, great. Here we go again.
P! BWOOP! BWOOP
What now? Is everybody going to be dinosaurs or something?
Johnny! Look alive, son!
BWOOP!
BWOOP! BWOOP! BWOOP
Just as the Probability Engine predicted, Dr. Doom is attacking us with his Doombots!
Okay... so far, so good...
Me, Ben, Sue and Reed are together... we all have our usual costumes and powers... and nobody has gills...
I am cautiously optimistic...
Bow down or be destroyed, Richards!
What did you say, Doom?
Huh? What's-- sounds like--swelling orchestral music!
But it's not coming out of the building's speaker-system--it's more like...
...this alterniverse has its own sound-track...

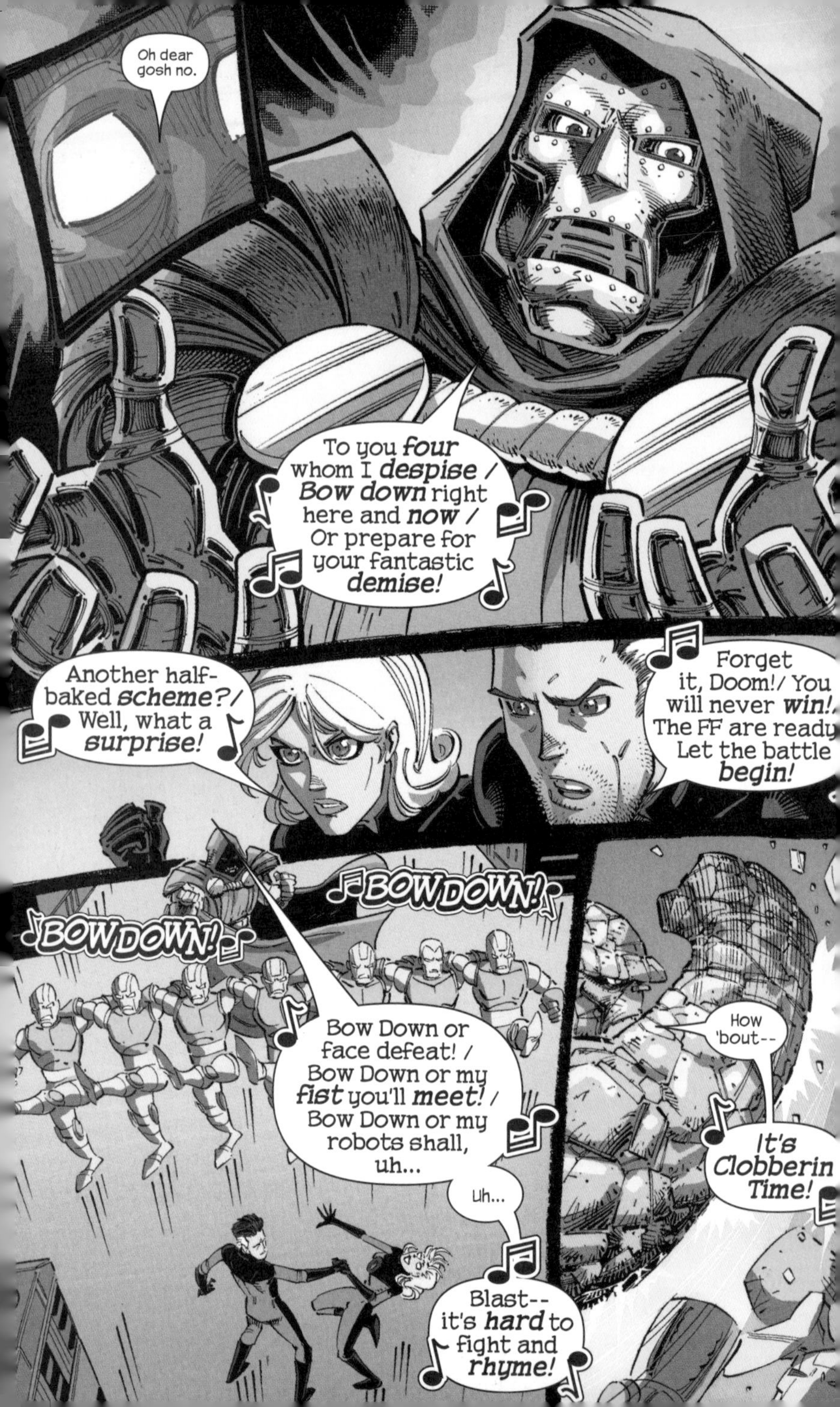

Oh dear gosh no.
To you four whom I despise / Bow down right here and now / Or prepare for your fantastic demise!
Another half-baked scheme?/ Well, what a surprise!
Forget it, Doom!/ You will never win!/ The FF are ready Let the battle begin!
BOWDOWN!
BOWDOWN!
Bow Down or face defeat! / Bow Down or my fist you'll meet! / Bow Down or my robots shall, uh...
Uh...
Blast-- it's hard to fight and rhyme!
How 'bout--
It's Clobberin Time!

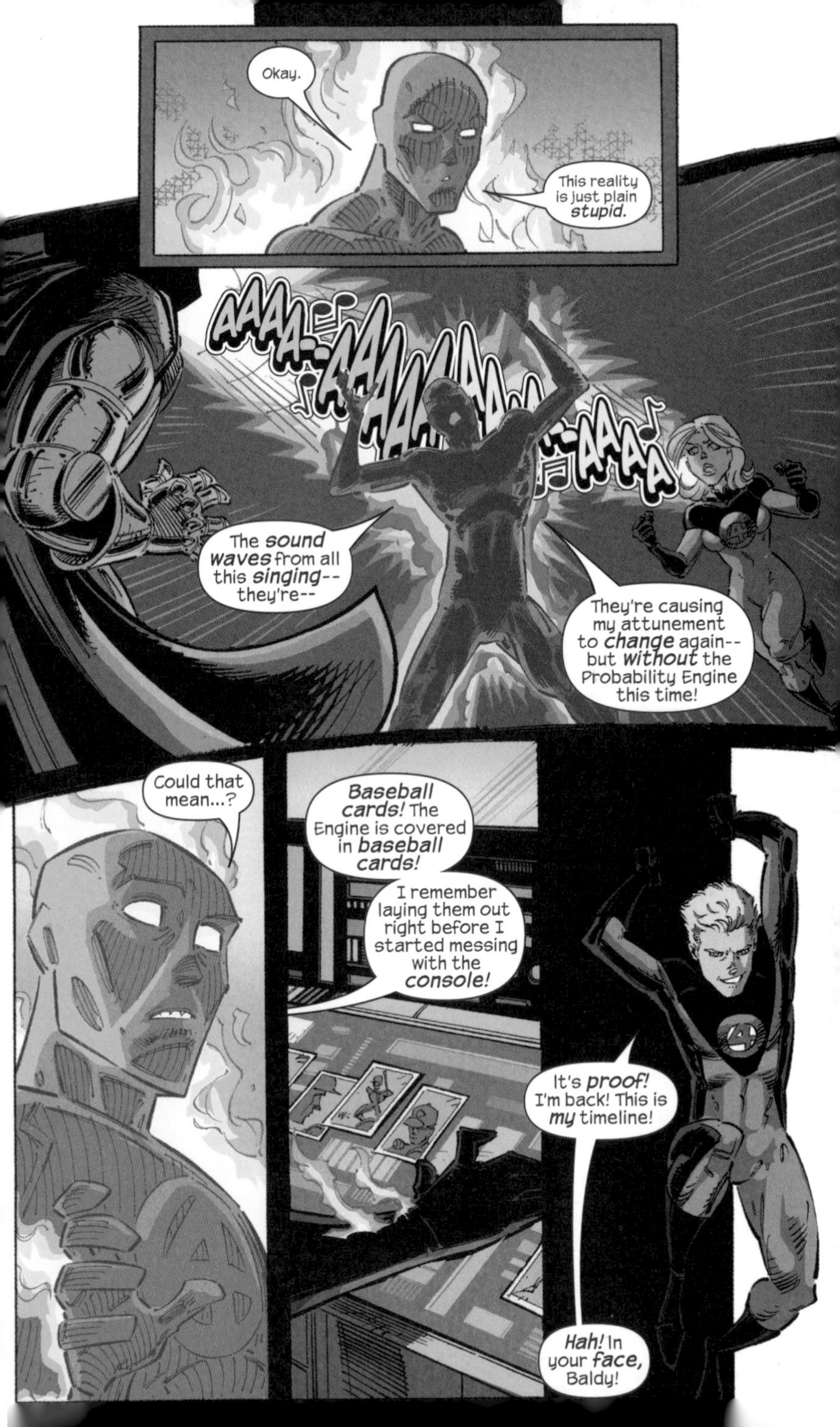
Okay.
This reality is just plain *stupid.*
AAAA--AAAAAAAA--AAAA
The *sound waves* from all this *singing*-- they're--
They're causing my attunement to *change* again-- but *without* the Probability Engine this time!
Could that mean...?
Baseball cards! The Engine is covered in *baseball cards!*
I remember laying them out right before I started messing with the *console!*
It's *proof!* I'm back! This is *my* timeline!
Hah! In your *face,* Baldy!

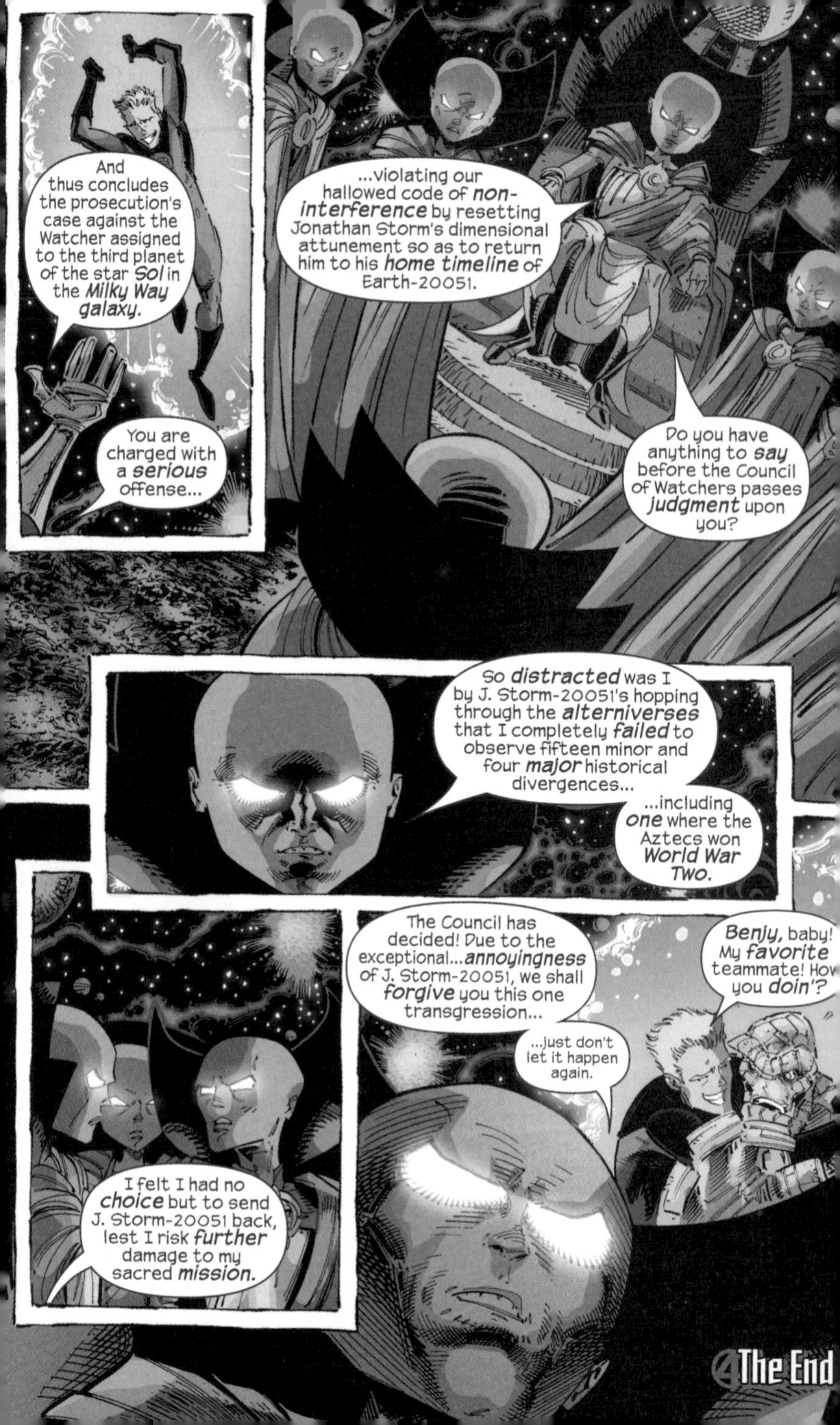
And thus concludes the prosecution's case against the Watcher assigned to the third planet of the star Sol in the Milky Way galaxy.
You are charged with a serious offense...
...violating our hallowed code of non-interference by resetting Jonathan Storm's dimensional attunement so as to return him to his home timeline of Earth-20051.
Do you have anything to say before the Council of Watchers passes judgment upon you?
So distracted was I by J. Storm-20051's hopping through the alterniverses that I completely failed to observe fifteen minor and four major historical divergences...
...including one where the Aztecs won World War Two.
I felt I had no choice but to send J. Storm-20051 back, lest I risk further damage to my sacred mission.
The Council has decided! Due to the exceptional...annoyingness of J. Storm-20051, we shall forgive you this one transgression...
...just don't let it happen again.
Benjy, baby! My favorite teammate! How you doin'?
The End

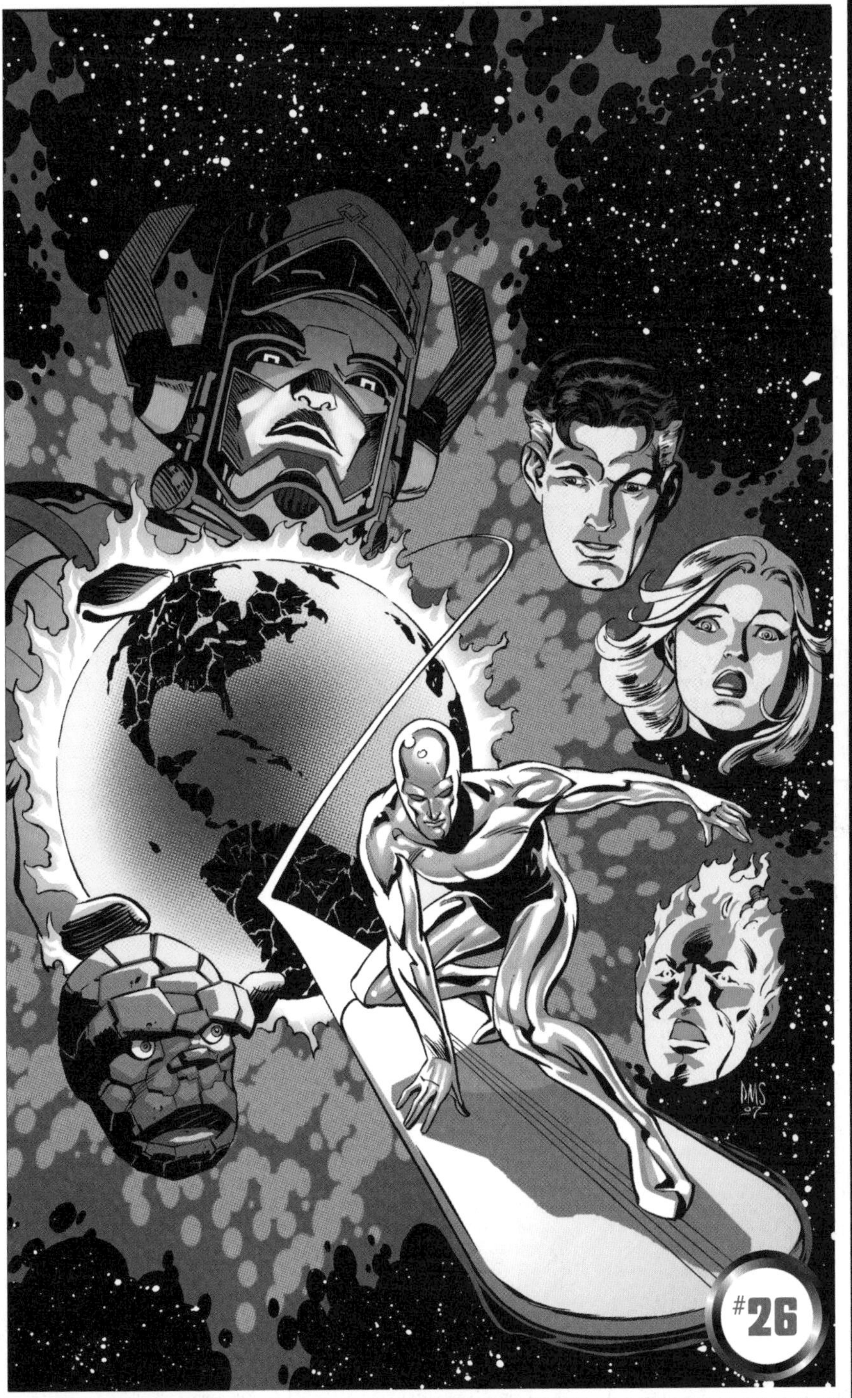
#26

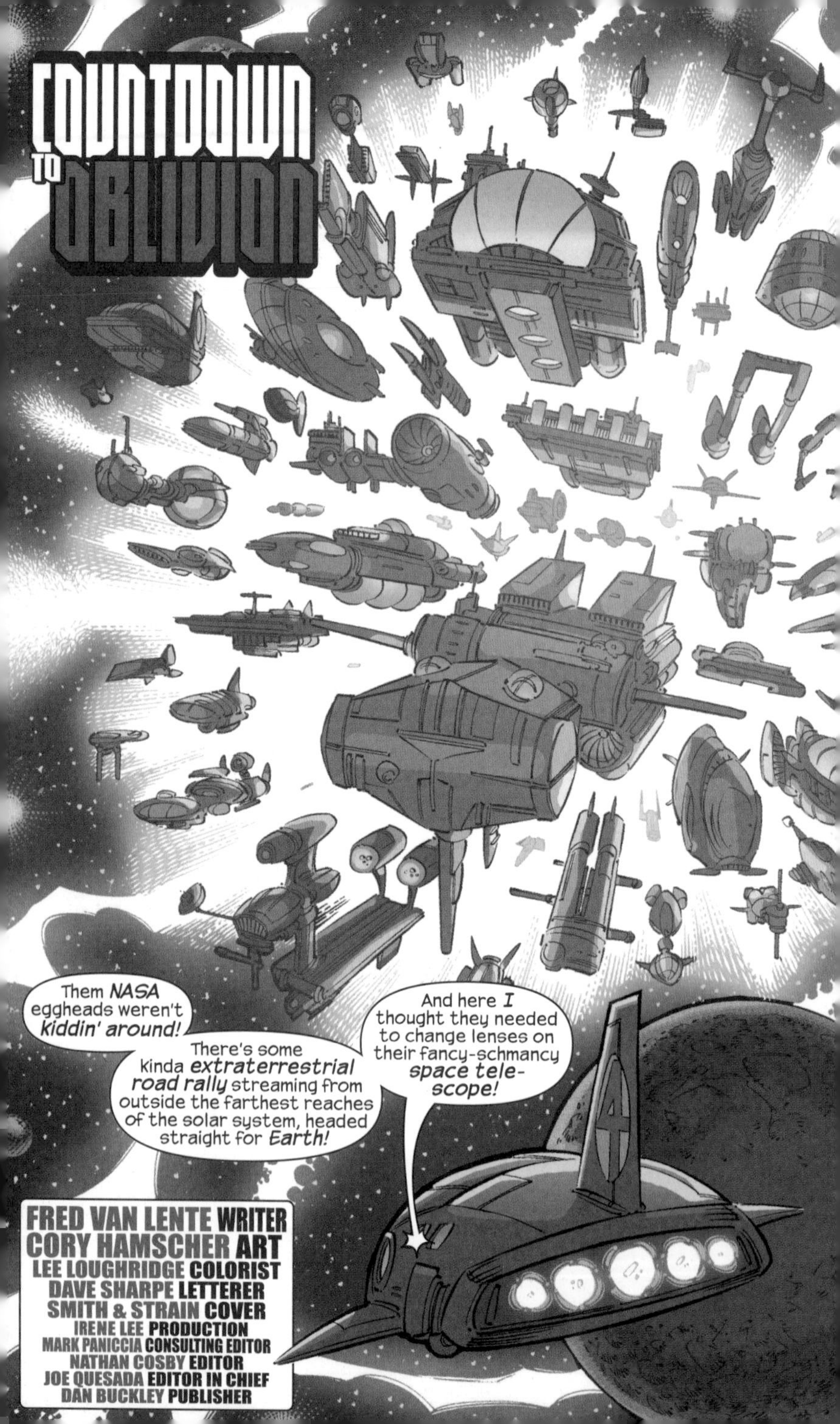
COUNTDOWN TO OBLIVION
Them NASA eggheads weren't kiddin' around!
There's some kinda extraterrestrial road rally streaming from outside the farthest reaches of the solar system, headed straight for Earth!
And here I thought they needed to change lenses on their fancy-schmancy space tele-scope!
FRED VAN LENTE WRITER
CORY HAMSCHER ART
LEE LOUGHRIDGE COLORIST
DAVE SHARPE LETTERER
SMITH & STRAIN COVER
IRENE LEE PRODUCTION
MARK PANICCIA CONSULTING EDITOR
NATHAN COSBY EDITOR
JOE QUESADA EDITOR IN CHIEF
DAN BUCKLEY PUBLISHER

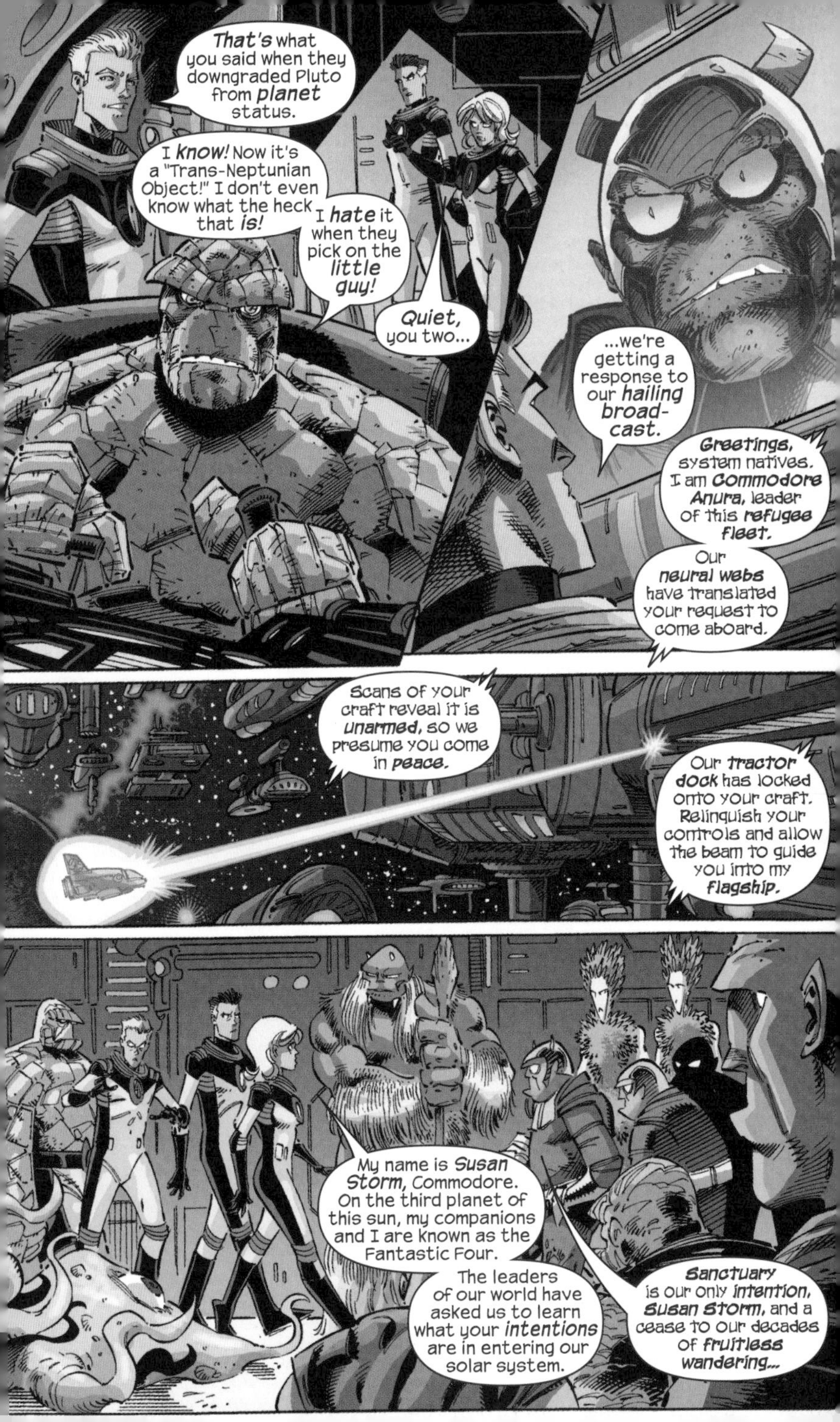

That's what you said when they downgraded Pluto from planet status.
I know! Now it's a "Trans-Neptunian Object!" I don't even know what the heck that is!
I hate it when they pick on the little guy!
Quiet, you two...
...we're getting a response to our hailing broad-cast.
Greetings, system natives. I am Commodore Anura, leader of this refugee fleet.
Our neural webs have translated your request to come aboard.
Scans of your craft reveal it is unarmed, so we presume you come in peace.
Our tractor dock has locked onto your craft. Relinquish your controls and allow the beam to guide you into my flagship.
My name is Susan Storm, Commodore. On the third planet of this sun, my companions and I are known as the Fantastic Four.
The leaders of our world have asked us to learn what your intentions are in entering our solar system.
Sanctuary is our only intention, Susan Storm, and a cease to our decades of fruitless wandering...

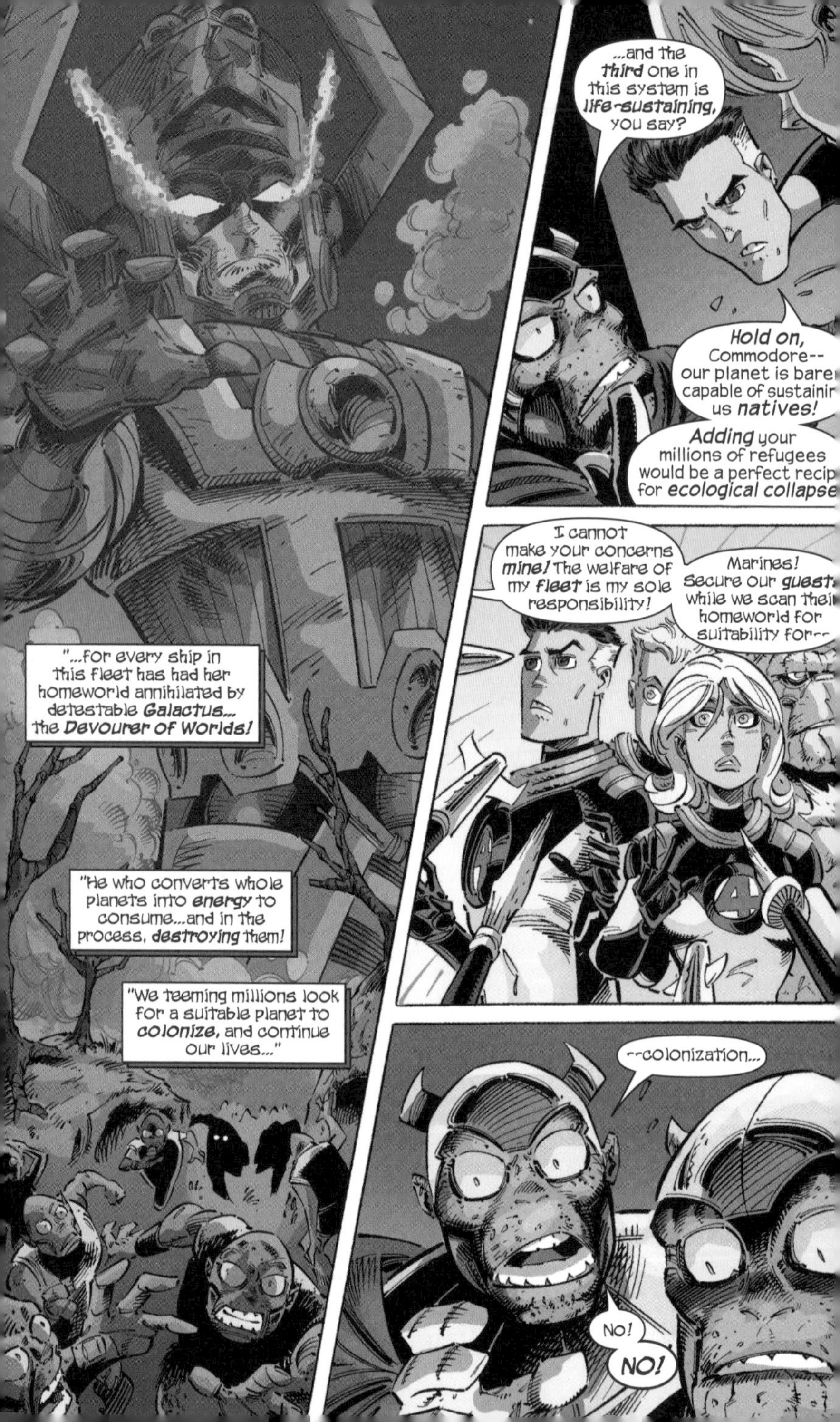

...and the third one in this system is life-sustaining, you say?
Hold on, Commodore-- our planet is bare capable of sustainir us natives!
Adding your millions of refugees would be a perfect recip for ecological collapse
"...for every ship in this fleet has had her homeworld annihilated by detestable Galactus... the Devourer of Worlds!
"He who converts whole planets into energy to consume...and in the process, destroying them!
"We teeming millions look for a suitable planet to colonize, and continue our lives..."
I cannot make your concerns mine! The welfare of my fleet is my sole responsibility!
Marines! Secure our guest while we scan thei homeworld for suitability for--
--colonization...
No!
NO!

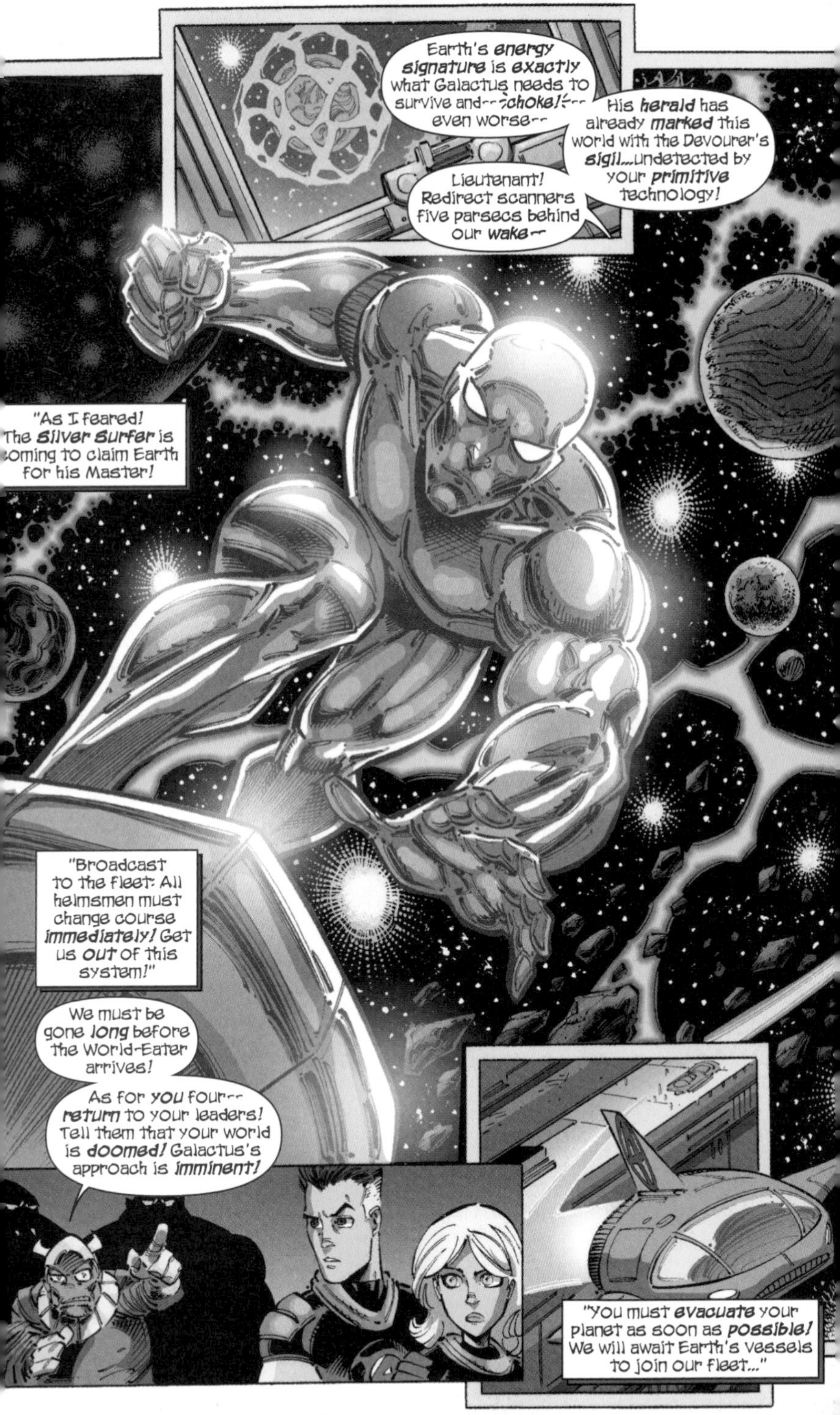
Earth's energy signature is exactly what Galactus needs to survive and-- *choke!* -- even worse--
His herald has already marked this world with the Devourer's sigil...undetected by your primitive technology!
Lieutenant! Redirect scanners five parsecs behind our wake--
"As I feared! The Silver Surfer is coming to claim Earth for his Master!
"Broadcast to the fleet: All helmsmen must change course immediately! Get us out of this system!"
We must be gone long before the World-Eater arrives!
As for you four-- return to your leaders! Tell them that your world is doomed! Galactus's approach is imminent!
"You must evacuate your planet as soon as possible! We will await Earth's vessels to join our fleet..."

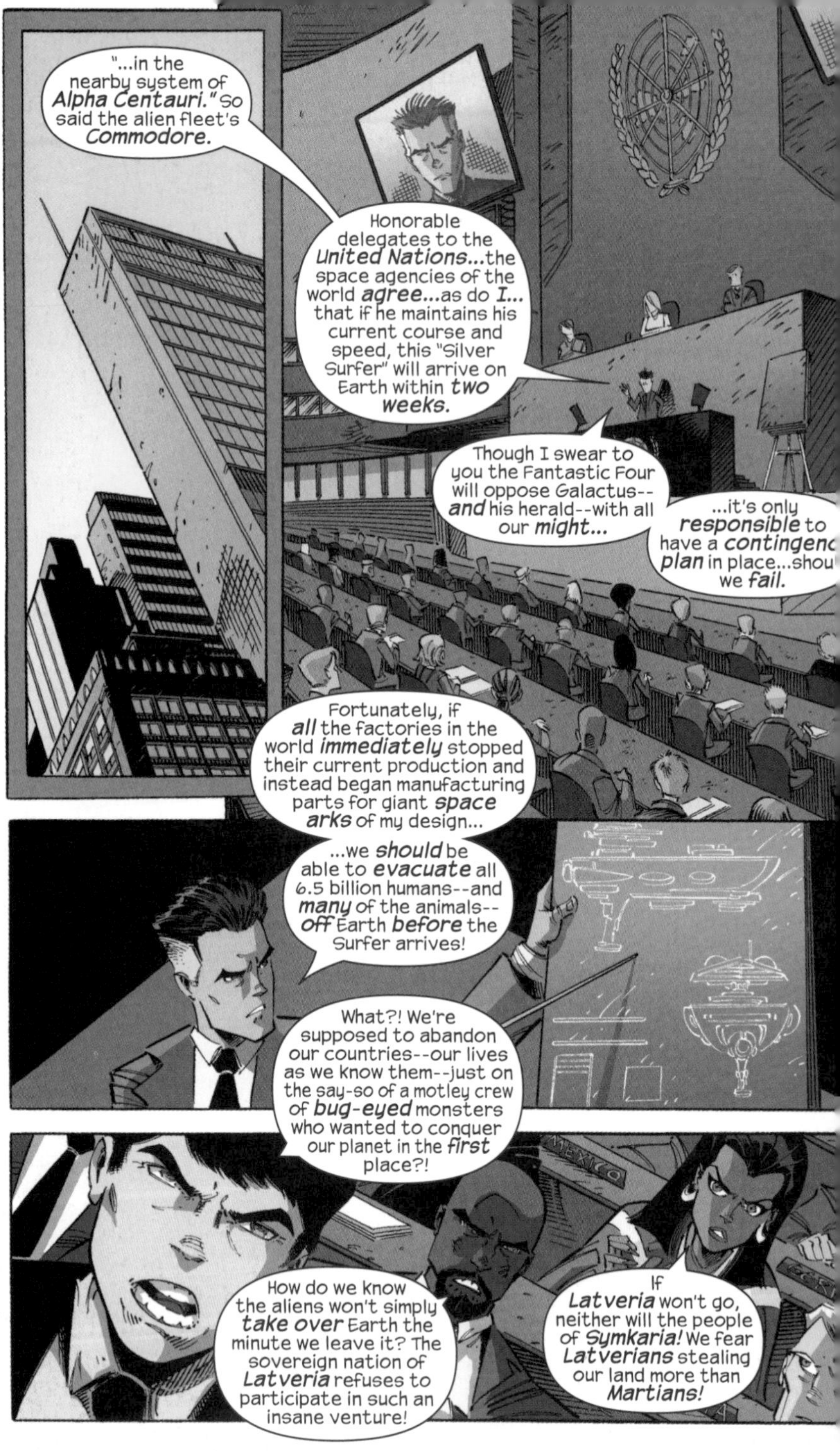
"...in the nearby system of Alpha Centauri." So said the alien fleet's Commodore.
Honorable delegates to the United Nations...the space agencies of the world agree...as do I... that if he maintains his current course and speed, this "Silver Surfer" will arrive on Earth within two weeks.
Though I swear to you the Fantastic Four will oppose Galactus-- and his herald--with all our might...
...it's only responsible to have a contingenc plan in place...shou we fail.
Fortunately, if all the factories in the world immediately stopped their current production and instead began manufacturing parts for giant space arks of my design...
...we should be able to evacuate all 6.5 billion humans--and many of the animals-- off Earth before the Surfer arrives!
What?! We're supposed to abandon our countries--our lives as we know them--just on the say-so of a motley crew of bug-eyed monsters who wanted to conquer our planet in the first place?!
MEXICO
How do we know the aliens won't simply take over Earth the minute we leave it? The sovereign nation of Latveria refuses to participate in such an insane venture!
If Latveria won't go, neither will the people of Symkaria! We fear Latverians stealing our land more than Martians!

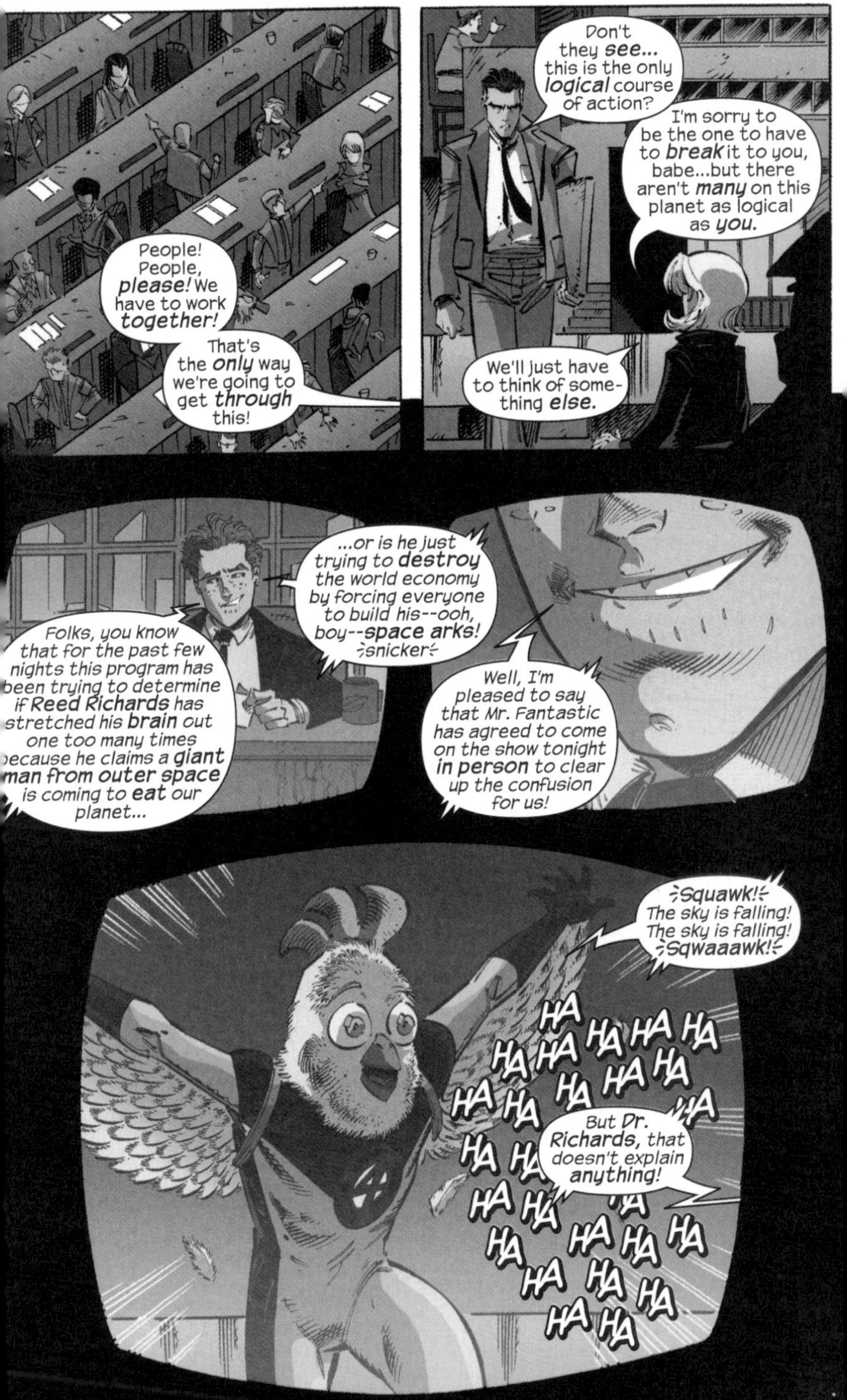
People! People, please! We have to work together!
That's the only way we're going to get through this!
Don't they see... this is the only logical course of action?
I'm sorry to be the one to have to break it to you, babe...but there aren't many on this planet as logical as you.
We'll just have to think of something else.
Folks, you know that for the past few nights this program has been trying to determine if Reed Richards has stretched his brain out one too many times because he claims a giant man from outer space is coming to eat our planet...
...or is he just trying to destroy the world economy by forcing everyone to build his--ooh, boy--space arks! snicker
Well, I'm pleased to say that Mr. Fantastic has agreed to come on the show tonight in person to clear up the confusion for us!
Squawk! The sky is falling! The sky is falling! Sqwaaawk!
HA HA HA HA HA HA HA HA HA HA HA HA HA HA HA HA HA HA HA HA HA HA HA HA HA HA HA HA HA HA HA HA
But Dr. Richards, that doesn't explain anything!

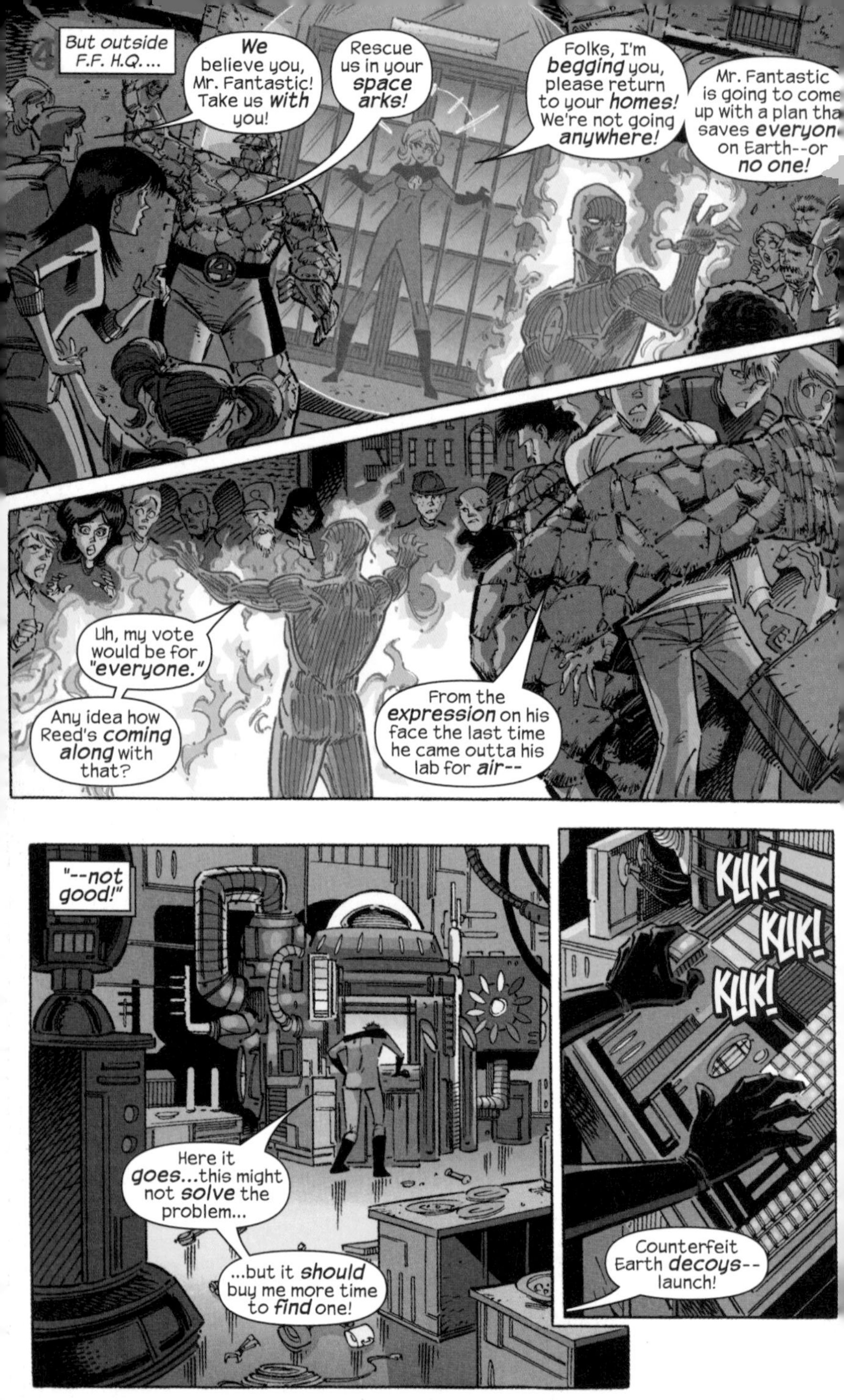
But outside F.F. H.Q....
We believe you, Mr. Fantastic! Take us with you!
Rescue us in your space arks!
Folks, I'm begging you, please return to your homes! We're not going anywhere!
Mr. Fantastic is going to come up with a plan that saves everyone on Earth--or no one!
Uh, my vote would be for "everyone."
Any idea how Reed's coming along with that?
From the expression on his face the last time he came outta his lab for air--
"--not good!"
Here it goes...this might not solve the problem...
...but it should buy me more time to find one!
KLIK! KLIK! KLIK!
Counterfeit Earth decoys--launch!

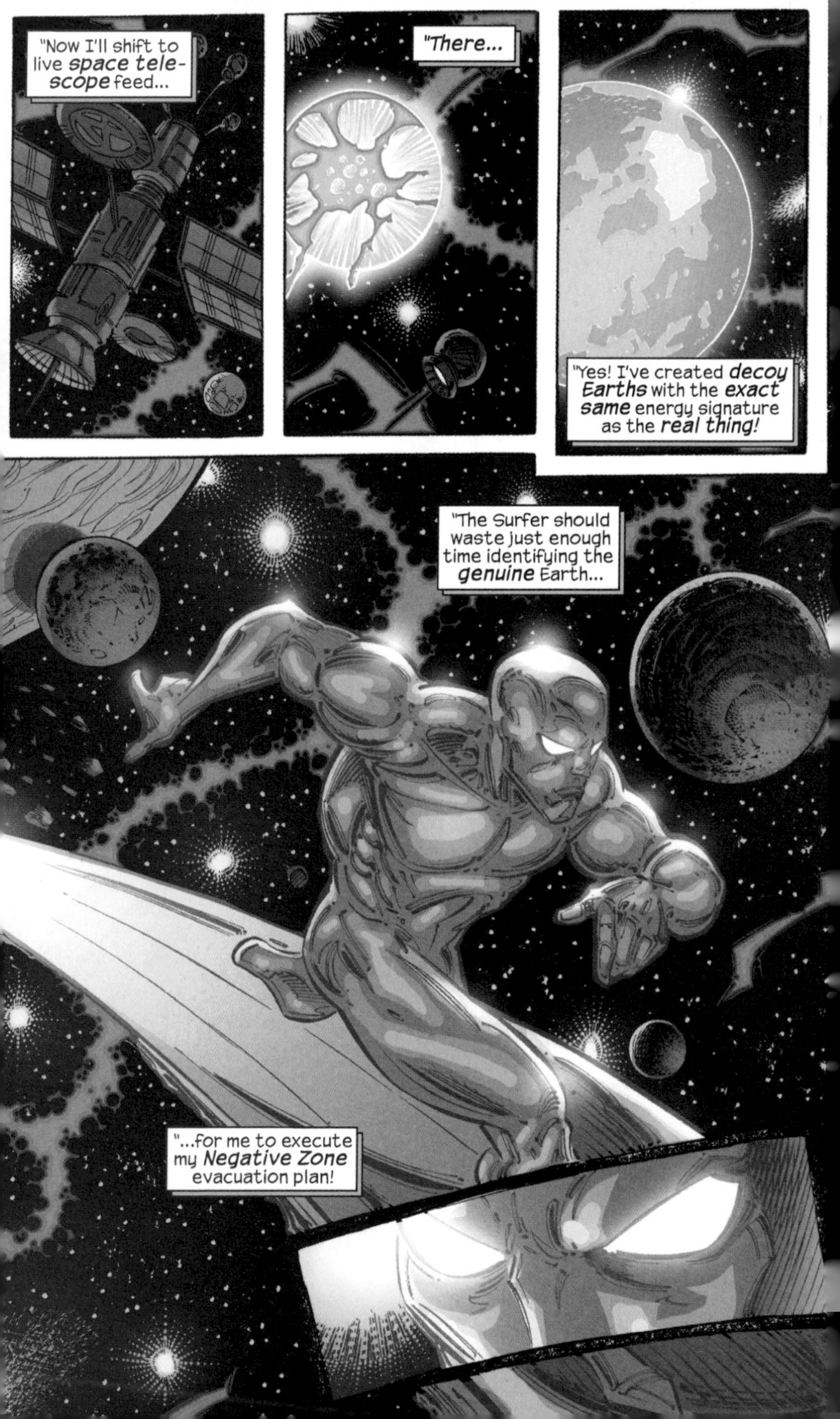
"Now I'll shift to live *space tele-scope* feed...
"There...
"Yes! I've created *decoy Earths* with the *exact same* energy signature as the *real thing!*
"The Surfer should waste just enough time identifying the *genuine* Earth...
"...for me to execute my *Negative Zone* evacuation plan!

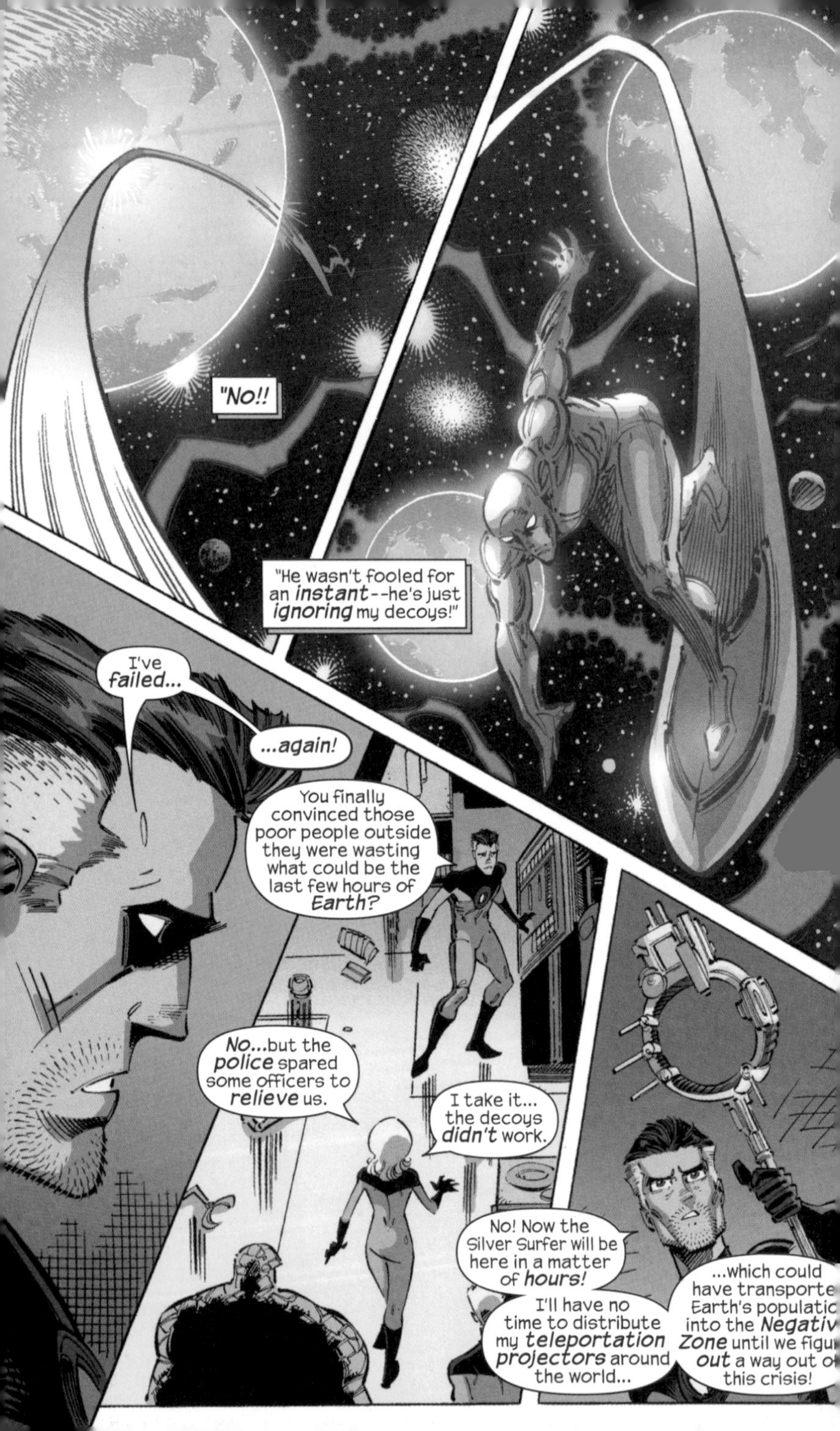
"No!!
"He wasn't fooled for an *instant*--he's just *ignoring* my decoys!"
I've *failed*...
...*again!*
You finally convinced those poor people outside they were wasting what could be the last few hours of *Earth?*
No...but the *police* spared some officers to *relieve* us.
I take it... the decoys *didn't* work.
No! Now the Silver Surfer will be here in a matter of *hours!*
I'll have no time to distribute my *teleportation projectors* around the world...
...which could have transporte Earth's populatic into the *Negativ Zone* until we figu *out* a way out o this crisis!

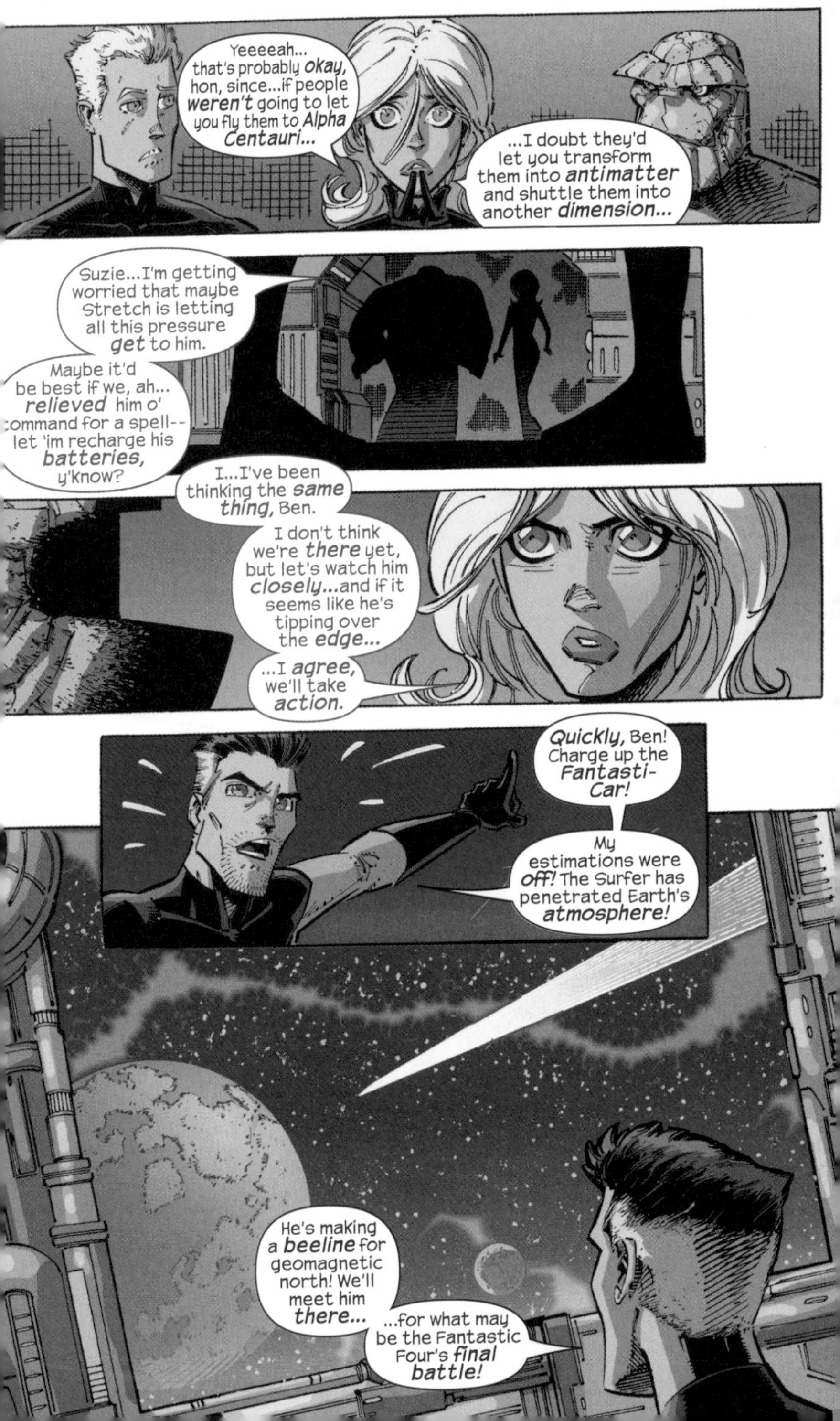
Yeeeeah... that's probably okay, hon, since...if people weren't going to let you fly them to Alpha Centauri...
...I doubt they'd let you transform them into antimatter and shuttle them into another dimension...
Suzie...I'm getting worried that maybe Stretch is letting all this pressure get to him.
Maybe it'd be best if we, ah... relieved him o' command for a spell-- let 'im recharge his batteries, y'know?
I...I've been thinking the same thing, Ben.
I don't think we're there yet, but let's watch him closely...and if it seems like he's tipping over the edge...
...I agree, we'll take action.
Quickly, Ben! Charge up the Fantasti-Car!
My estimations were off! The Surfer has penetrated Earth's atmosphere!
He's making a beeline for geomagnetic north! We'll meet him there...
...for what may be the Fantastic Four's final battle!

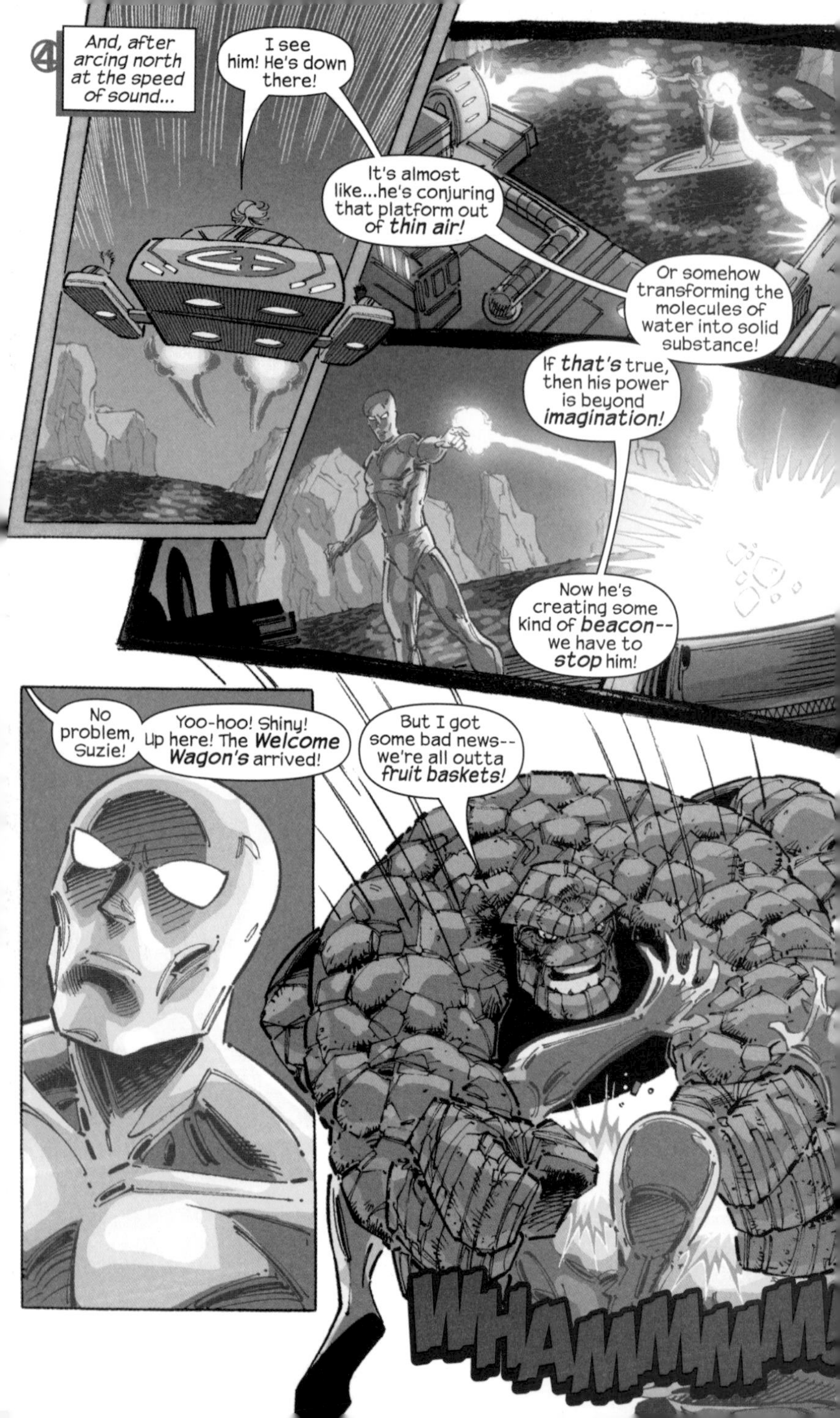
And, after arcing north at the speed of sound...
I see him! He's down there!
It's almost like...he's conjuring that platform out of thin air!
Or somehow transforming the molecules of water into solid substance!
If that's true, then his power is beyond imagination!
Now he's creating some kind of beacon-- we have to stop him!
No problem, Suzie!
Yoo-hoo! Shiny! Up here! The Welcome Wagon's arrived!
But I got some bad news-- we're all outta fruit baskets!
WHAMMMMM

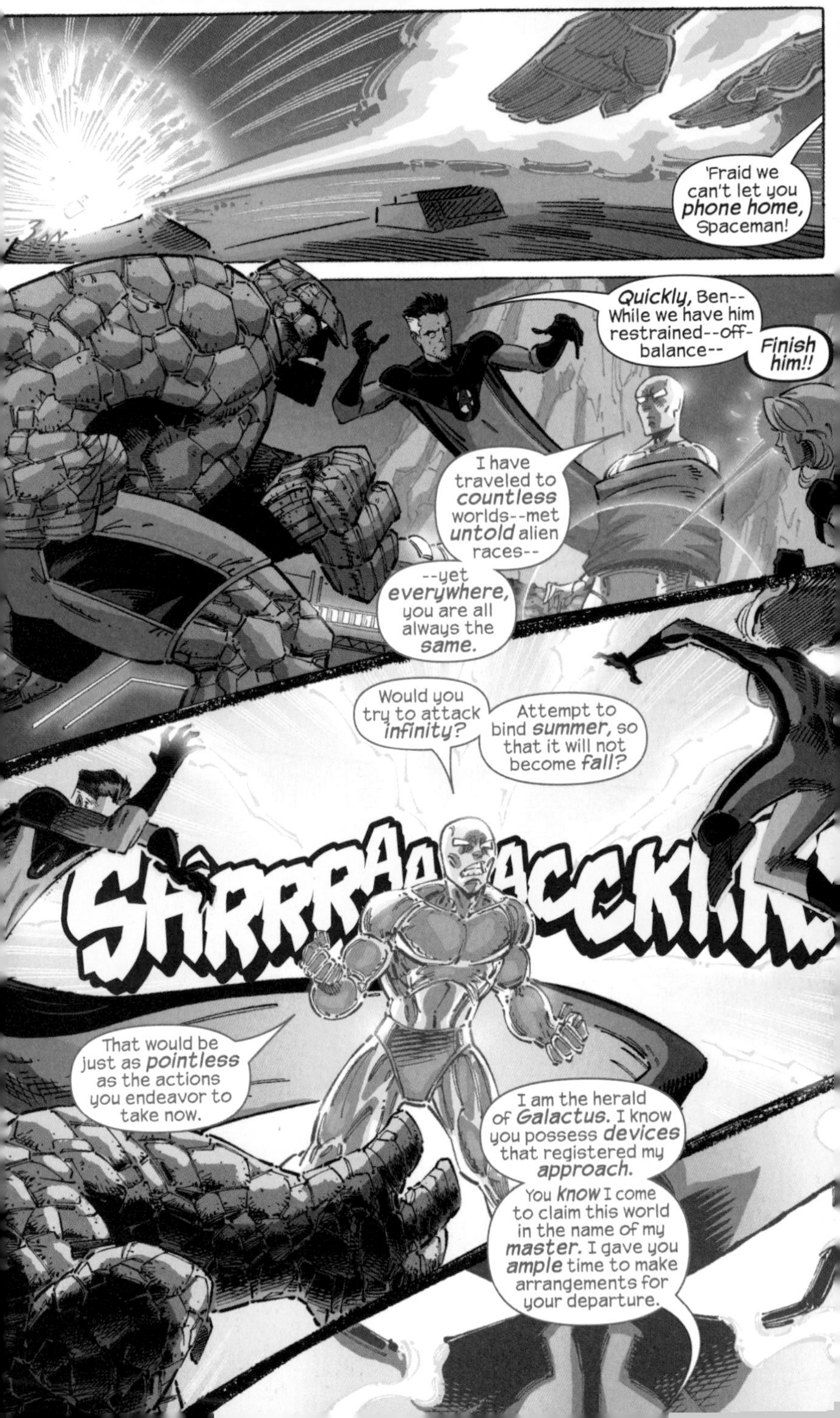

'Fraid we can't let you *phone home,* Spaceman!
Quickly, Ben-- While we have him restrained--off-balance--
Finish him!!
I have traveled to *countless* worlds--met *untold* alien races--
--yet *everywhere,* you are all always the *same.*
Would you try to attack *infinity?*
Attempt to bind *summer,* so that it will not become *fall?*
SHRRRAAAACCKKK
That would be just as *pointless* as the actions you endeavor to take now.
I am the herald of *Galactus.* I know you possess *devices* that registered my *approach.*
You *know* I come to claim this world in the name of my *master.* I gave you *ample* time to make arrangements for your departure.

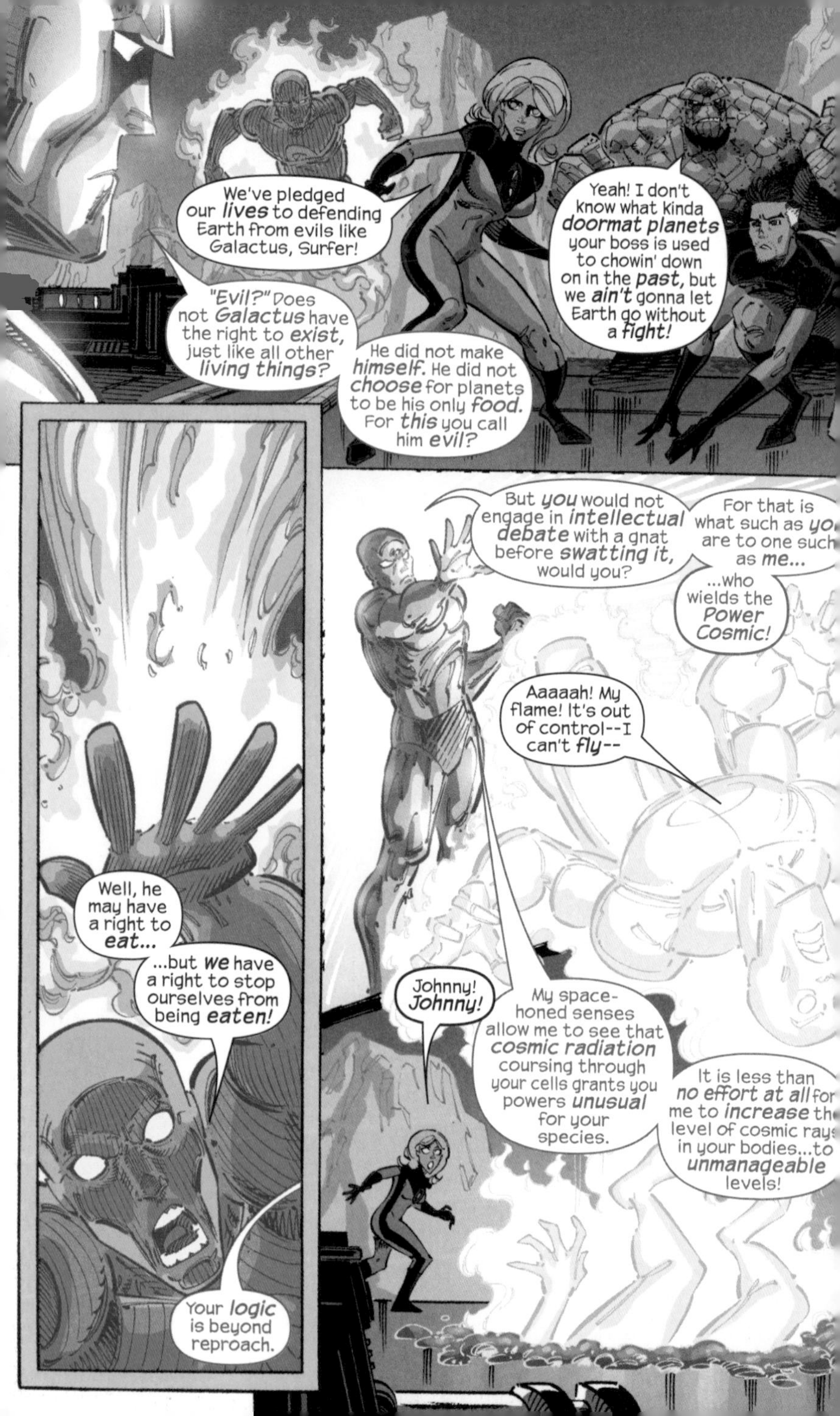

We've pledged our lives to defending Earth from evils like Galactus, Surfer!
Yeah! I don't know what kinda doormat planets your boss is used to chowin' down on in the past, but we ain't gonna let Earth go without a fight!
"Evil?" Does not Galactus have the right to exist, just like all other living things?
He did not make himself. He did not choose for planets to be his only food. For this you call him evil?
Well, he may have a right to eat...
...but we have a right to stop ourselves from being eaten!
Your logic is beyond reproach.
But you would not engage in intellectual debate with a gnat before swatting it, would you?
For that is what such as yo are to one such as me...
...who wields the Power Cosmic!
Aaaaah! My flame! It's out of control--I can't fly--
Johnny! Johnny!
My space-honed senses allow me to see that cosmic radiation coursing through your cells grants you powers unusual for your species.
It is less than no effort at all for me to increase th level of cosmic ray in your bodies...to unmanageable levels!

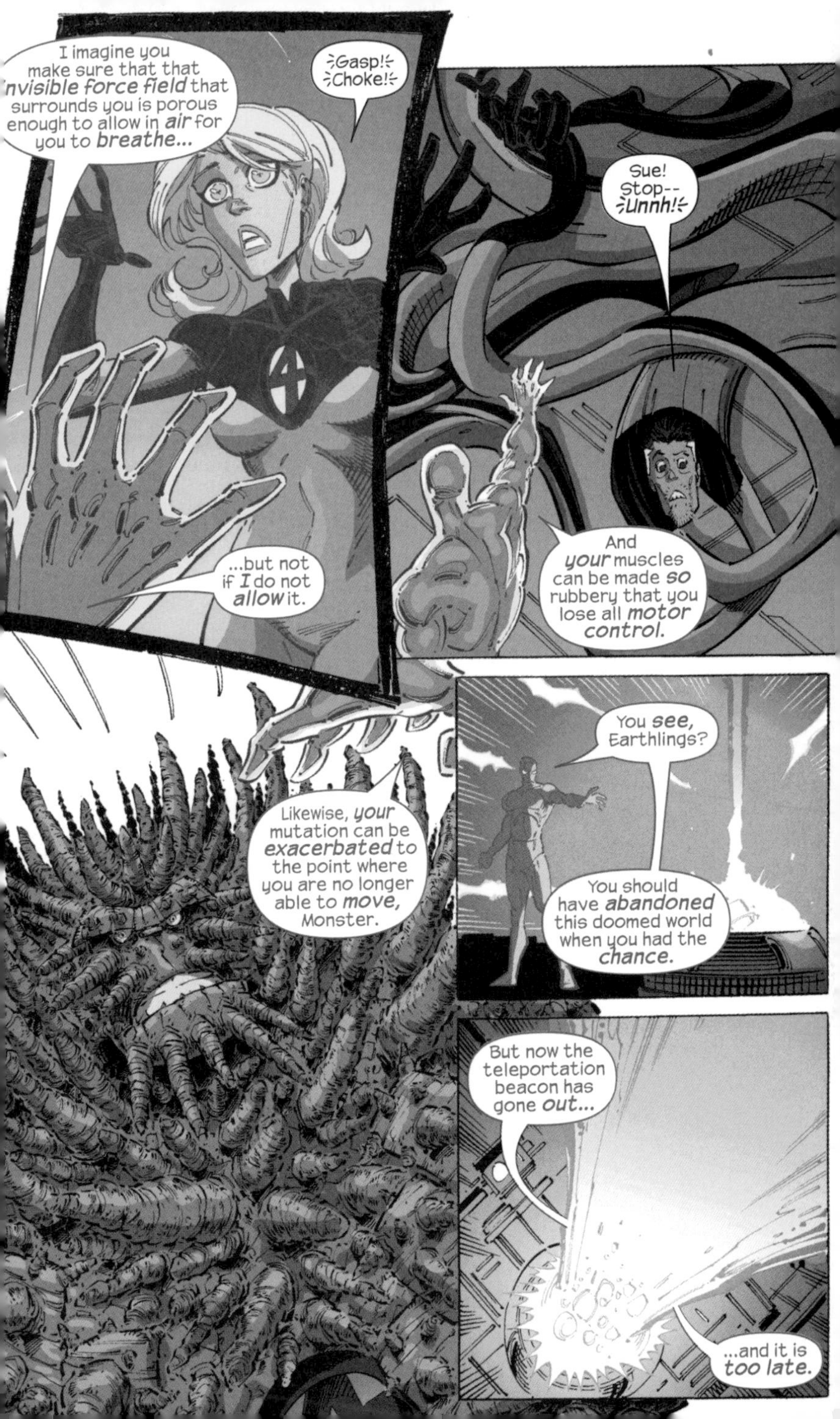
I imagine you make sure that that invisible force field that surrounds you is porous enough to allow in air for you to breathe...
Gasp! Choke!
...but not if I do not allow it.
Sue! Stop-- Unnh!
And your muscles can be made so rubbery that you lose all motor control.
Likewise, your mutation can be exacerbated to the point where you are no longer able to move, Monster.
You see, Earthlings?
You should have abandoned this doomed world when you had the chance.
But now the teleportation beacon has gone out...
...and it is too late.

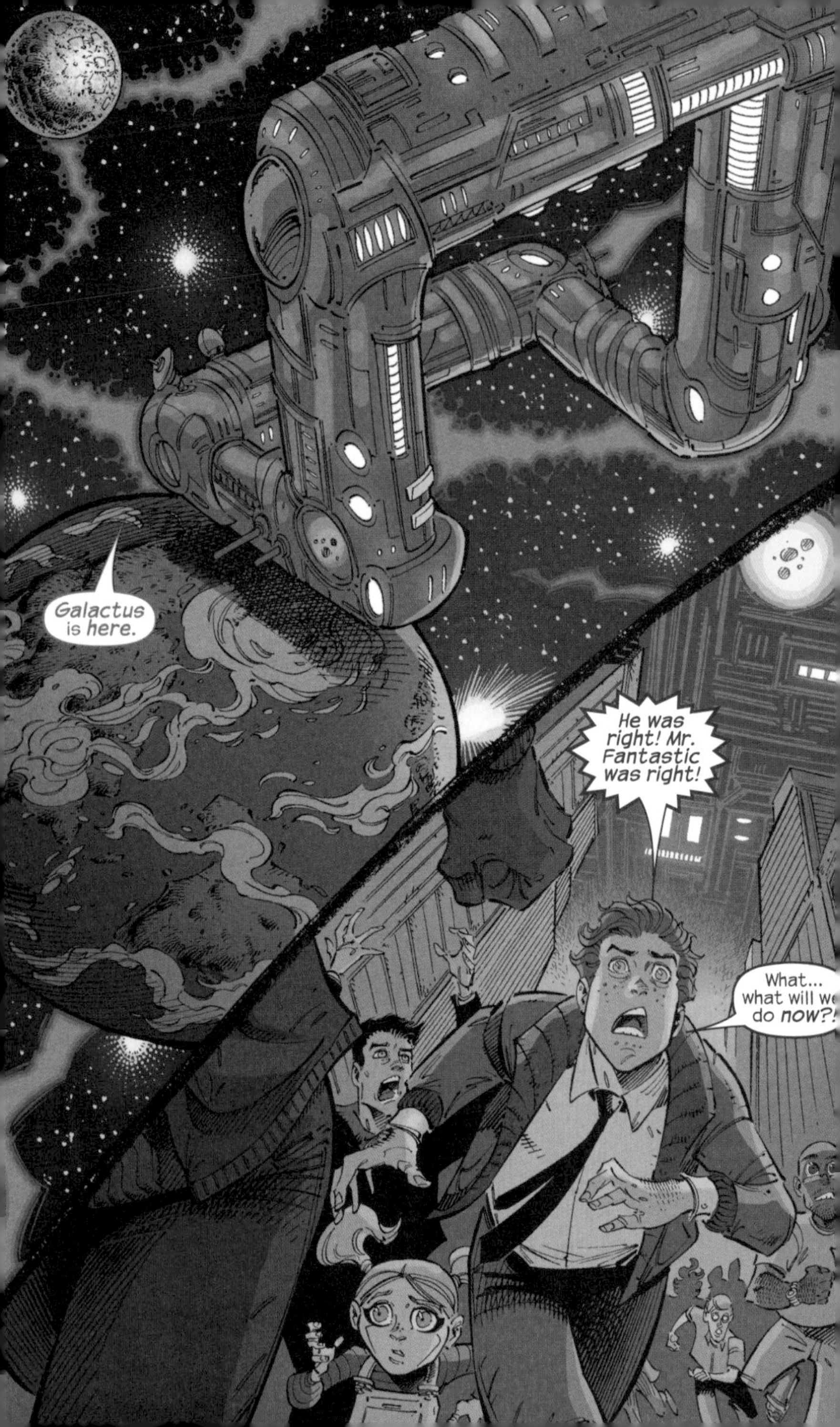
Galactus is here.
He was right! Mr. Fantastic was right!
What... what will we do now?!

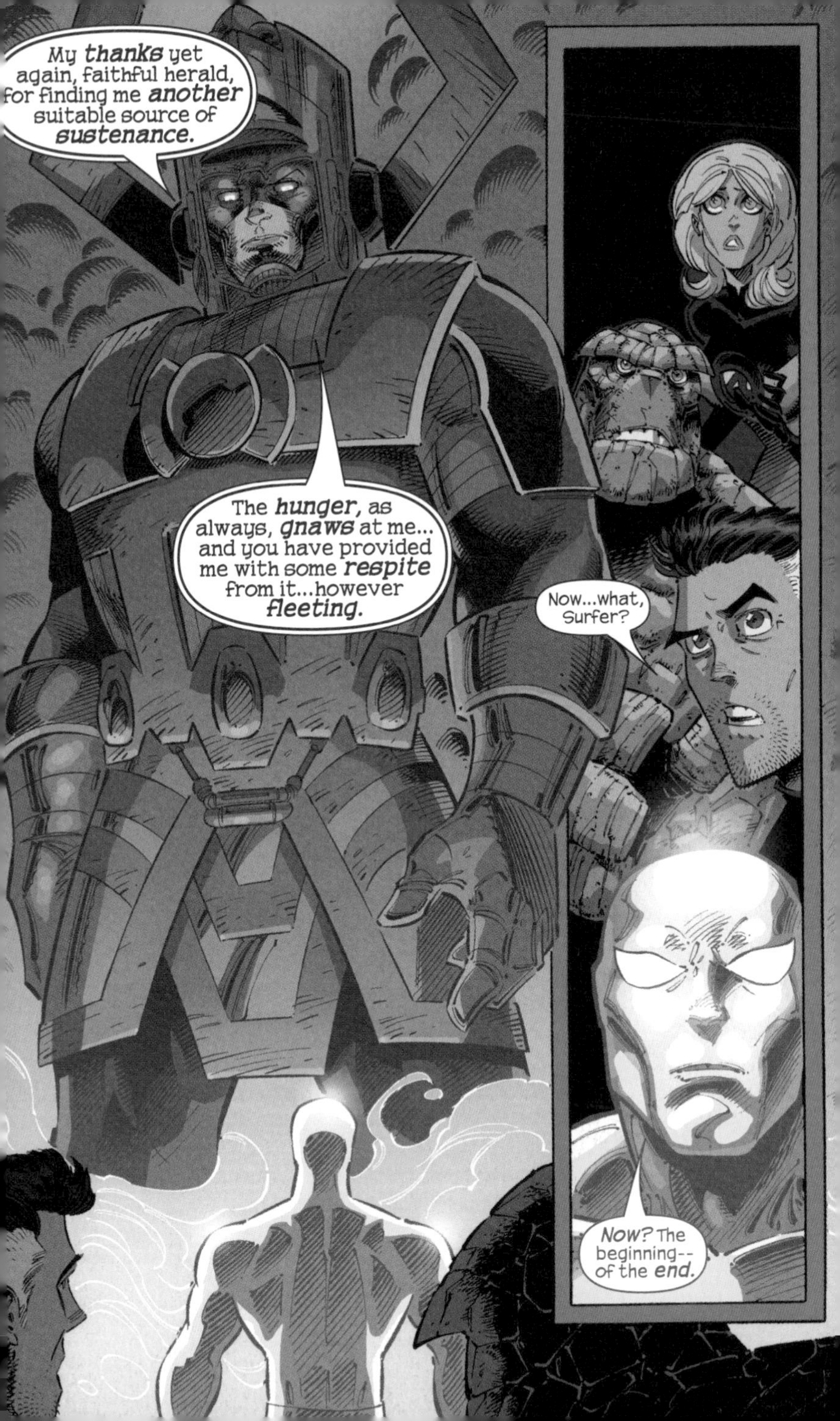

My thanks yet again, faithful herald, for finding me another suitable source of sustenance.
The hunger, as always, gnaws at me... and you have provided me with some respite from it...however fleeting.
Now...what, Surfer?
Now? The beginning-- of the end.

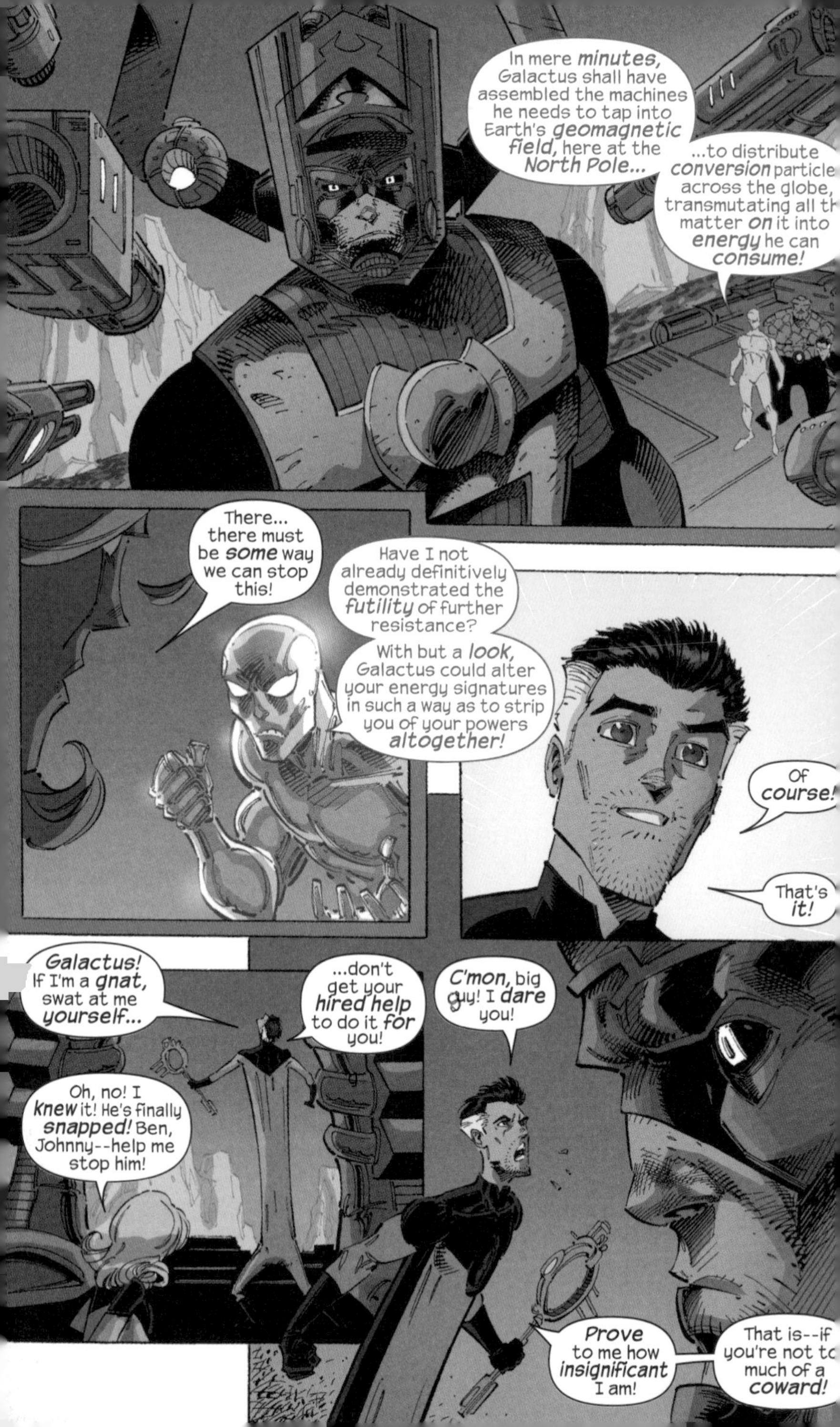
In mere minutes, Galactus shall have assembled the machines he needs to tap into Earth's geomagnetic field, here at the North Pole...
...to distribute conversion particle across the globe, transmutating all th matter on it into energy he can consume!
There... there must be some way we can stop this!
Have I not already definitively demonstrated the futility of further resistance?
With but a look, Galactus could alter your energy signatures in such a way as to strip you of your powers altogether!
Of course!
That's it!
Galactus! If I'm a gnat, swat at me yourself...
...don't get your hired help to do it for you!
C'mon, big guy! I dare you!
Oh, no! I knew it! He's finally snapped! Ben, Johnny--help me stop him!
Prove to me how insignificant I am!
That is--if you're not to much of a coward!

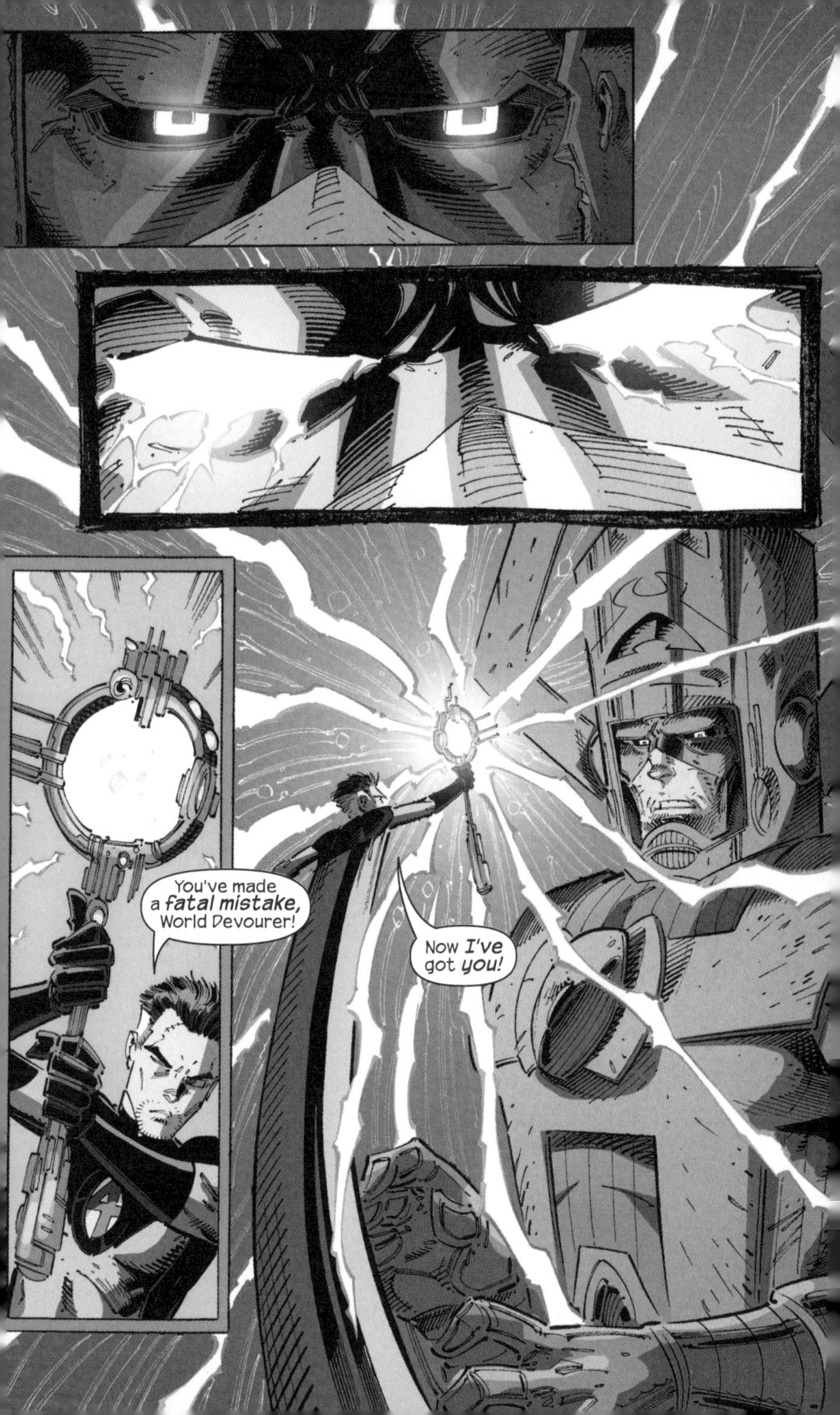
You've made a *fatal mistake,* World Devourer!
Now *I've* got *you!*

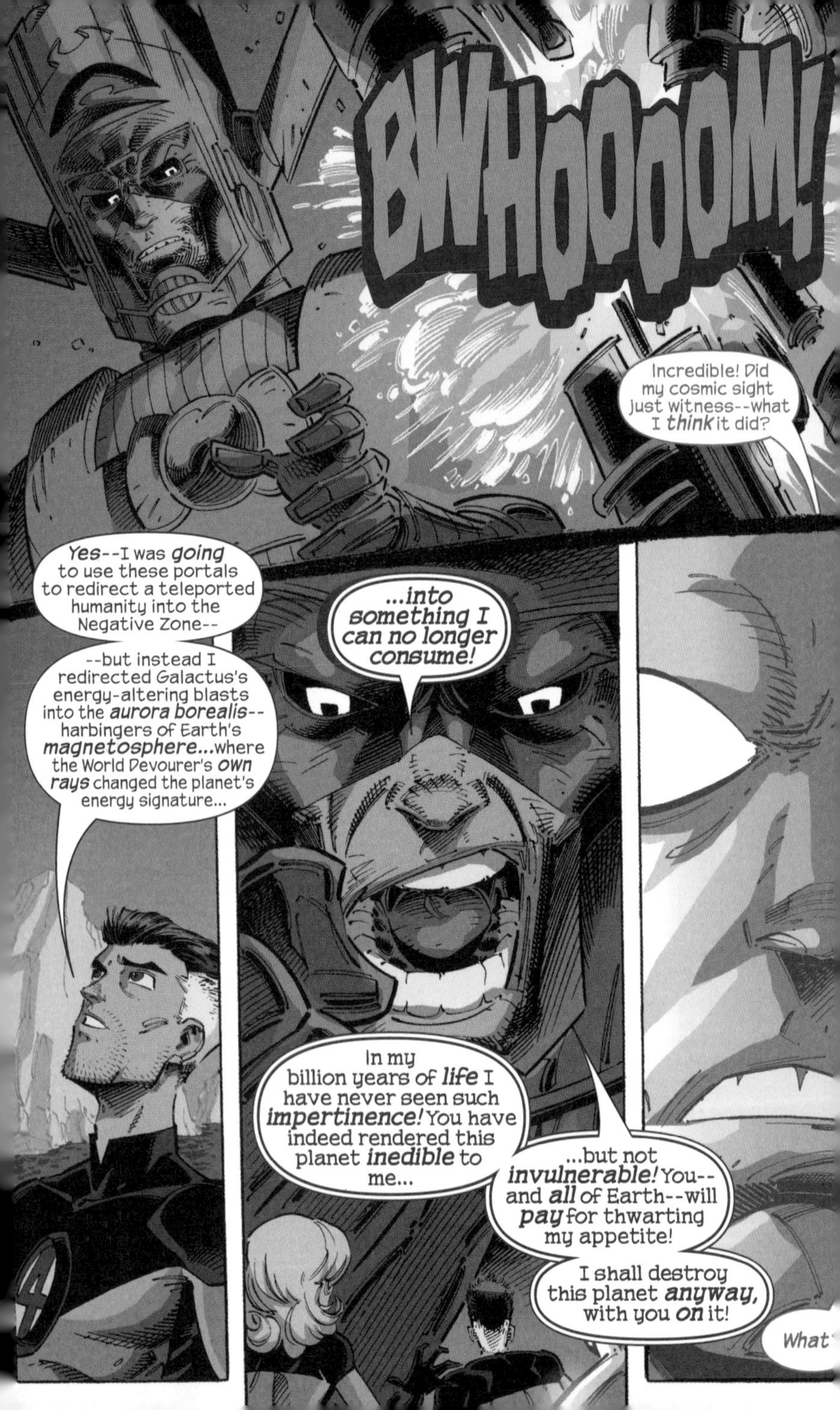
BWHOOOOOM!
Incredible! Did my cosmic sight just witness--what I *think* it did?
Yes--I was *going* to use these portals to redirect a teleported humanity into the Negative Zone--
--but instead I redirected Galactus's energy-altering blasts into the *aurora borealis*--harbingers of Earth's *magnetosphere...*where the World Devourer's *own rays* changed the planet's energy signature...
...into something I can no longer consume!
In my billion years of *life* I have never seen such *impertinence!* You have indeed rendered this planet *inedible* to me...
...but not *invulnerable!* You--and *all* of Earth--will *pay* for thwarting my appetite!
I shall destroy this planet *anyway,* with you *on* it!
What

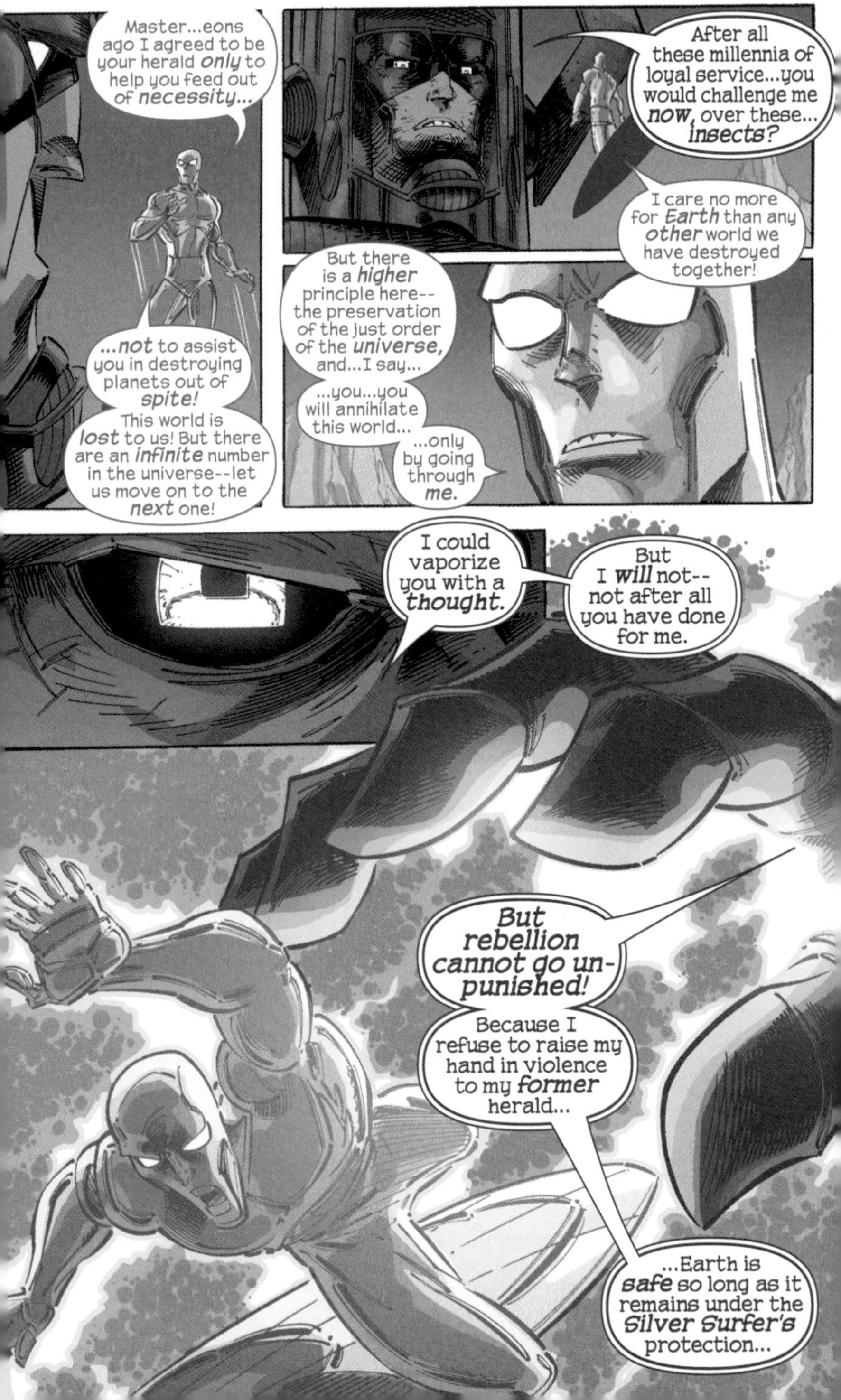

Master...eons ago I agreed to be your herald only to help you feed out of necessity...
...not to assist you in destroying planets out of spite!
This world is lost to us! But there are an infinite number in the universe--let us move on to the next one!
After all these millennia of loyal service...you would challenge me now, over these... insects?
I care no more for Earth than any other world we have destroyed together!
But there is a higher principle here--the preservation of the just order of the universe, and...I say...
...you...you will annihilate this world...
...only by going through me.
I could vaporize you with a thought.
But I will not--not after all you have done for me.
But rebellion cannot go un-punished!
Because I refuse to raise my hand in violence to my former herald...
...Earth is safe so long as it remains under the Silver Surfer's protection...

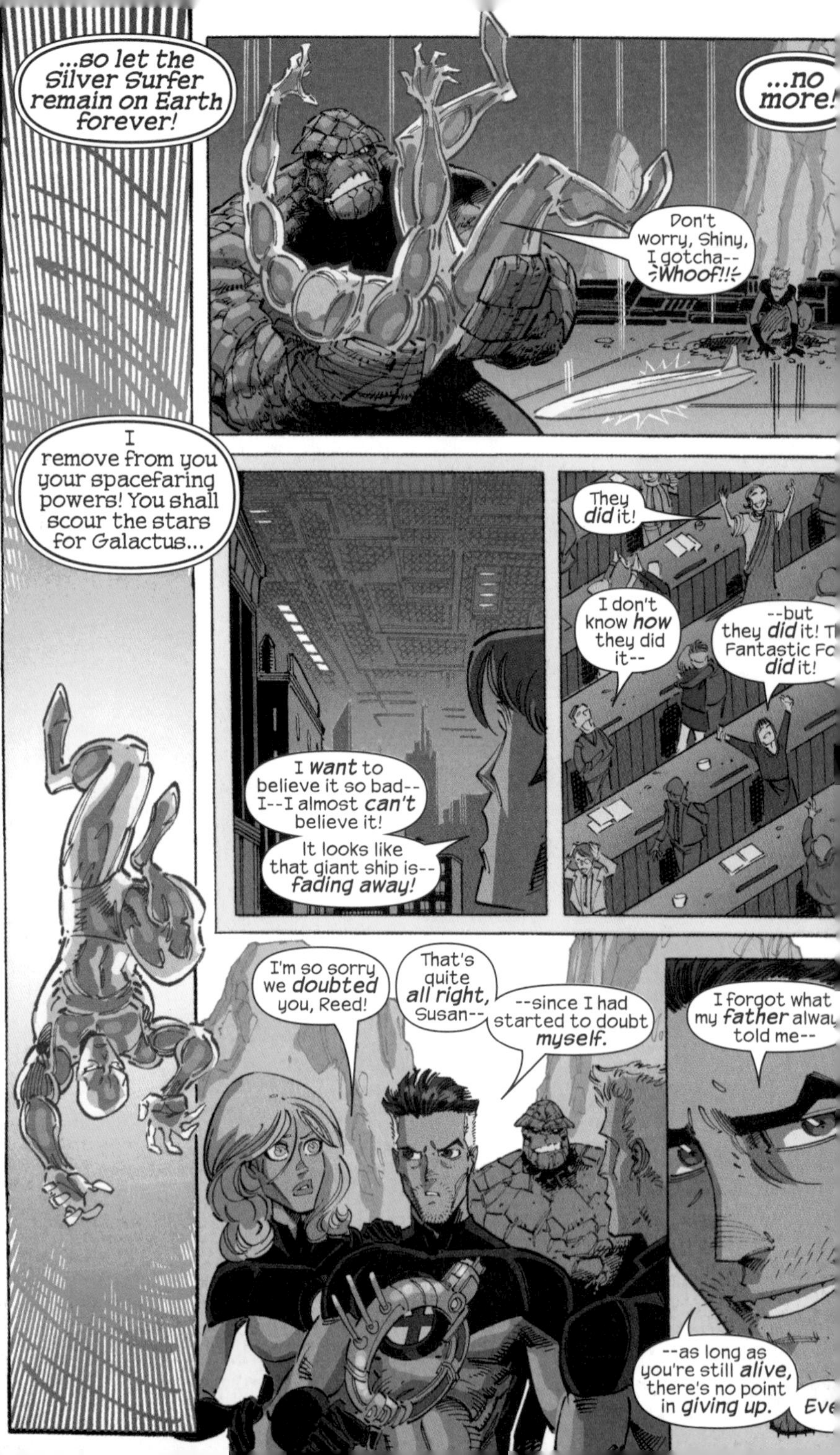
...so let the Silver Surfer remain on Earth forever!
...no more!
Don't worry, Shiny, I gotcha-- Whoof!!!
I remove from you your spacefaring powers! You shall scour the stars for Galactus...
I want to believe it so bad-- I--I almost can't believe it!
It looks like that giant ship is-- fading away!
They did it!
I don't know how they did it--
--but they did it!
I'm so sorry we doubted you, Reed!
That's quite all right, Susan--
--since I had started to doubt myself.
I forgot what my father always told me--
--as long as you're still alive, there's no point in giving up.

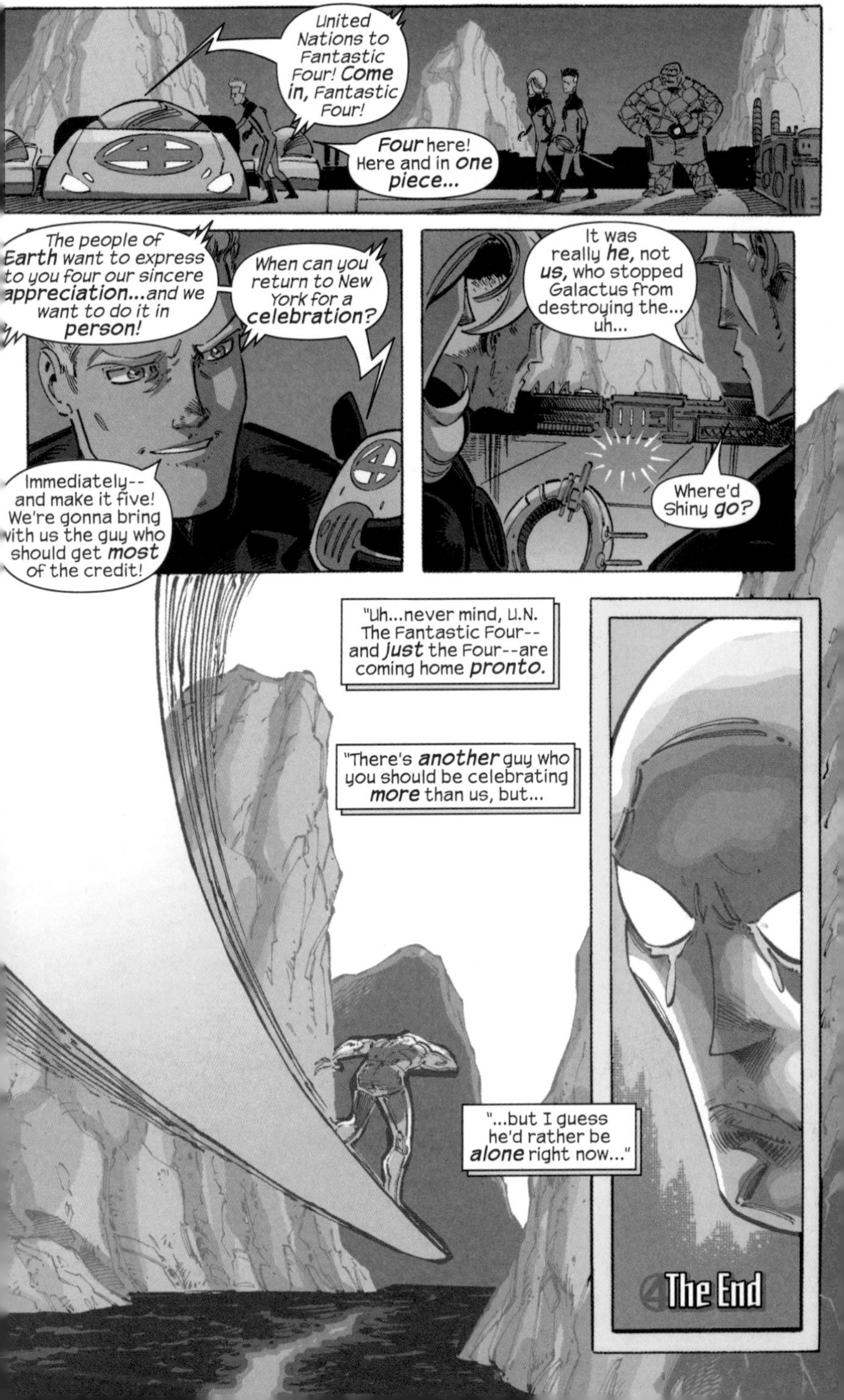
United Nations to Fantastic Four! Come in, Fantastic Four!
Four here! Here and in one piece...
The people of Earth want to express to you four our sincere appreciation...and we want to do it in person!
When can you return to New York for a celebration?
Immediately-- and make it five! We're gonna bring with us the guy who should get most of the credit!
It was really he, not us, who stopped Galactus from destroying the... uh...
Where'd Shiny go?
"Uh...never mind, U.N. The Fantastic Four-- and just the Four--are coming home pronto.
"There's another guy who you should be celebrating more than us, but...
"...but I guess he'd rather be alone right now..."
The End

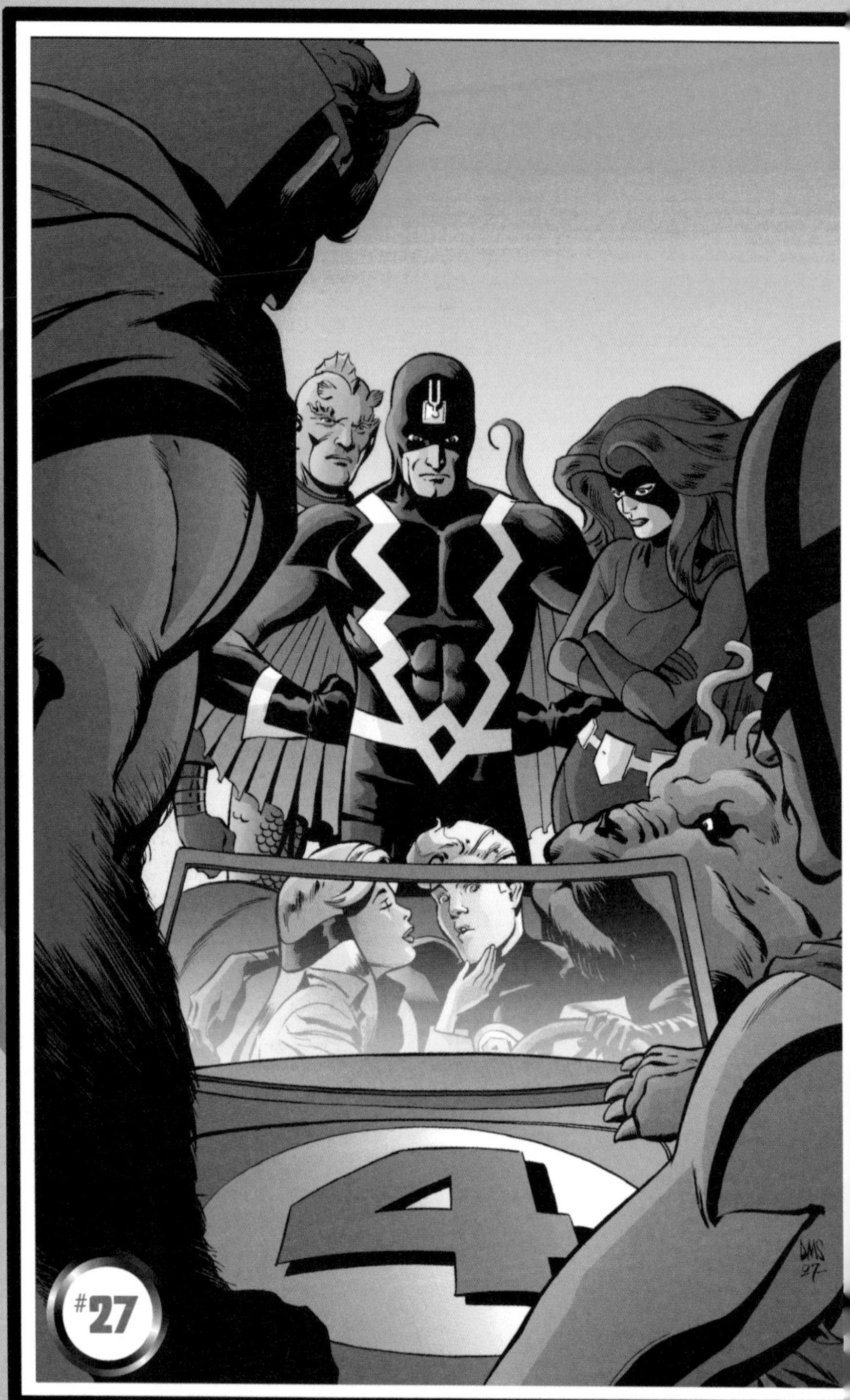
#27
DMS 07

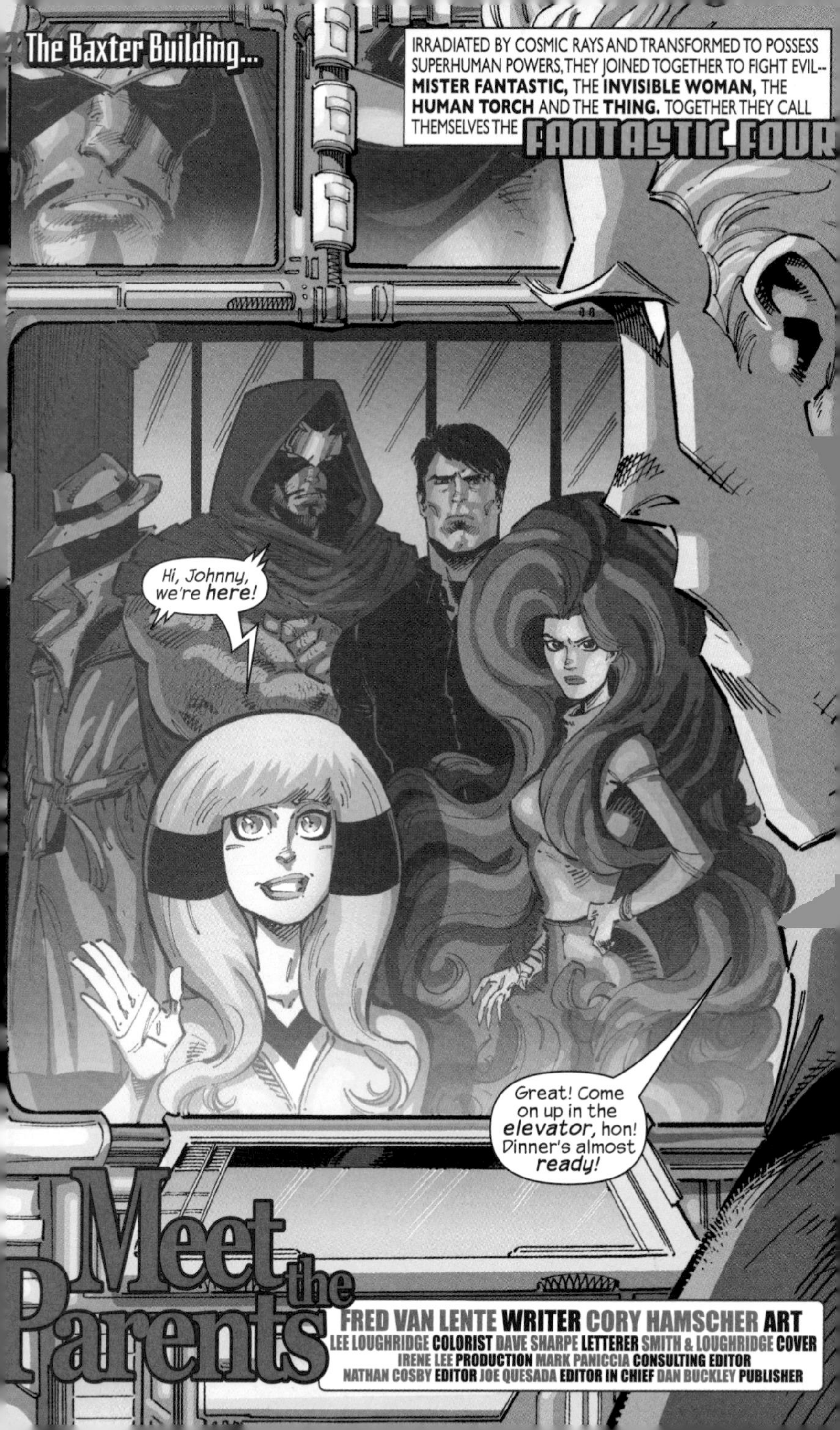

The Baxter Building...
IRRADIATED BY COSMIC RAYS AND TRANSFORMED TO POSSESS SUPERHUMAN POWERS, THEY JOINED TOGETHER TO FIGHT EVIL-- MISTER FANTASTIC, THE INVISIBLE WOMAN, THE HUMAN TORCH AND THE THING. TOGETHER THEY CALL THEMSELVES THE FANTASTIC FOUR
Hi, Johnny, we're here!
Great! Come on up in the elevator, hon! Dinner's almost ready!
Meet the Parents
FRED VAN LENTE WRITER CORY HAMSCHER ART
LEE LOUGHRIDGE COLORIST DAVE SHARPE LETTERER SMITH & LOUGHRIDGE COVER
IRENE LEE PRODUCTION MARK PANICCIA CONSULTING EDITOR
NATHAN COSBY EDITOR JOE QUESADA EDITOR IN CHIEF DAN BUCKLEY PUBLISHER

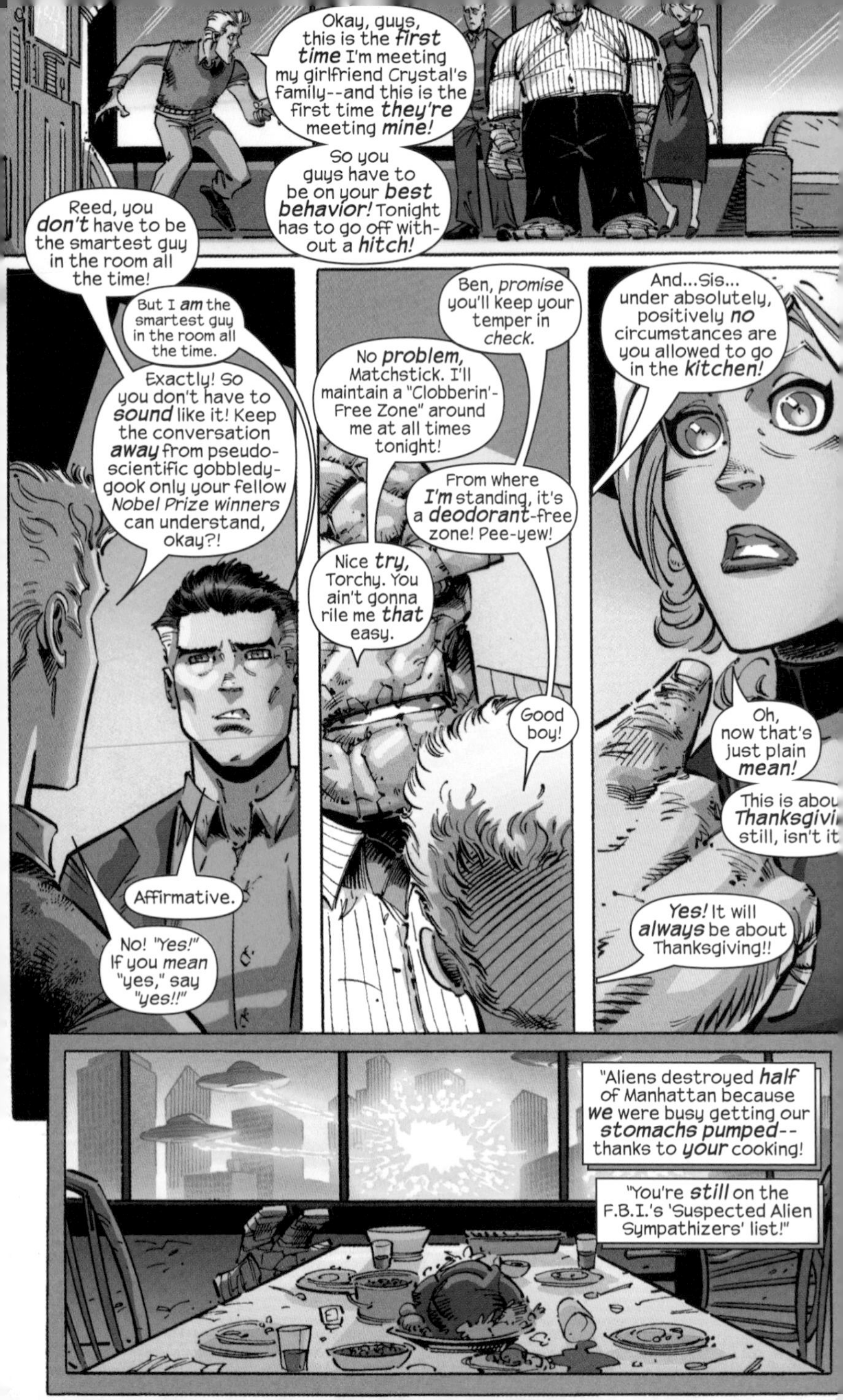

Okay, guys, this is the first time I'm meeting my girlfriend Crystal's family--and this is the first time they're meeting mine!
So you guys have to be on your best behavior! Tonight has to go off without a hitch!
Reed, you don't have to be the smartest guy in the room all the time!
But I am the smartest guy in the room all the time.
Exactly! So you don't have to sound like it! Keep the conversation away from pseudo-scientific gobbledygook only your fellow Nobel Prize winners can understand, okay?!
Affirmative.
No! "Yes!" If you mean "yes," say "yes!!"
Ben, promise you'll keep your temper in check.
No problem, Matchstick. I'll maintain a "Clobberin'-Free Zone" around me at all times tonight!
From where I'm standing, it's a deodorant-free zone! Pee-yew!
Nice try, Torchy. You ain't gonna rile me that easy.
Good boy!
And...Sis... under absolutely, positively no circumstances are you allowed to go in the kitchen!
Oh, now that's just plain mean!
This is abou Thanksgivi still, isn't it
Yes! It will always be about Thanksgiving!!
"Aliens destroyed half of Manhattan because we were busy getting our stomachs pumped--thanks to your cooking!
"You're still on the F.B.I.'s 'Suspected Alien Sympathizers' list!"

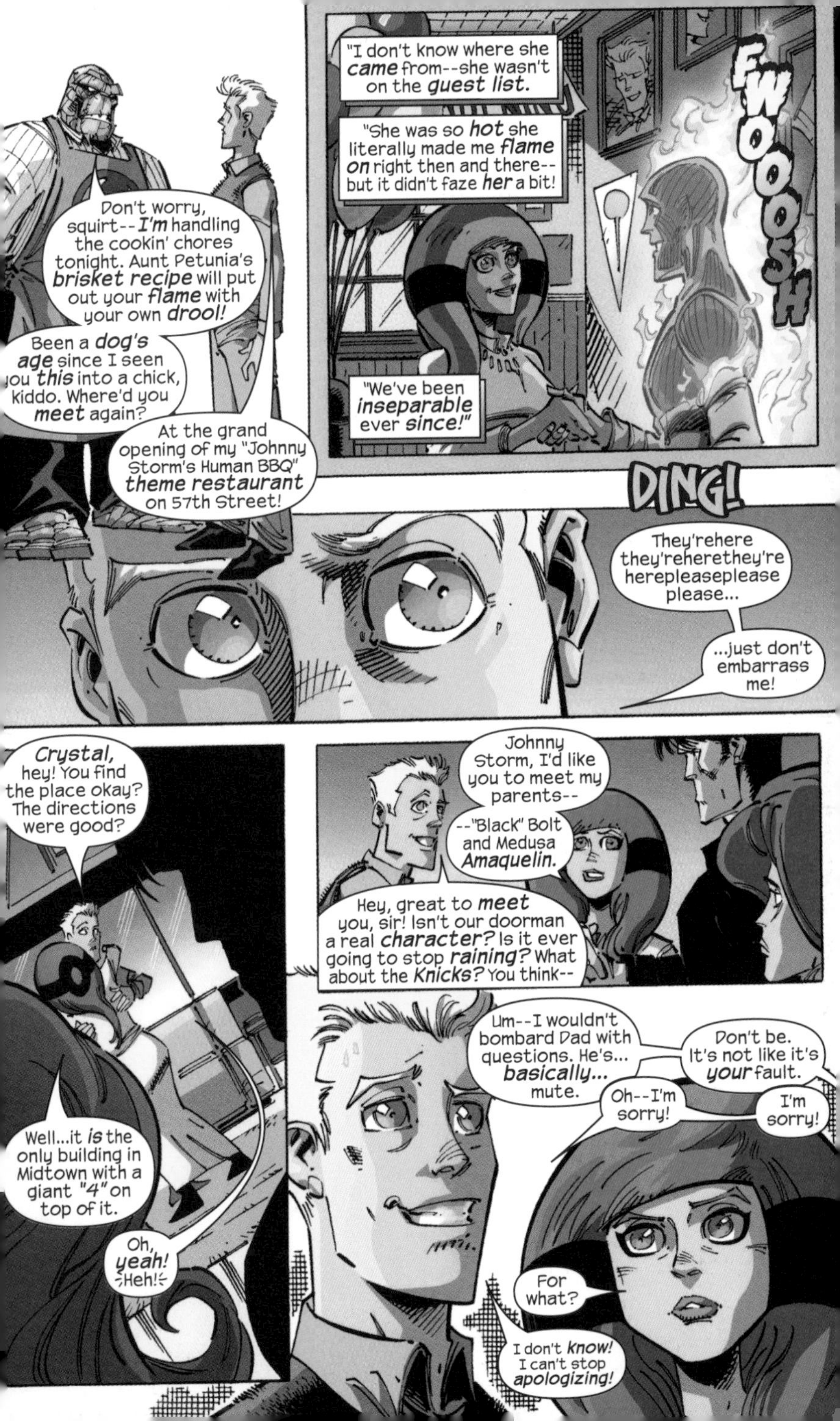

Don't worry, squirt--I'm handling the cookin' chores tonight. Aunt Petunia's brisket recipe will put out your flame with your own drool!
Been a dog's age since I seen you this into a chick, kiddo. Where'd you meet again?
At the grand opening of my "Johnny Storm's Human BBQ" theme restaurant on 57th Street!
"I don't know where she came from--she wasn't on the guest list.
"She was so hot she literally made me flame on right then and there--but it didn't faze her a bit!
FWOOOOSH
"We've been inseparable ever since!"
DING!
They'rehere they'reherethey're herepleaseplease please...
...just don't embarrass me!
Crystal, hey! You find the place okay? The directions were good?
Well...it is the only building in Midtown with a giant "4" on top of it.
Oh, yeah! Heh!
Johnny Storm, I'd like you to meet my parents--
--"Black" Bolt and Medusa Amaquelin.
Hey, great to meet you, sir! Isn't our doorman a real character? Is it ever going to stop raining? What about the Knicks? You think--
Um--I wouldn't bombard Dad with questions. He's... basically... mute.
Oh--I'm sorry!
Don't be. It's not like it's your fault.
I'm sorry!
For what?
I don't know! I can't stop apologizing!

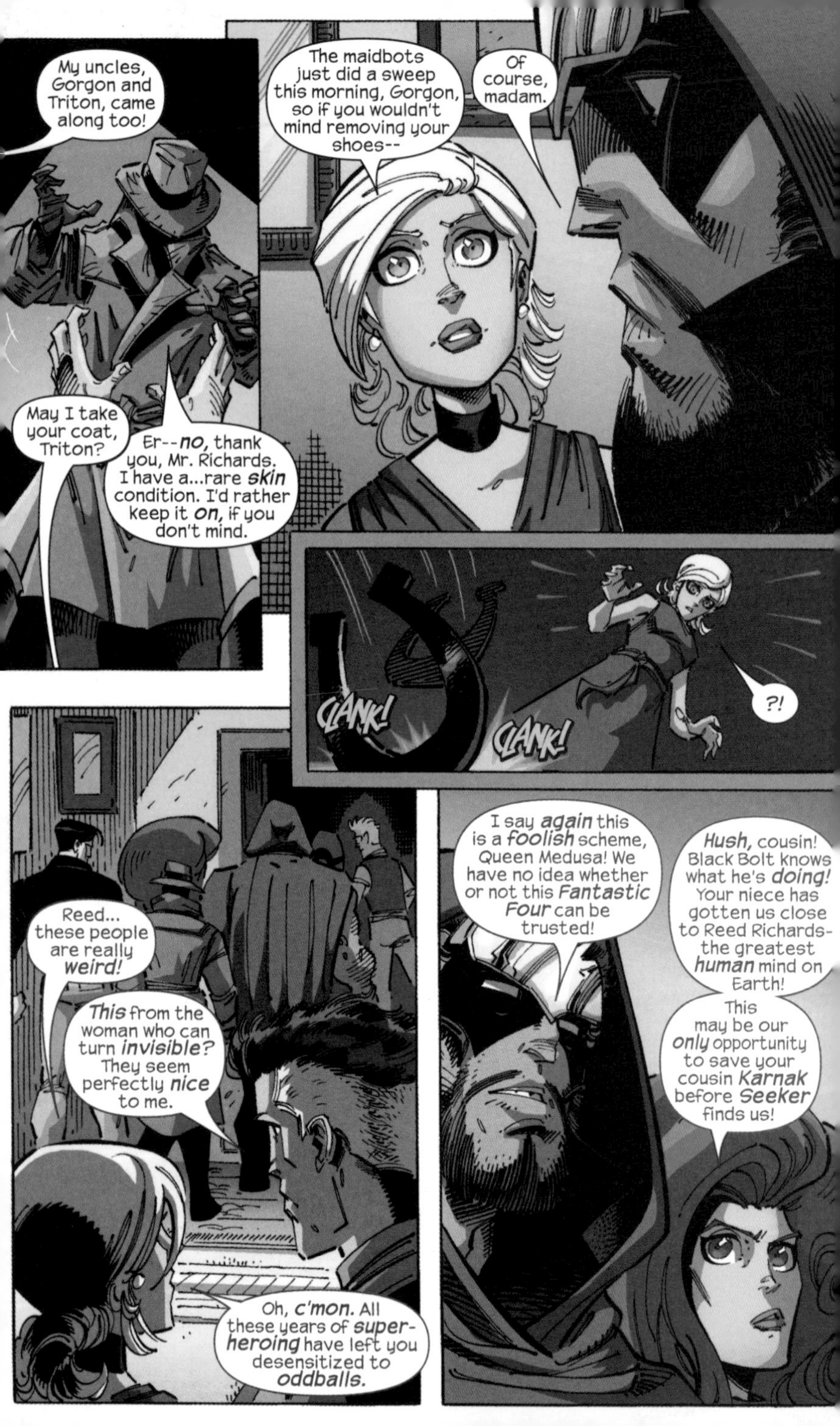

My uncles, Gorgon and Triton, came along too!
The maidbots just did a sweep this morning, Gorgon, so if you wouldn't mind removing your shoes--
Of course, madam.
May I take your coat, Triton?
Er--no, thank you, Mr. Richards. I have a...rare skin condition. I'd rather keep it on, if you don't mind.
CLANK!
CLANK!
?!
Reed... these people are really weird!
This from the woman who can turn invisible? They seem perfectly nice to me.
Oh, c'mon. All these years of super-heroing have left you desensitized to oddballs.
I say again this is a foolish scheme, Queen Medusa! We have no idea whether or not this Fantastic Four can be trusted!
Hush, cousin! Black Bolt knows what he's doing! Your niece has gotten us close to Reed Richards-the greatest human mind on Earth!
This may be our only opportunity to save your cousin Karnak before Seeker finds us!

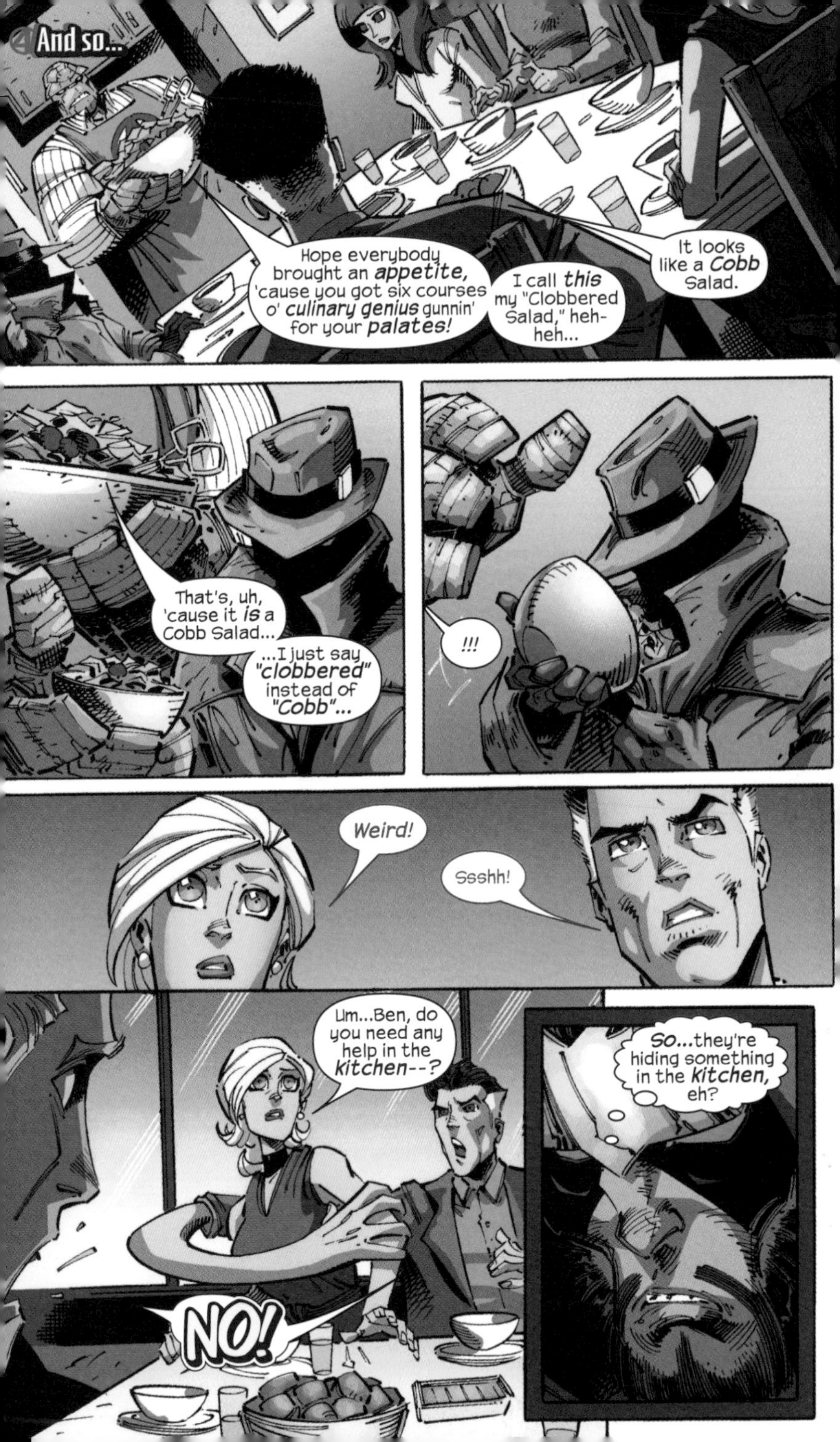

And so...
Hope everybody brought an *appetite,* 'cause you got six courses o' *culinary genius* gunnin' for your *palates!*
I call *this* my "Clobbered Salad," heh-heh...
It looks like a *Cobb* Salad.
That's, uh, 'cause it *is* a Cobb Salad...
...I just say *"clobbered"* instead of *"Cobb"*...
!!!
Weird!
Ssshh!
Um...Ben, do you need any help in the *kitchen--?*
NO!
*So...*they're hiding something in the *kitchen,* eh?

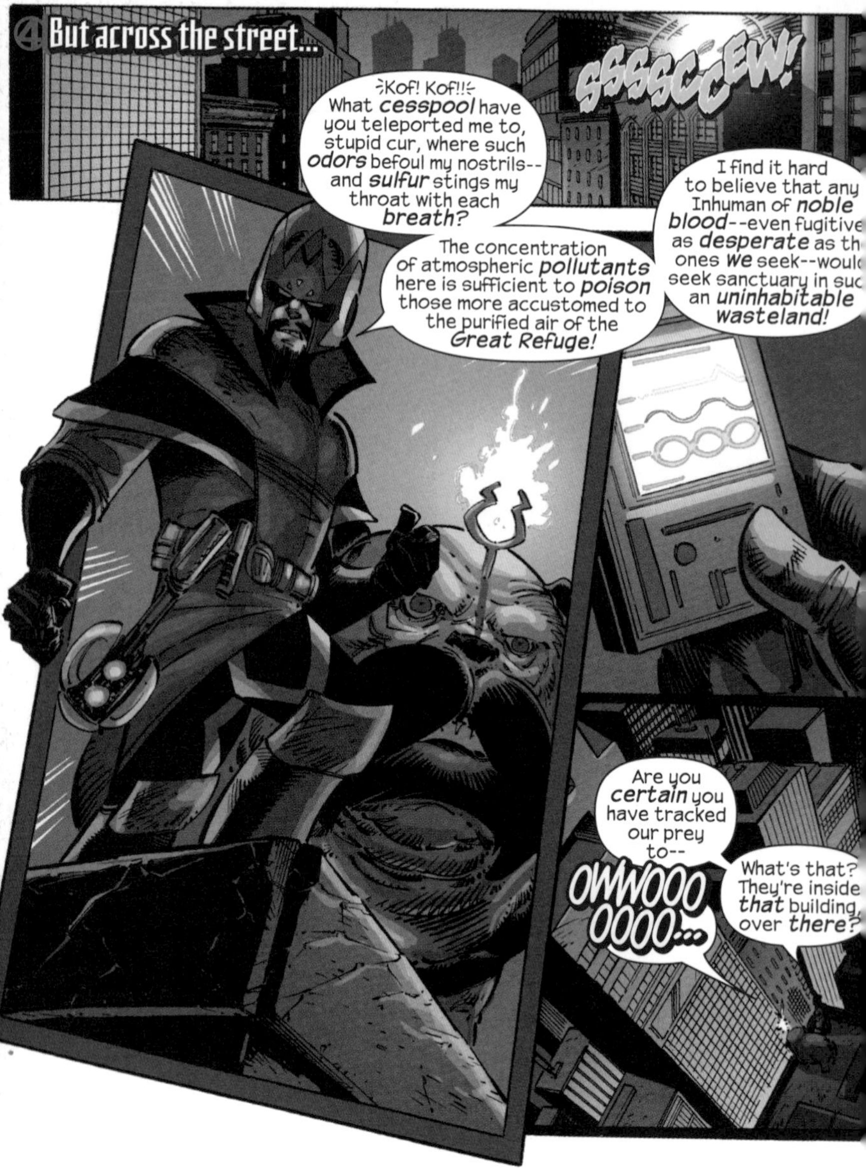
But across the street...
SSSSCCEW!
Kof! Kof!! What cesspool have you teleported me to, stupid cur, where such odors befoul my nostrils--and sulfur stings my throat with each breath?
The concentration of atmospheric pollutants here is sufficient to poison those more accustomed to the purified air of the Great Refuge!
I find it hard to believe that any Inhuman of noble blood--even fugitive as desperate as th ones we seek--woul seek sanctuary in suc an uninhabitable wasteland!
Are you certain you have tracked our prey to--
OWWOOO OOOO...
What's that? They're inside that building, over there?

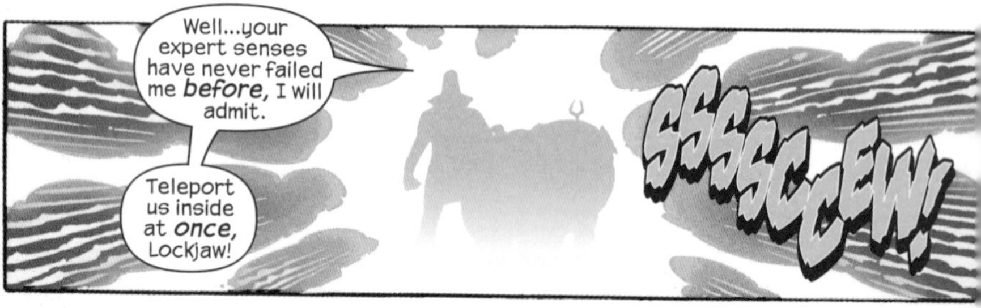
Well...your expert senses have never failed me before, I will admit.
Teleport us inside at once, Lockjaw!
SSSSCCEW!

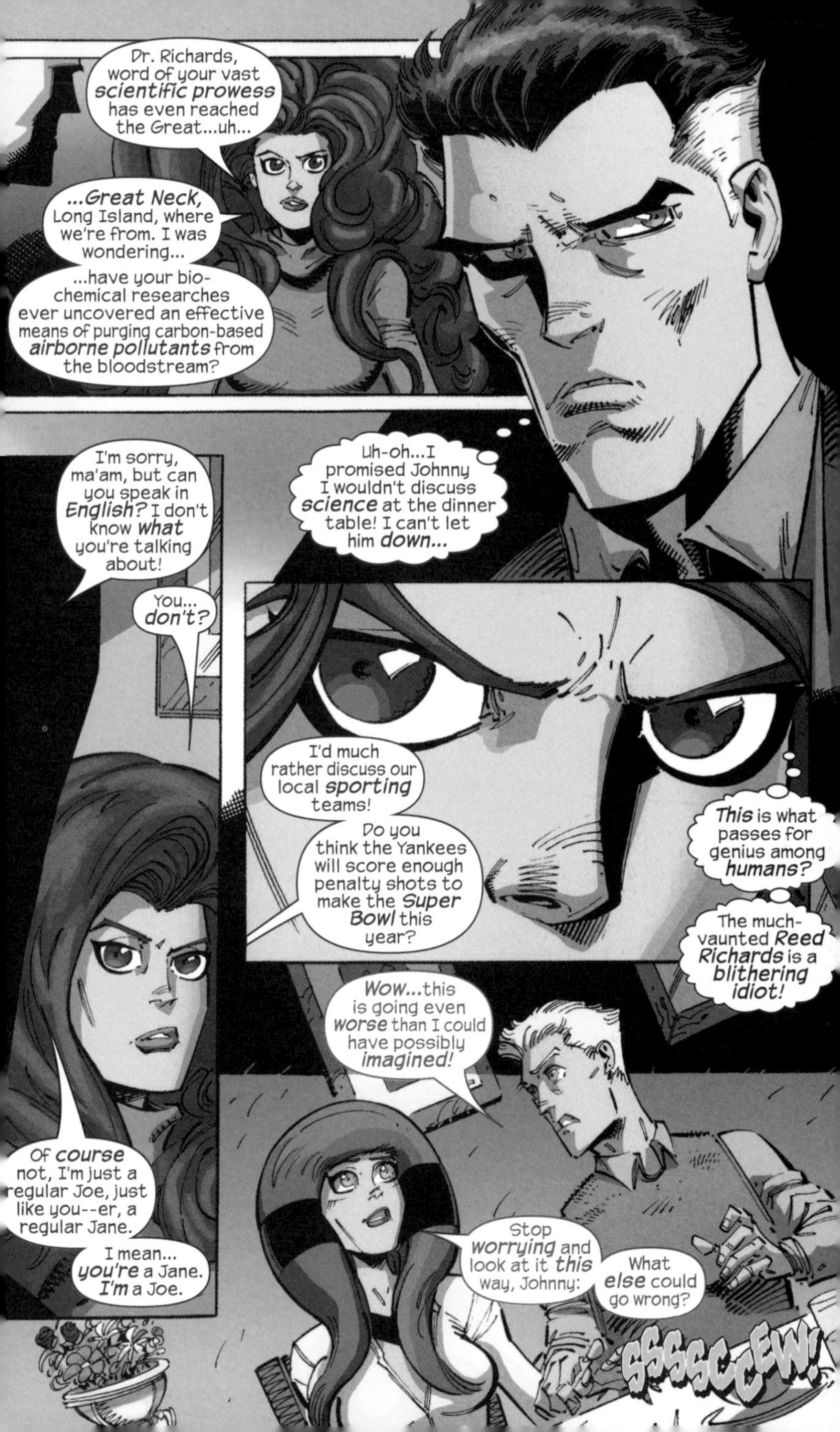
Dr. Richards, word of your vast scientific prowess has even reached the Great...uh...
...Great Neck, Long Island, where we're from. I was wondering...
...have your bio-chemical researches ever uncovered an effective means of purging carbon-based airborne pollutants from the bloodstream?
Uh-oh...I promised Johnny I wouldn't discuss science at the dinner table! I can't let him down...
I'm sorry, ma'am, but can you speak in English? I don't know what you're talking about!
You... don't?
I'd much rather discuss our local sporting teams!
Do you think the Yankees will score enough penalty shots to make the Super Bowl this year?
This is what passes for genius among humans?
The much-vaunted Reed Richards is a blithering idiot!
Of course not, I'm just a regular Joe, just like you--er, a regular Jane.
I mean... you're a Jane. I'm a Joe.
Wow...this is going even worse than I could have possibly imagined!
Stop worrying and look at it this way, Johnny:
What else could go wrong?
SSSSCCEW!

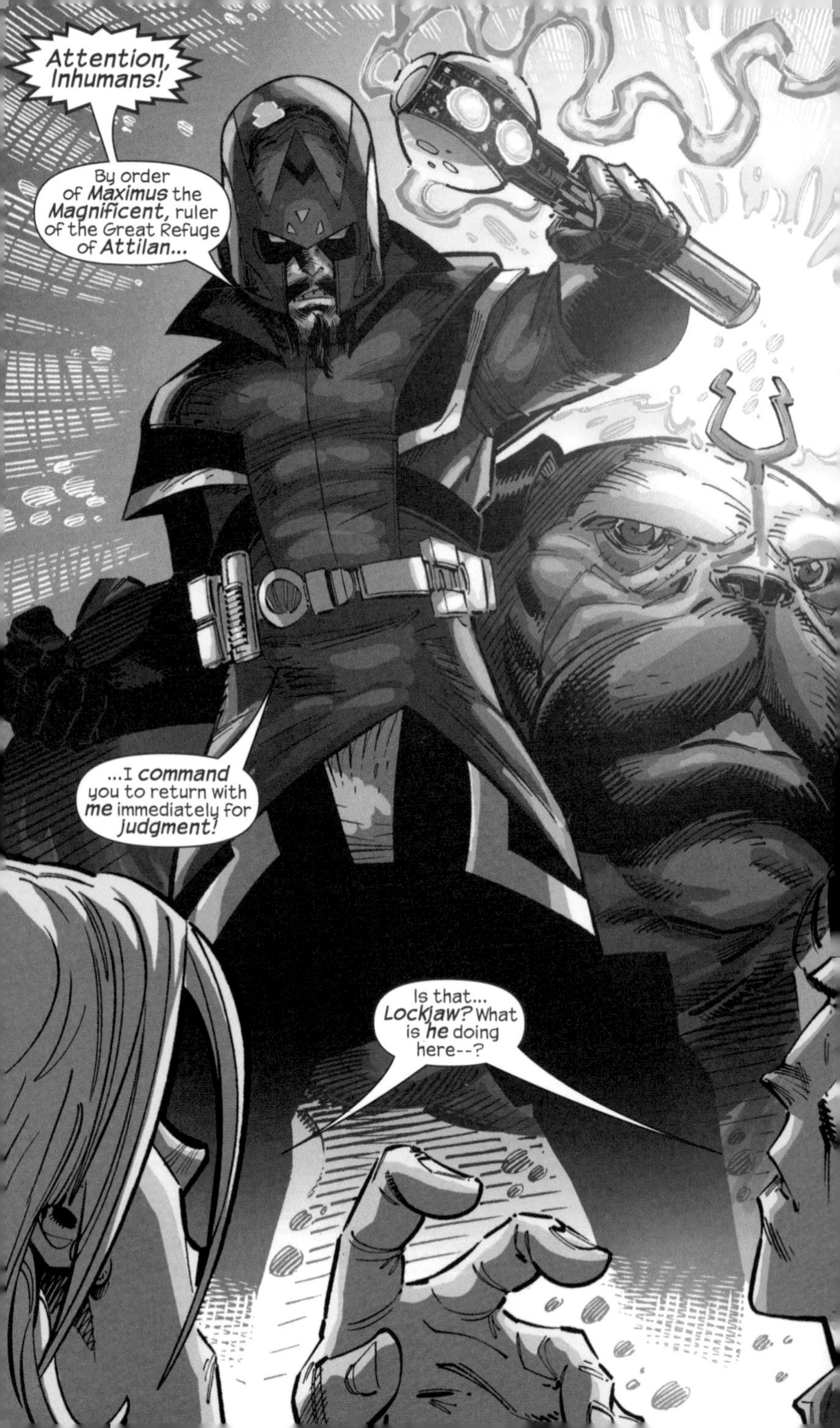
Attention, Inhumans!
By order of Maximus the Magnificent, ruler of the Great Refuge of Attilan...
...I command you to return with me immediately for judgment!
Is that... Lockjaw? What is he doing here--?

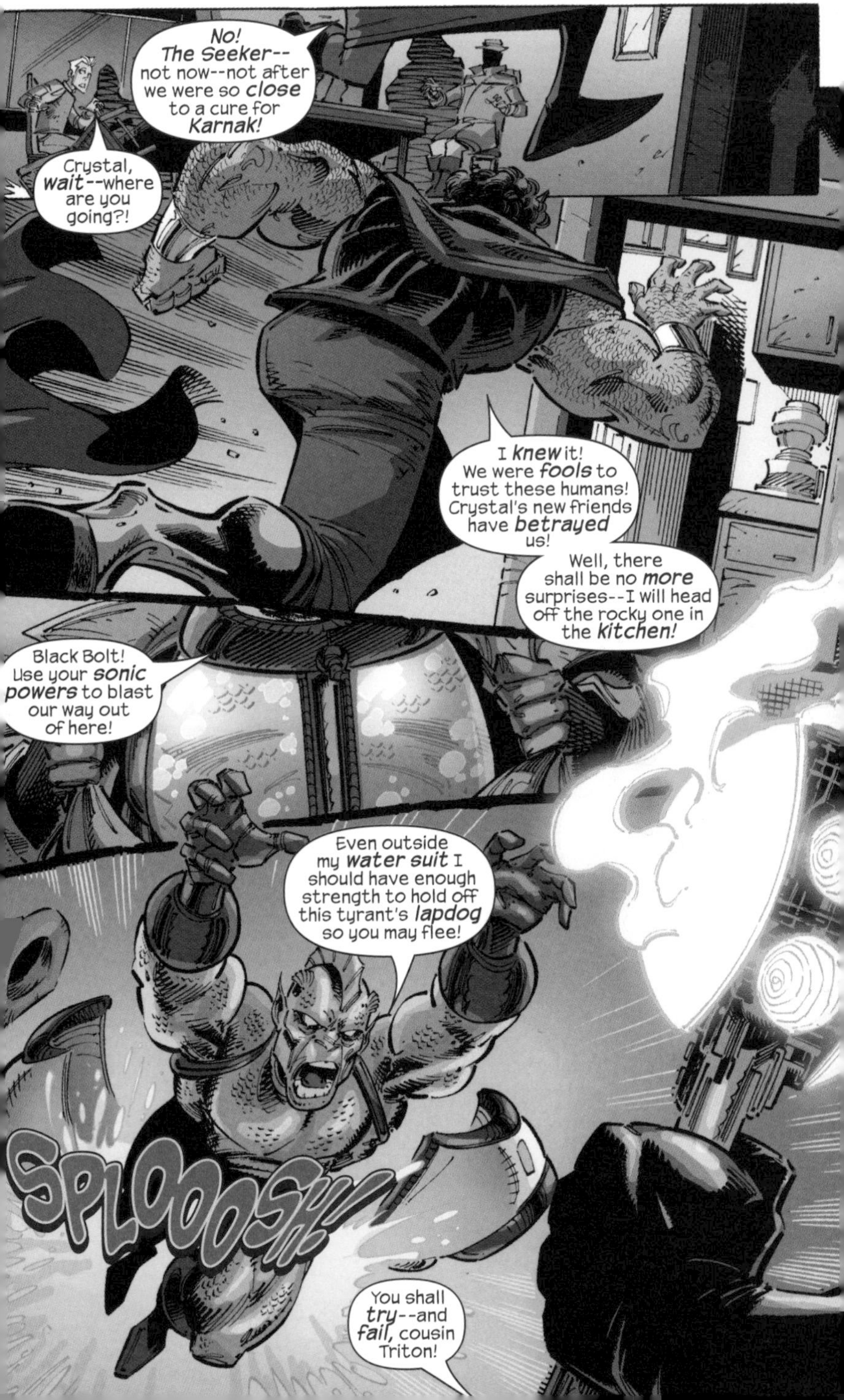
No! The Seeker-- not now--not after we were so close to a cure for Karnak!
Crystal, wait--where are you going?!
I knew it! We were fools to trust these humans! Crystal's new friends have betrayed us!
Well, there shall be no more surprises--I will head off the rocky one in the kitchen!
Black Bolt! Use your sonic powers to blast our way out of here!
Even outside my water suit I should have enough strength to hold off this tyrant's lapdog so you may flee!
SPLOOOSH!
You shall try--and fail, cousin Triton!

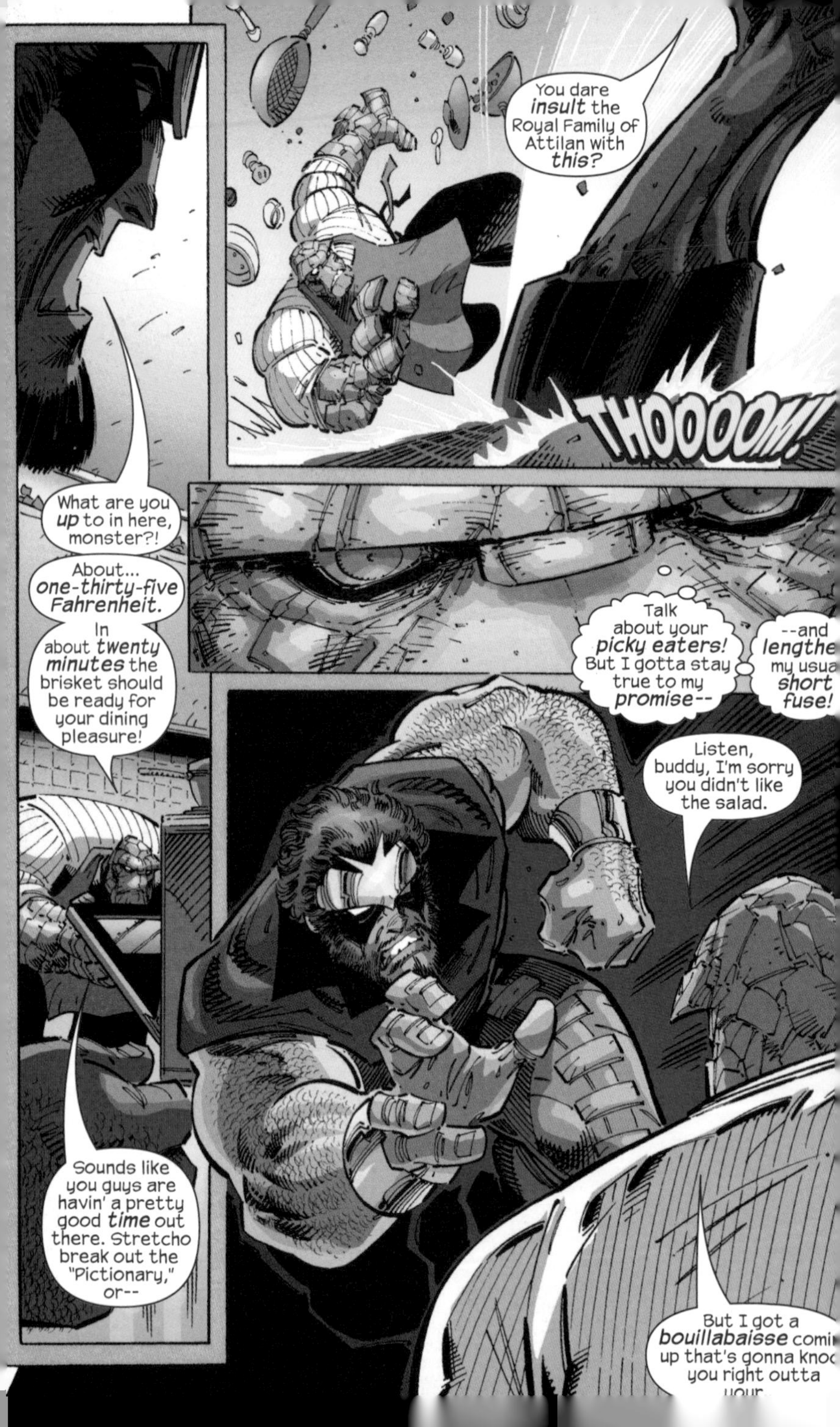

What are you *up* to in here, monster?!
About... *one-thirty-five Fahrenheit.*
In about *twenty minutes* the brisket should be ready for your dining pleasure!
Sounds like you guys are havin' a pretty good *time* out there. Stretcho break out the "Pictionary," or--
You dare *insult* the Royal Family of Attilan with *this?*
THOOOOM!
Talk about your *picky eaters!* But I gotta stay true to my *promise--*
--and *lengthe* my usua *short fuse!*
Listen, buddy, I'm sorry you didn't like the salad.
But I got a *bouillabaisse* comi up that's gonna knoc you right outta

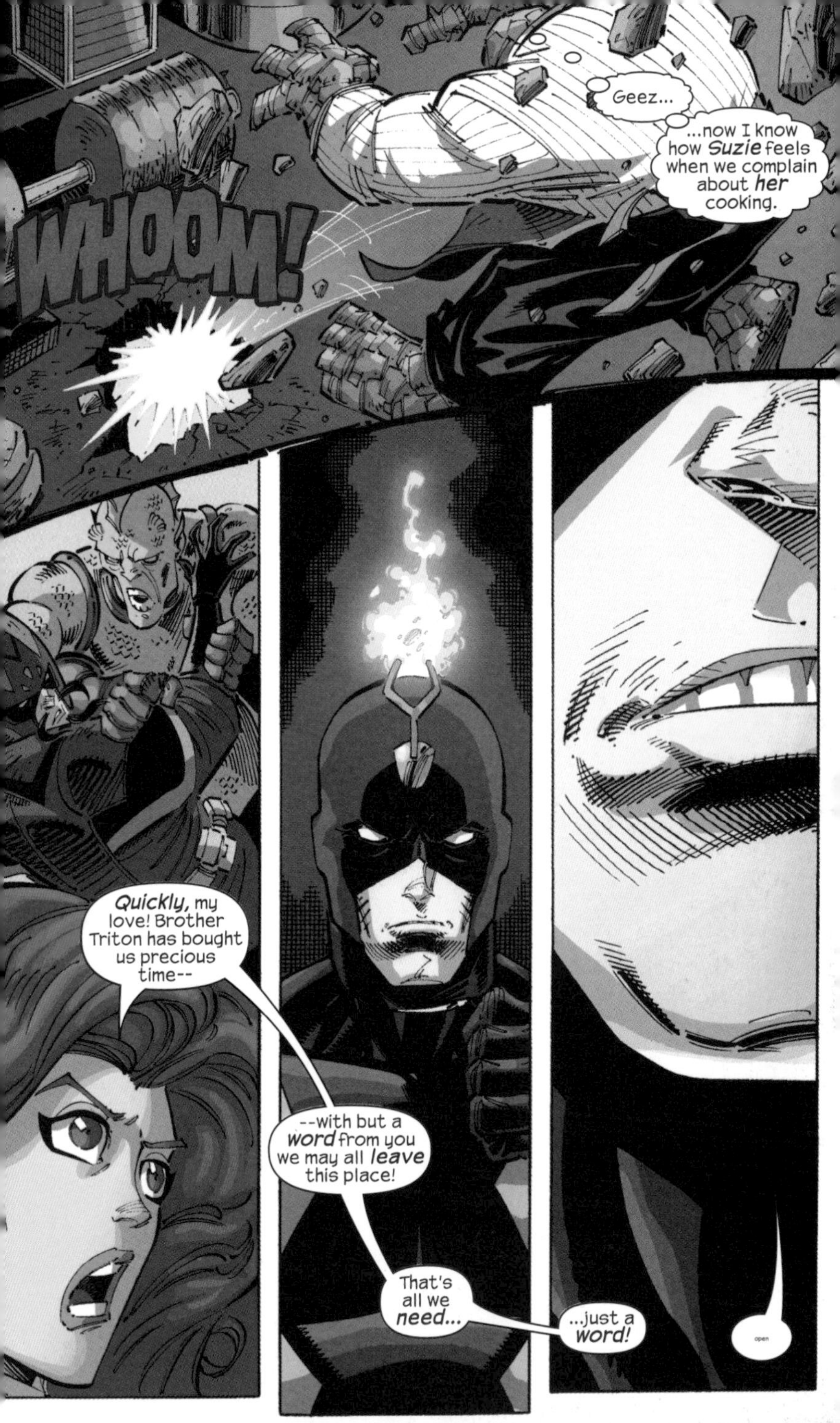
WHOOM!
Geez...
...now I know how Suzie feels when we complain about her cooking.
Quickly, my love! Brother Triton has bought us precious time--
--with but a word from you we may all leave this place!
That's all we need...
...just a word!

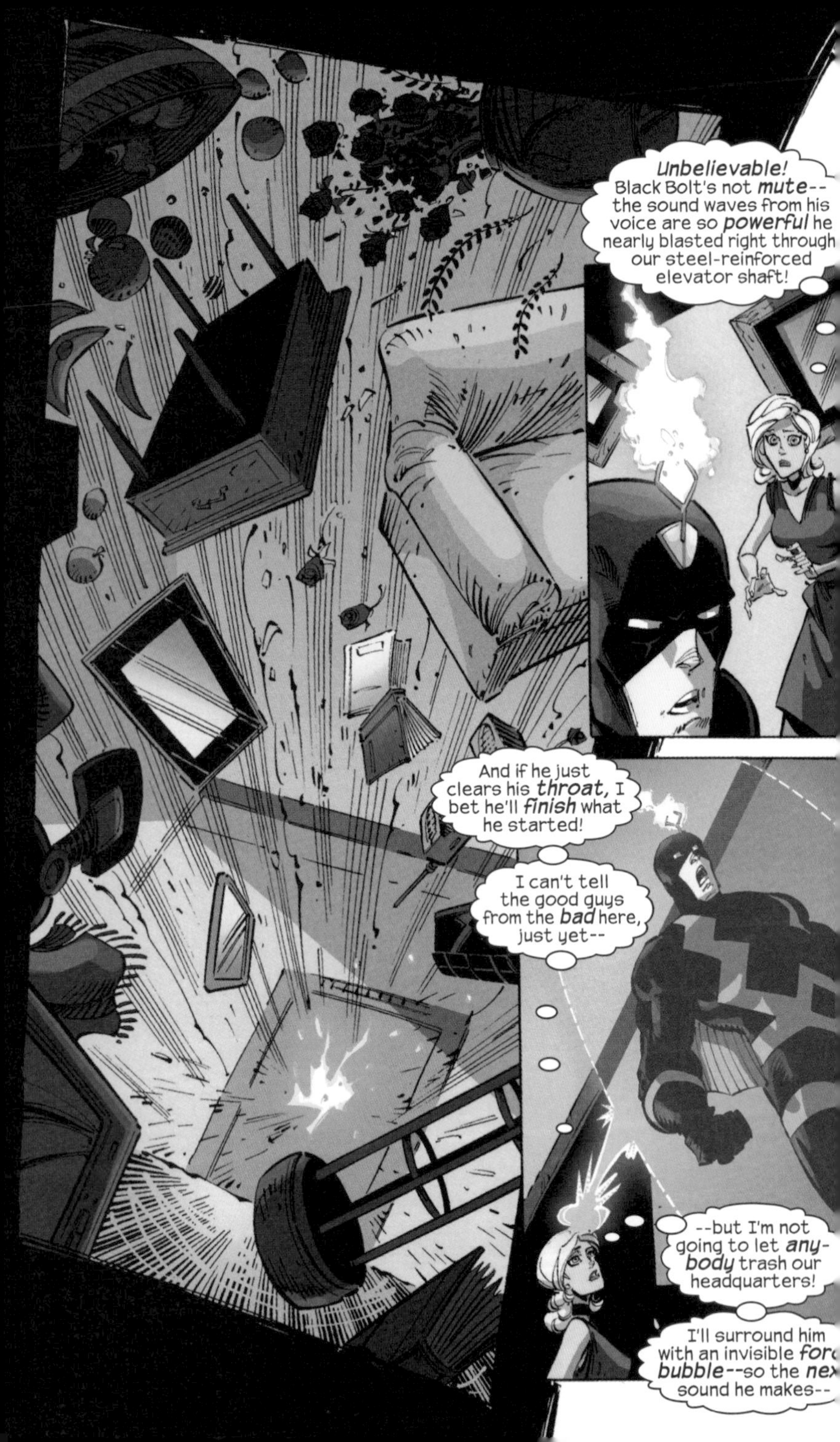
Unbelievable! Black Bolt's not mute-- the sound waves from his voice are so powerful he nearly blasted right through our steel-reinforced elevator shaft!
And if he just clears his throat, I bet he'll finish what he started!
I can't tell the good guys from the bad here, just yet--
--but I'm not going to let any-body trash our headquarters!
I'll surround him with an invisible forc bubble--so the nex sound he makes--

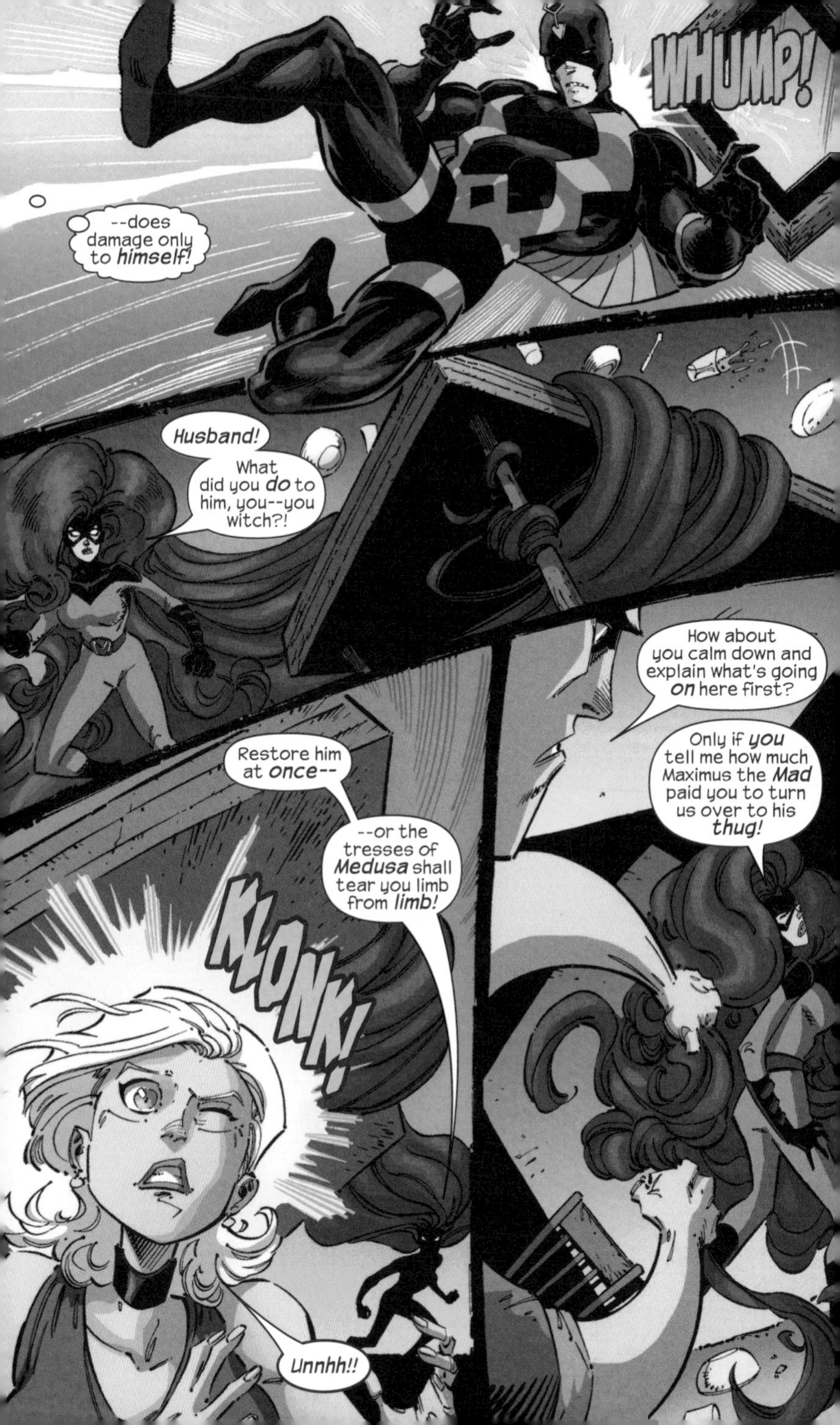
WHUMP!
--does damage only to *himself!*
Husband!
What did you *do* to him, you--you witch?!
How about you calm down and explain what's going *on* here first?
Only if *you* tell me how much Maximus the *Mad* paid you to turn us over to his *thug!*
Restore him at *once--*
--or the tresses of *Medusa* shall tear you limb from *limb!*
KLONK!
Unnhh!!

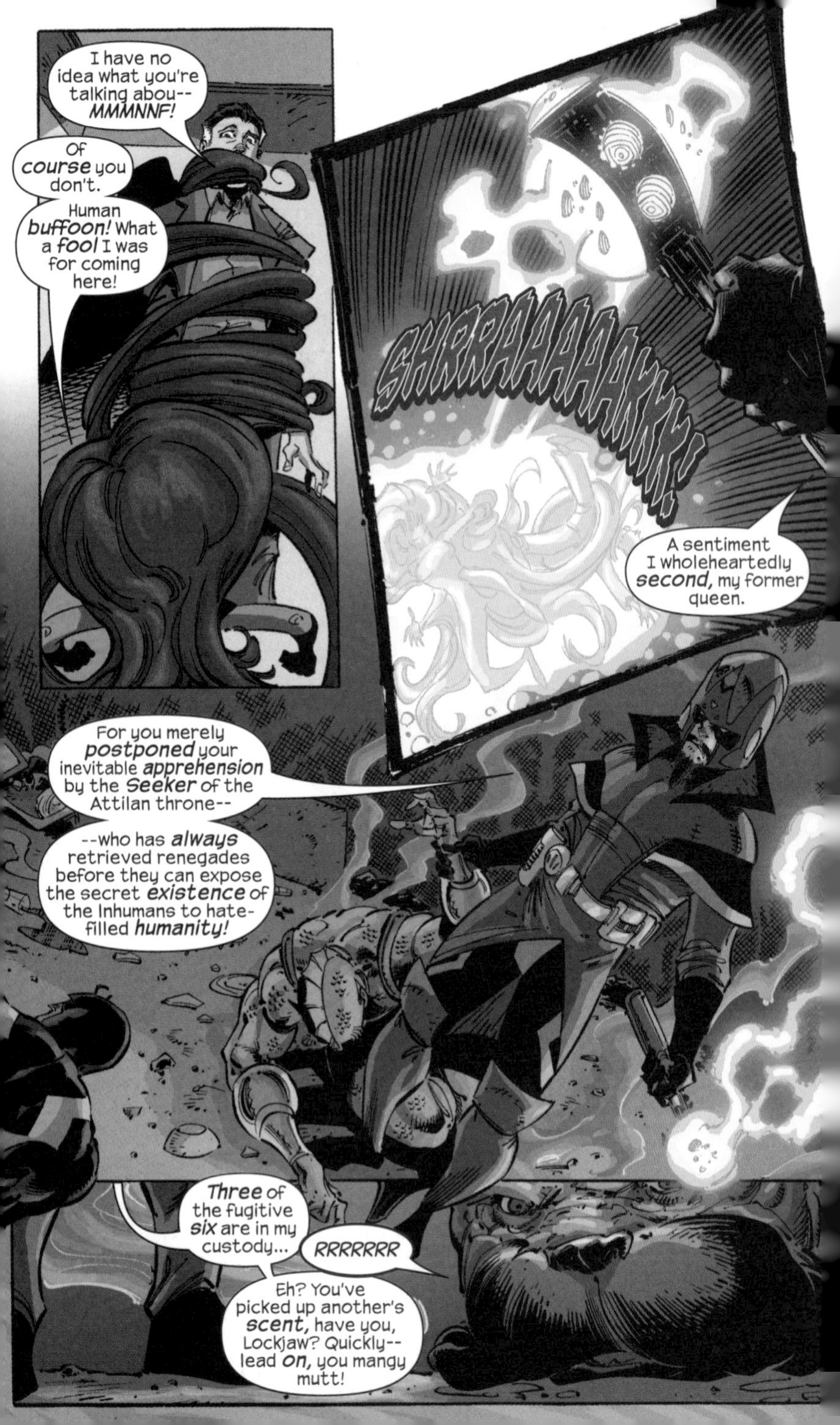
I have no idea what you're talking abou-- MMMNNF!
Of course you don't.
Human buffoon! What a fool I was for coming here!
SHRAAAAAAKK!
A sentiment I wholeheartedly second, my former queen.
For you merely postponed your inevitable apprehension by the Seeker of the Attilan throne--
--who has always retrieved renegades before they can expose the secret existence of the Inhumans to hate-filled humanity!
Three of the fugitive six are in my custody...
RRRRRRR
Eh? You've picked up another's scent, have you, Lockjaw? Quickly-- lead on, you mangy mutt!

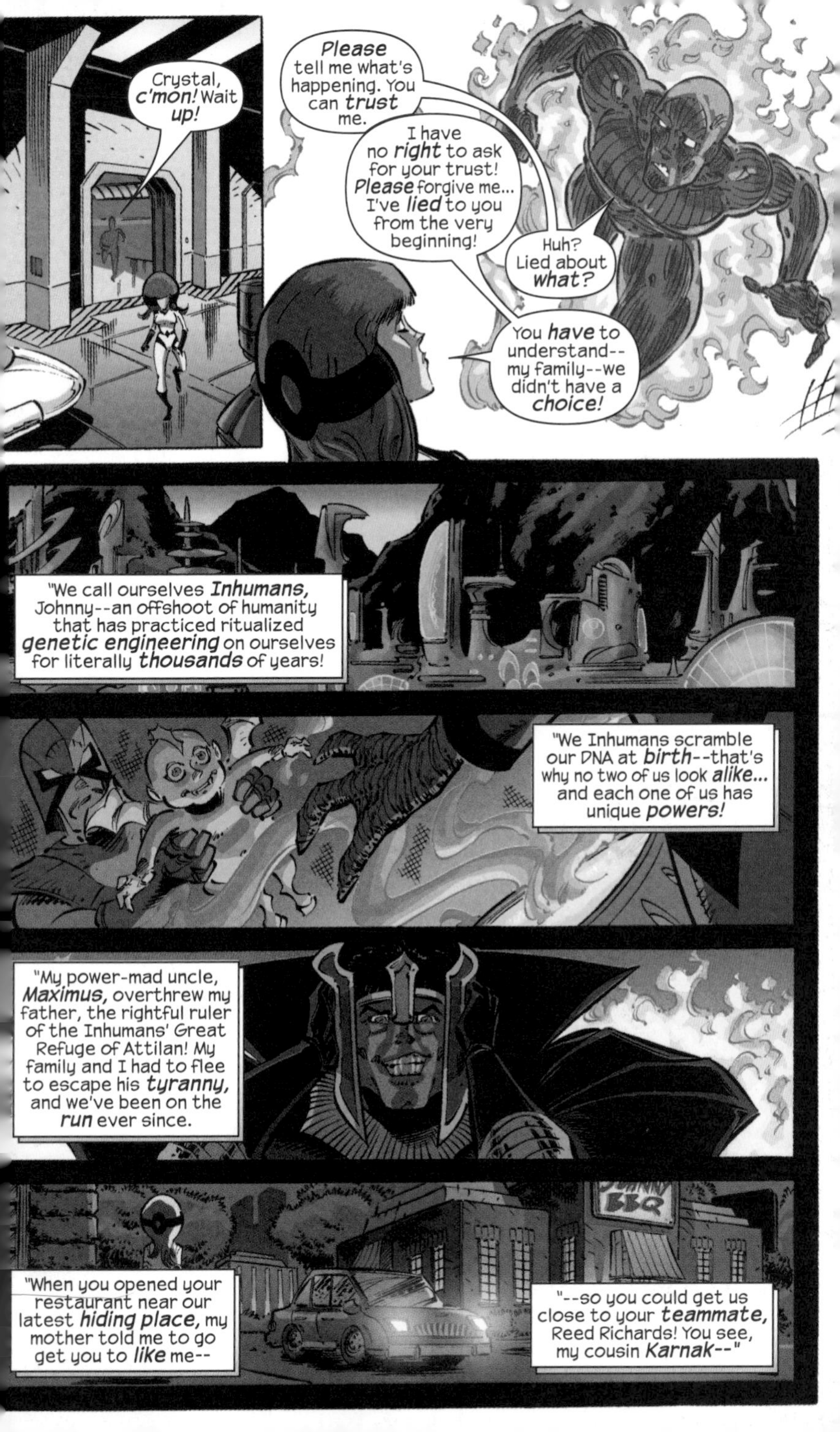

Crystal, c'mon! Wait up!
Please tell me what's happening. You can trust me.
I have no right to ask for your trust! Please forgive me... I've lied to you from the very beginning!
Huh? Lied about what?
You have to understand--my family--we didn't have a choice!
"We call ourselves Inhumans, Johnny--an offshoot of humanity that has practiced ritualized genetic engineering on ourselves for literally thousands of years!
"We Inhumans scramble our DNA at birth--that's why no two of us look alike... and each one of us has unique powers!
"My power-mad uncle, Maximus, overthrew my father, the rightful ruler of the Inhumans' Great Refuge of Attilan! My family and I had to flee to escape his tyranny, and we've been on the run ever since.
BBQ
"When you opened your restaurant near our latest hiding place, my mother told me to go get you to like me--
"--so you could get us close to your teammate, Reed Richards! You see, my cousin Karnak--"

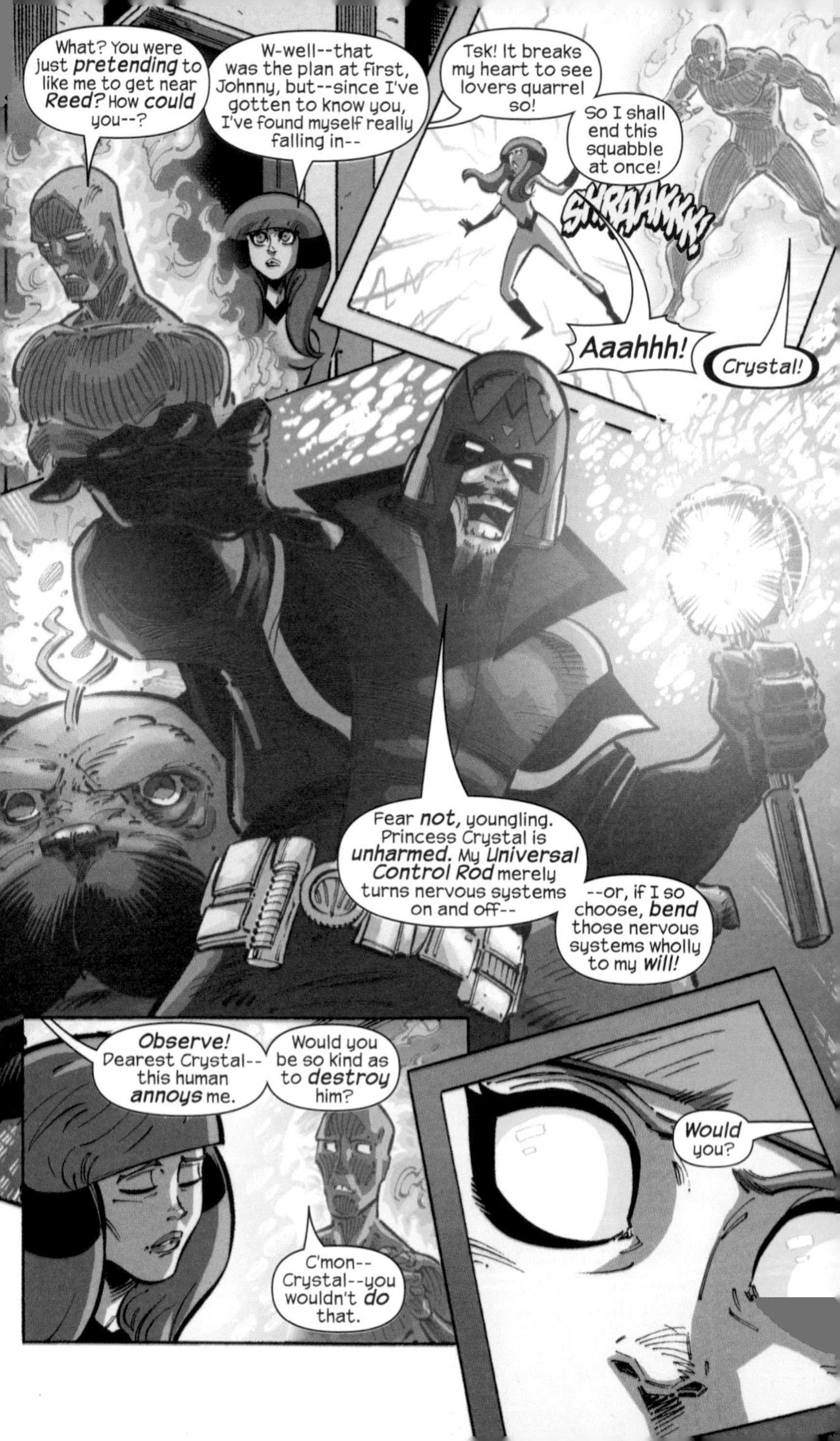
What? You were just *pretending* to like me to get near *Reed?* How *could* you--?
W-well--that was the plan at first, Johnny, but--since I've gotten to know you, I've found myself really falling in--
Tsk! It breaks my heart to see lovers quarrel so!
So I shall end this squabble at once!
SHRAAKKK!
Aaahhh!
Crystal!
Fear *not,* youngling. Princess Crystal is *unharmed.* My *Universal Control Rod* merely turns nervous systems on and off--
--or, if I so choose, *bend* those nervous systems wholly to my *will!*
Observe! Dearest Crystal--this human *annoys* me.
Would you be so kind as to *destroy* him?
C'mon--Crystal--you wouldn't *do* that.
Would you?

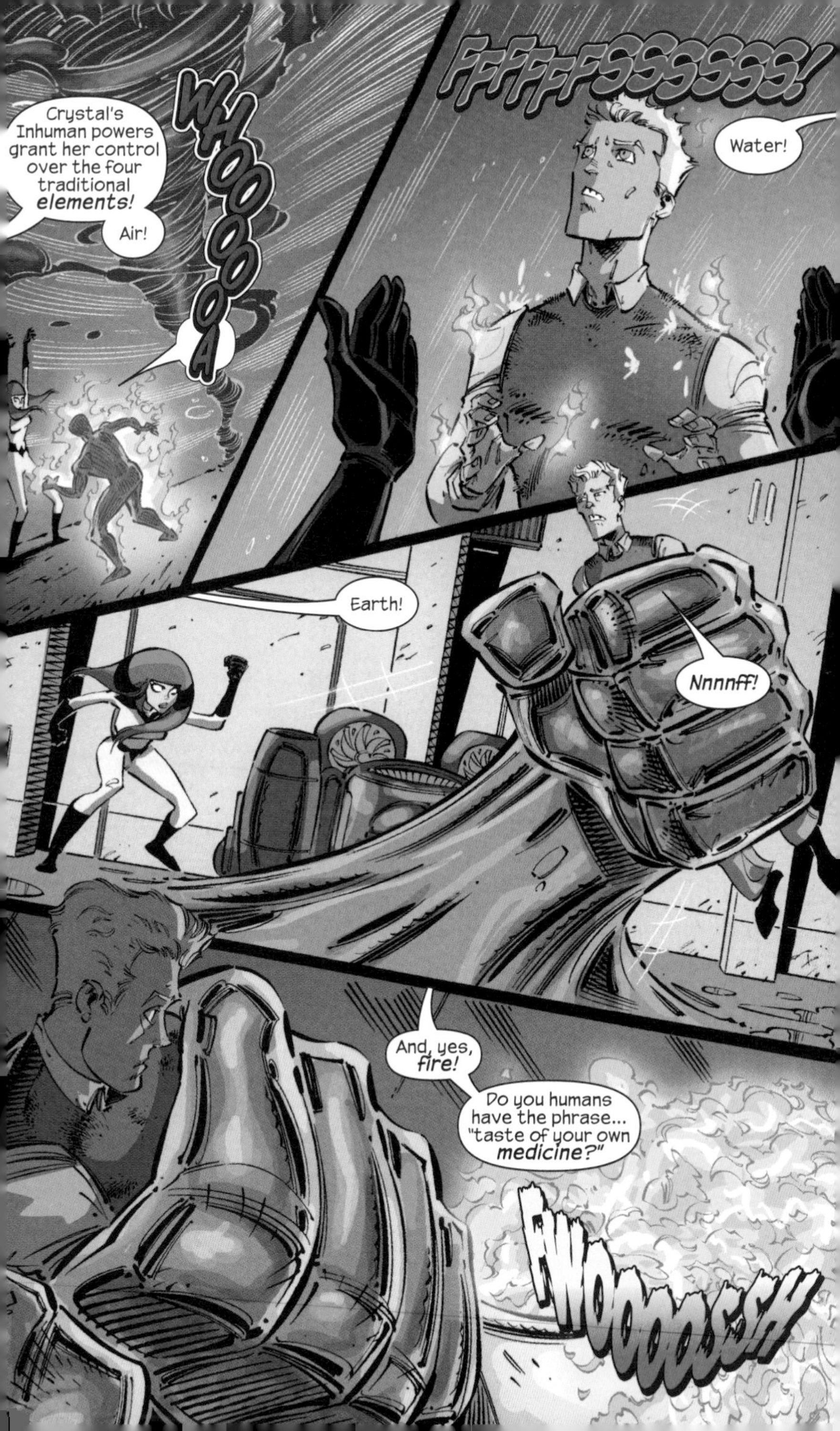

Crystal's Inhuman powers grant her control over the four traditional *elements!*
Air!
WHOOOOOOA
FFFFFFSSSSSSS!
Water!
Earth!
Nnnnff!
And, yes, *fire!*
Do you humans have the phrase... "taste of your own *medicine?*"
FWOOOOOSH

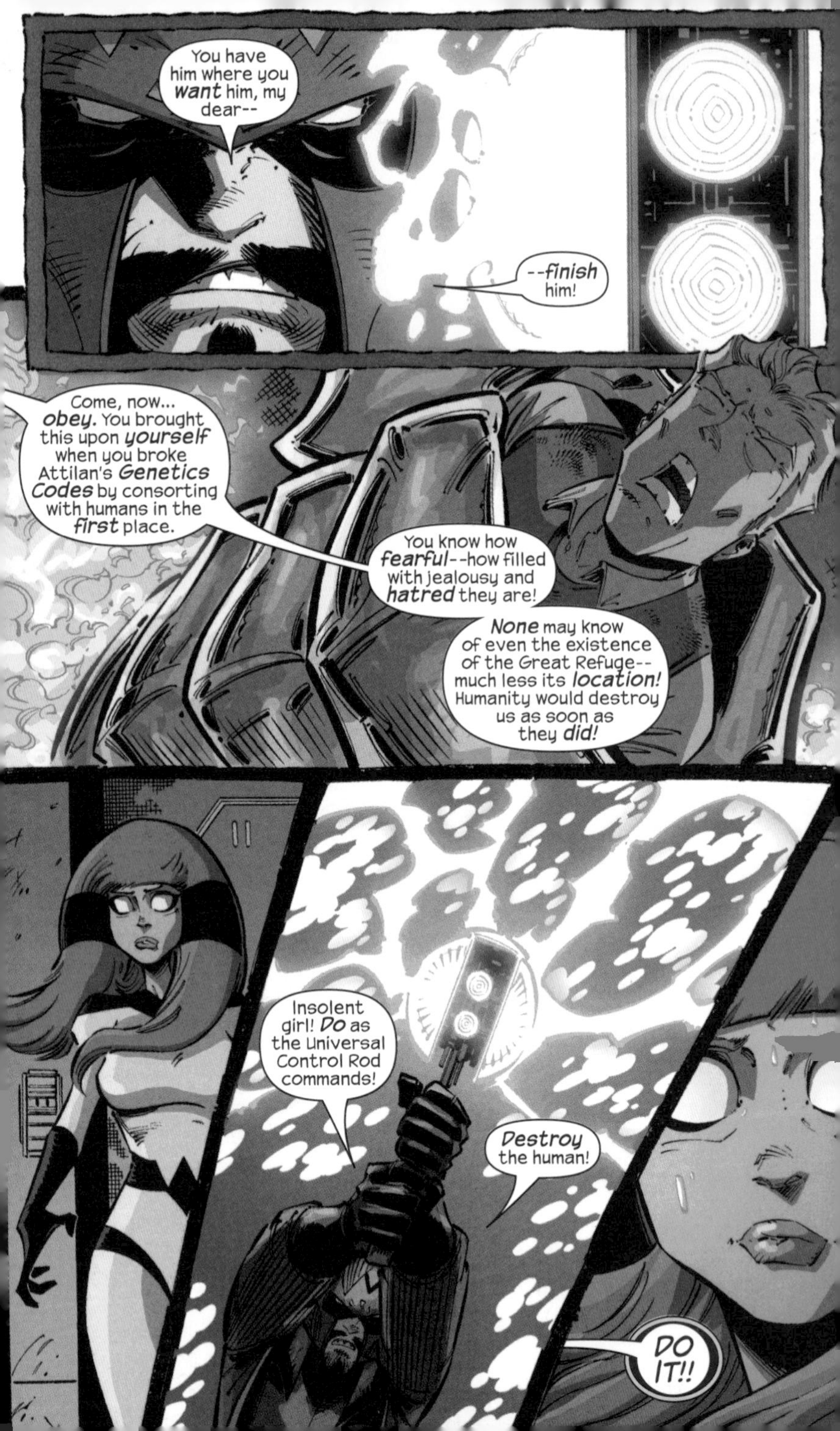
You have him where you want him, my dear--
--finish him!
Come, now... obey. You brought this upon yourself when you broke Attilan's Genetics Codes by consorting with humans in the first place.
You know how fearful--how filled with jealousy and hatred they are!
None may know of even the existence of the Great Refuge--much less its location! Humanity would destroy us as soon as they did!
Insolent girl! Do as the Universal Control Rod commands!
Destroy the human!
DO IT!!

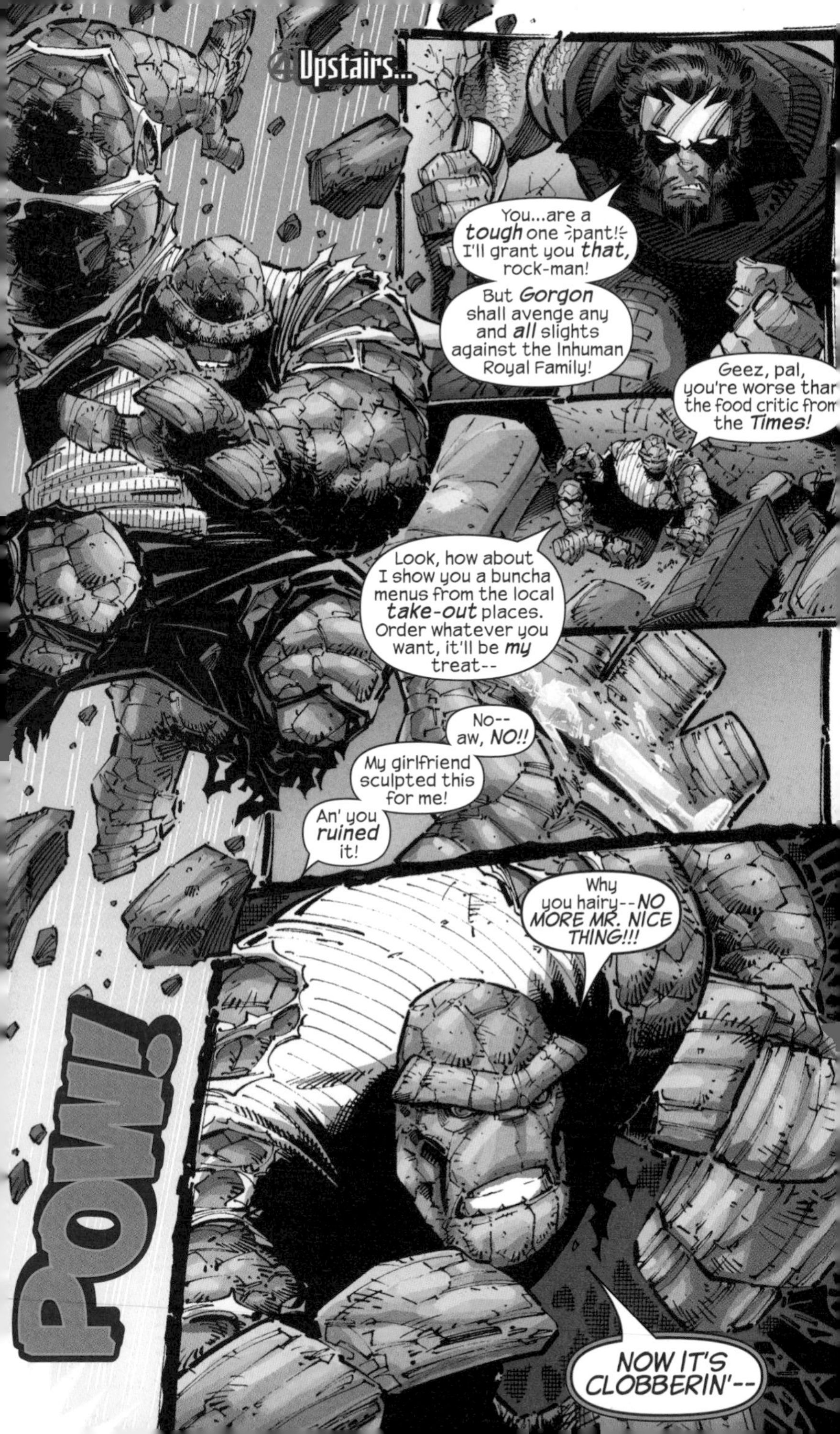
Upstairs...
You...are a tough one -pant!- I'll grant you that, rock-man!
But Gorgon shall avenge any and all slights against the Inhuman Royal Family!
Geez, pal, you're worse than the food critic from the Times!
Look, how about I show you a buncha menus from the local take-out places. Order whatever you want, it'll be my treat--
No-- aw, NO!!
My girlfriend sculpted this for me!
An' you ruined it!
Why you hairy--NO MORE MR. NICE THING!!!
NOW IT'S CLOBBERIN'--
POW!

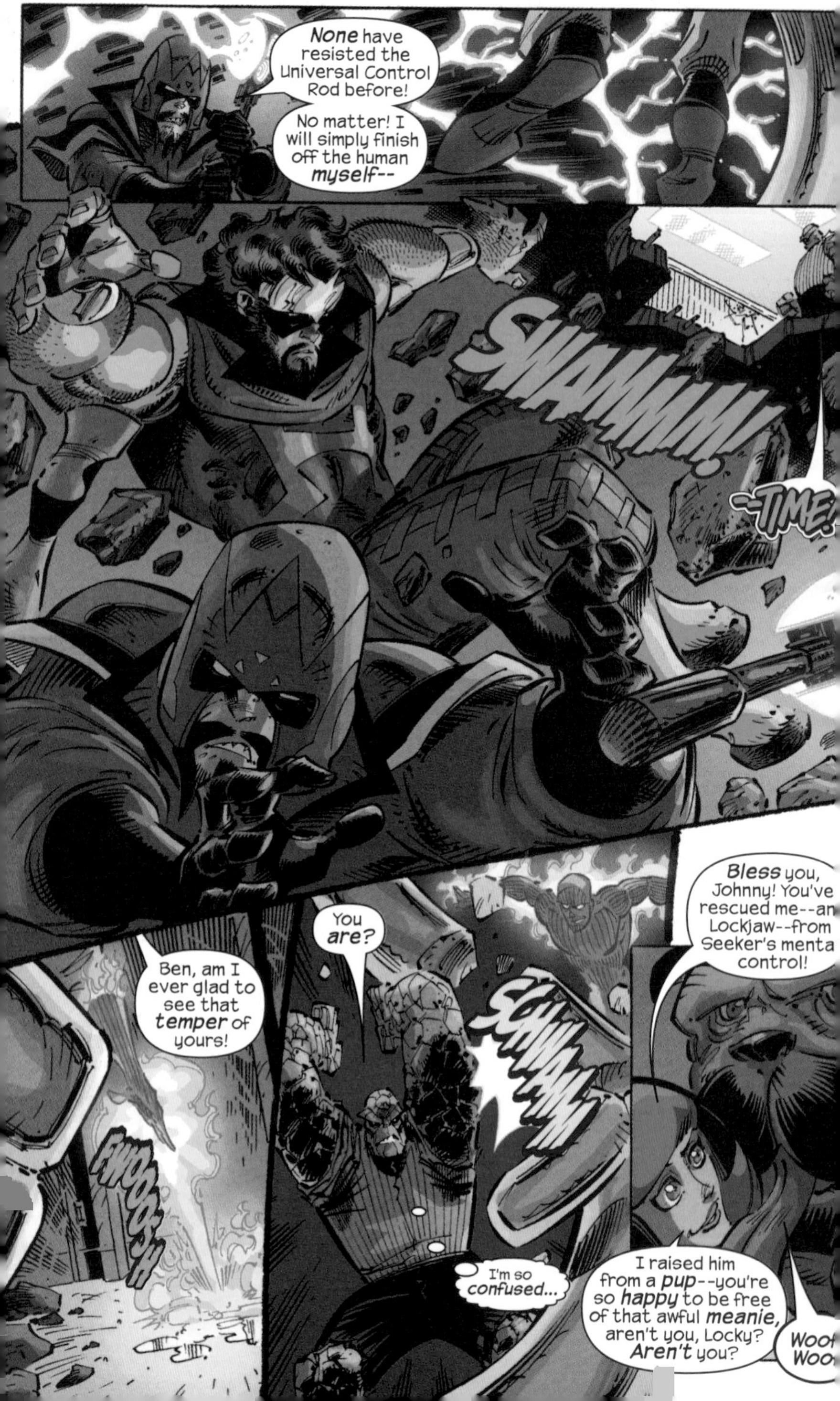

None have resisted the Universal Control Rod before!
No matter! I will simply finish off the human myself--
SHAMMM!
--TIME!
Bless you, Johnny! You've rescued me--an Lockjaw--from Seeker's menta control!
You are?
Ben, am I ever glad to see that temper of yours!
SCHWAM
FWOOOSH
I'm so confused...
I raised him from a pup--you're so happy to be free of that awful meanie, aren't you, Locky? Aren't you?
Woo Woo

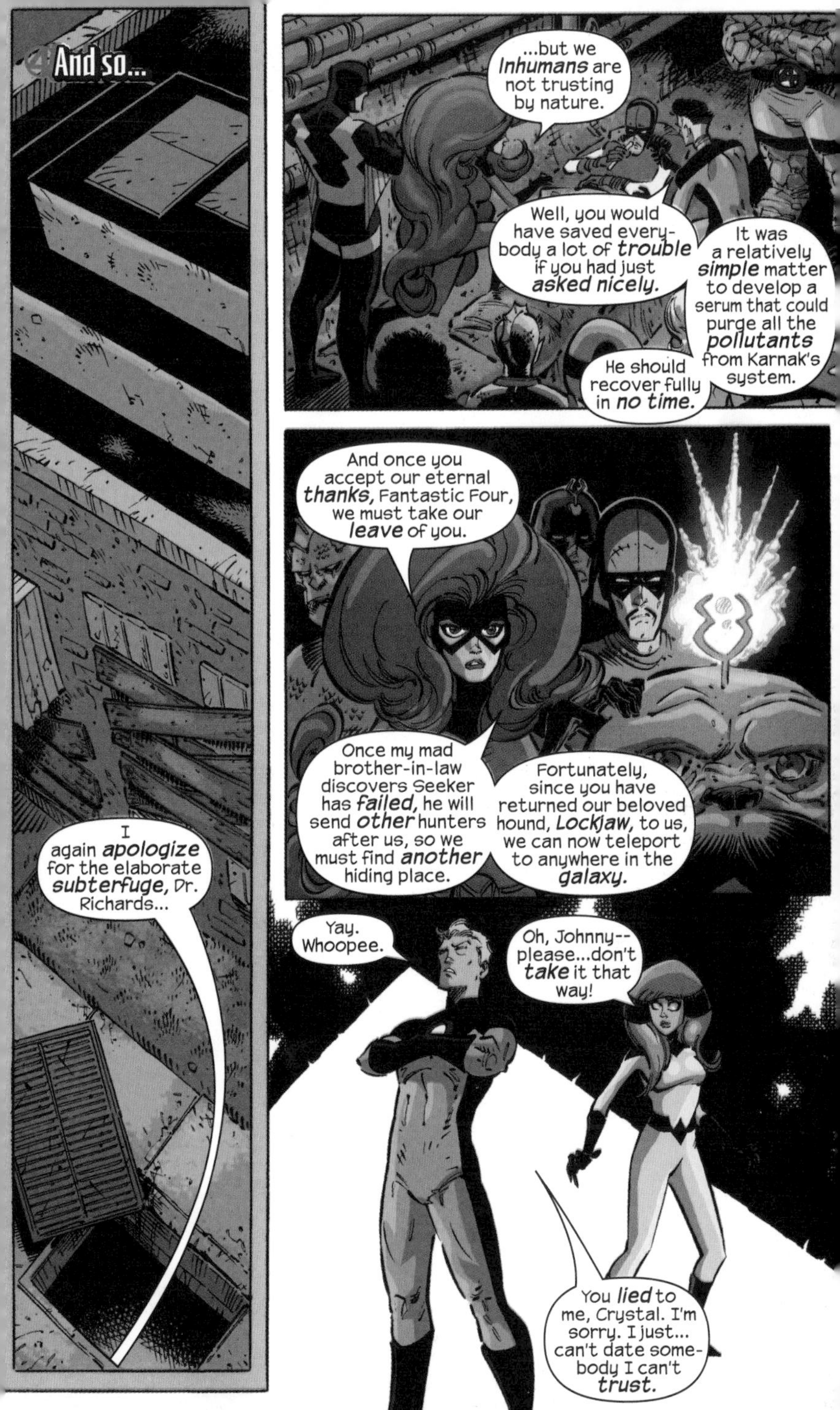
And so...
I again apologize for the elaborate subterfuge, Dr. Richards...
...but we Inhumans are not trusting by nature.
Well, you would have saved every-body a lot of trouble if you had just asked nicely.
It was a relatively simple matter to develop a serum that could purge all the pollutants from Karnak's system.
He should recover fully in no time.
And once you accept our eternal thanks, Fantastic Four, we must take our leave of you.
Once my mad brother-in-law discovers Seeker has failed, he will send other hunters after us, so we must find another hiding place.
Fortunately, since you have returned our beloved hound, Lockjaw, to us, we can now teleport to anywhere in the galaxy.
Yay. Whoopee.
Oh, Johnny-- please...don't take it that way!
You lied to me, Crystal. I'm sorry. I just... can't date some-body I can't trust.

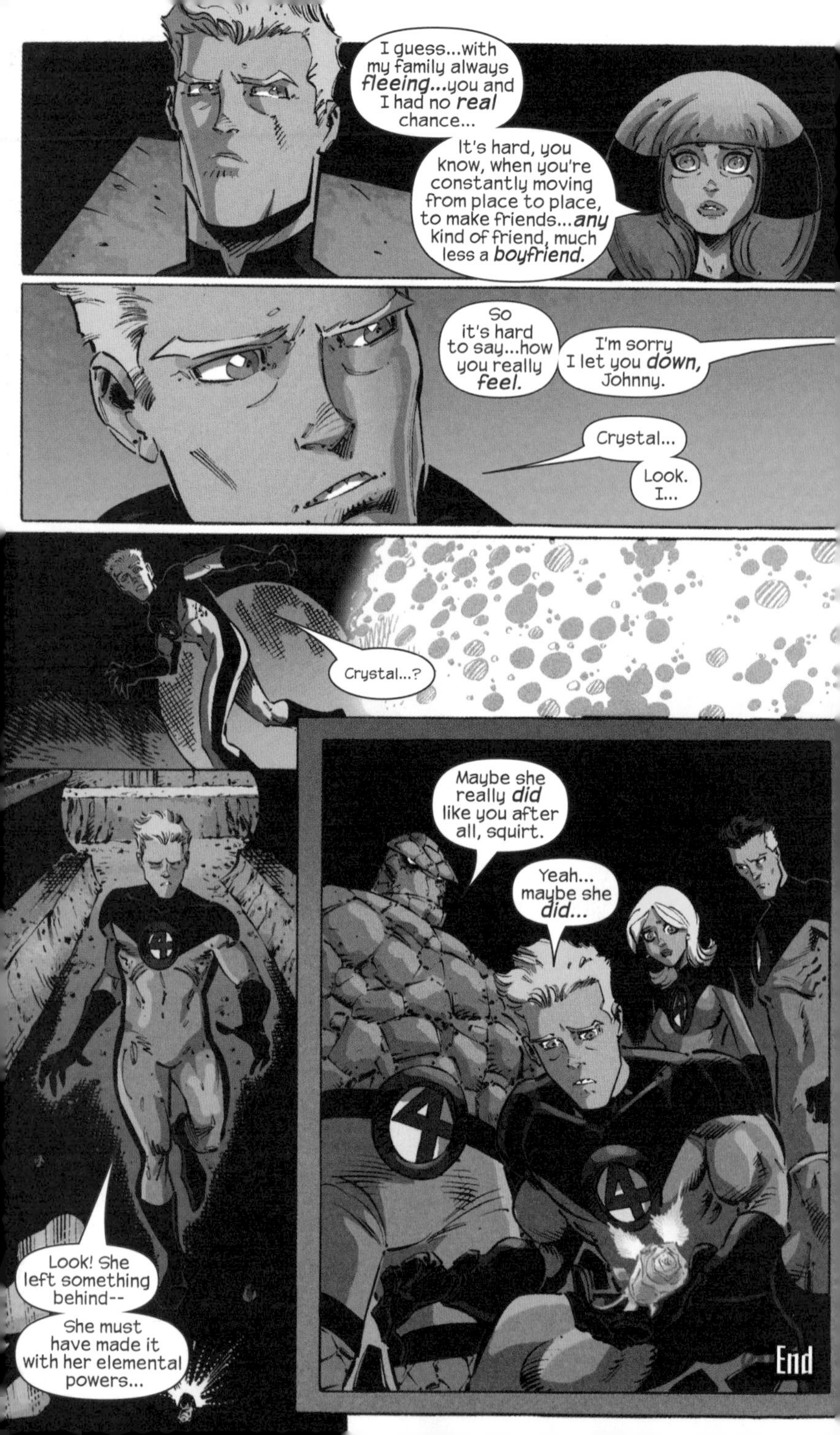
I guess...with my family always fleeing...you and I had no real chance...
It's hard, you know, when you're constantly moving from place to place, to make friends...any kind of friend, much less a boyfriend.
So it's hard to say...how you really feel.
I'm sorry I let you down, Johnny.
Crystal...
Look. I...
Crystal...?
Look! She left something behind--
She must have made it with her elemental powers...
Maybe she really did like you after all, squirt.
Yeah... maybe she did...
End

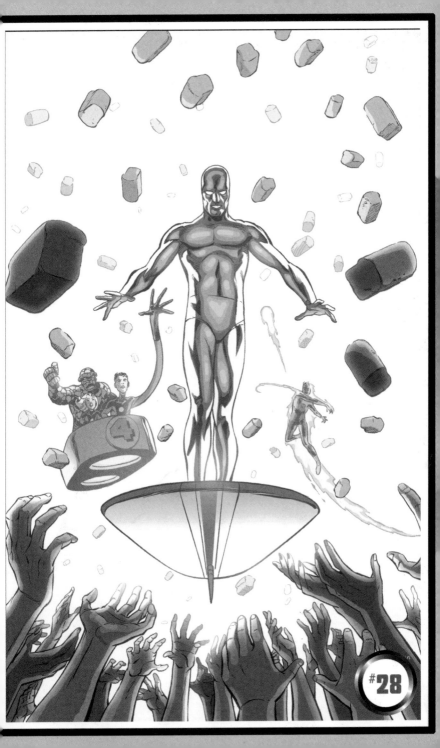

#28

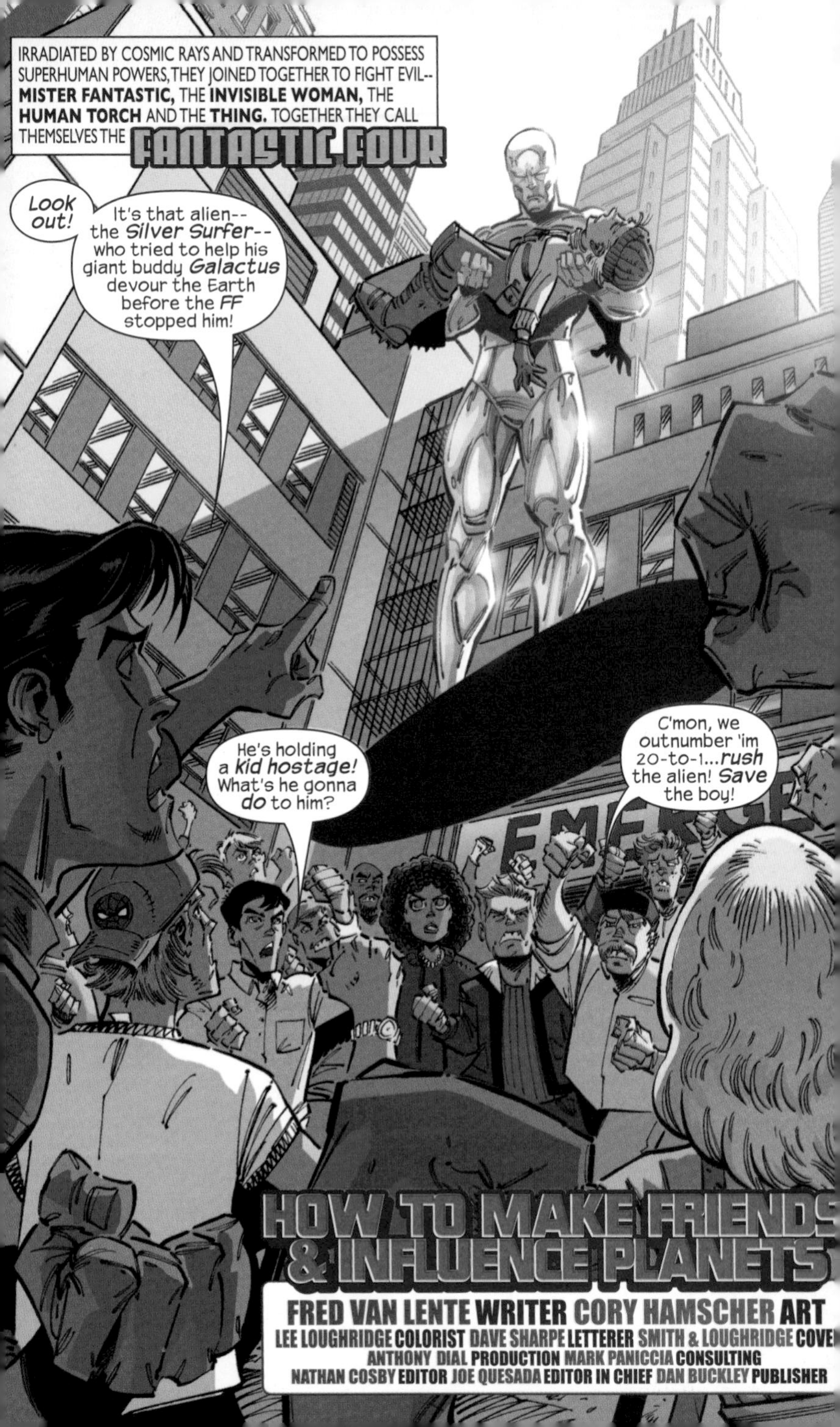
IRRADIATED BY COSMIC RAYS AND TRANSFORMED TO POSSESS SUPERHUMAN POWERS, THEY JOINED TOGETHER TO FIGHT EVIL-- **MISTER FANTASTIC,** THE **INVISIBLE WOMAN,** THE **HUMAN TORCH** AND THE **THING.** TOGETHER THEY CALL THEMSELVES THE FANTASTIC FOUR
Look out!
It's that alien-- the *Silver Surfer*-- who tried to help his giant buddy *Galactus* devour the Earth before the *FF* stopped him!
He's holding a *kid hostage!* What's he gonna *do* to him?
C'mon, we outnumber 'im 20-to-1...*rush* the alien! *Save* the boy!
HOW TO MAKE FRIENDS & INFLUENCE PLANETS
FRED VAN LENTE WRITER CORY HAMSCHER ART
LEE LOUGHRIDGE COLORIST DAVE SHARPE LETTERER SMITH & LOUGHRIDGE COVER
ANTHONY DIAL PRODUCTION MARK PANICCIA CONSULTING
NATHAN COSBY EDITOR JOE QUESADA EDITOR IN CHIEF DAN BUCKLEY PUBLISHER

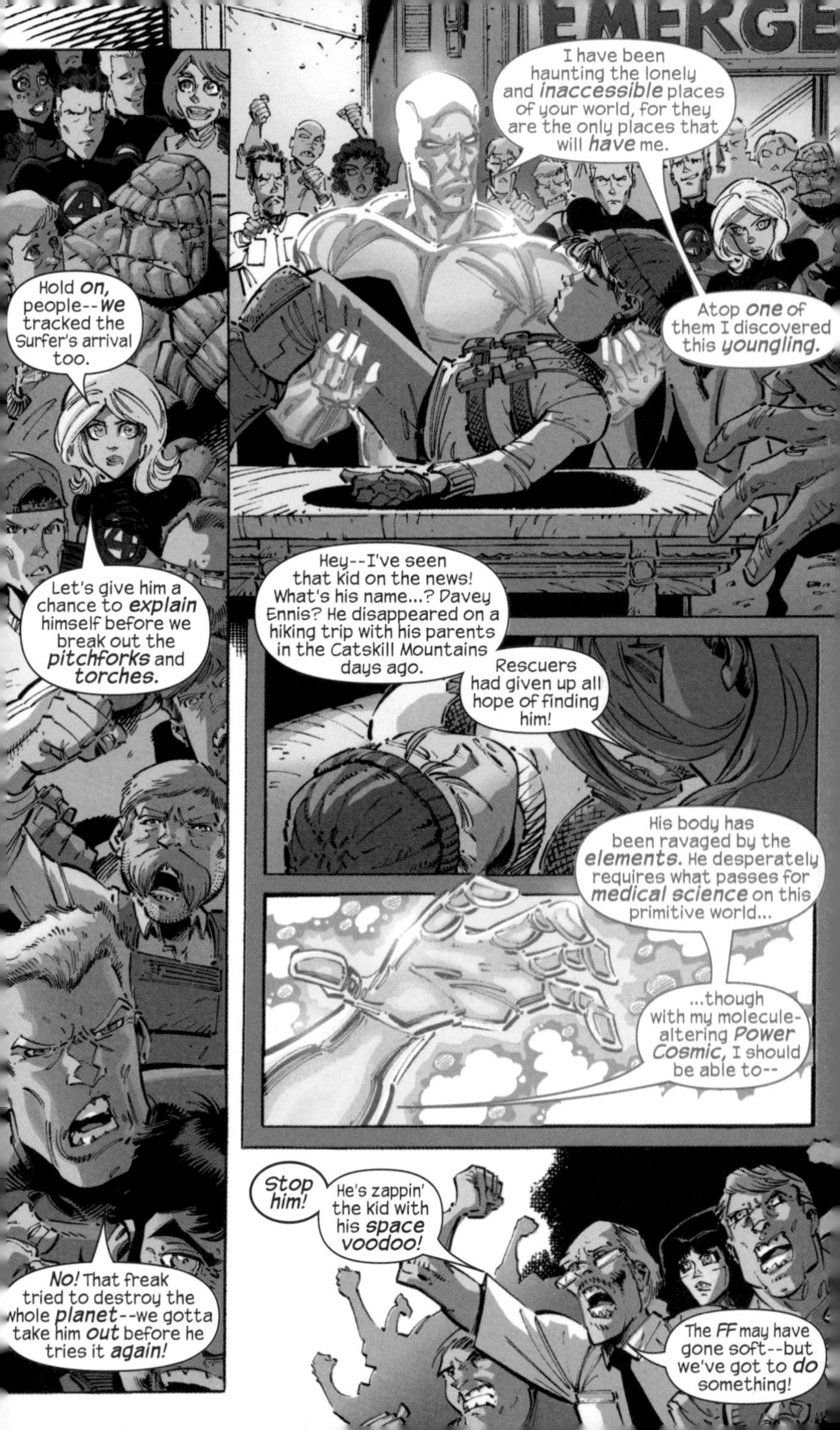
EMERGE
I have been haunting the lonely and inaccessible places of your world, for they are the only places that will have me.
Atop one of them I discovered this youngling.
Hold on, people--we tracked the Surfer's arrival too.
Let's give him a chance to explain himself before we break out the pitchforks and torches.
Hey--I've seen that kid on the news! What's his name...? Davey Ennis? He disappeared on a hiking trip with his parents in the Catskill Mountains days ago.
Rescuers had given up all hope of finding him!
His body has been ravaged by the elements. He desperately requires what passes for medical science on this primitive world...
...though with my molecule-altering Power Cosmic, I should be able to--
No! That freak tried to destroy the whole planet--we gotta take him out before he tries it again!
Stop him!
He's zappin' the kid with his space voodoo!
The FF may have gone soft--but we've got to do something!

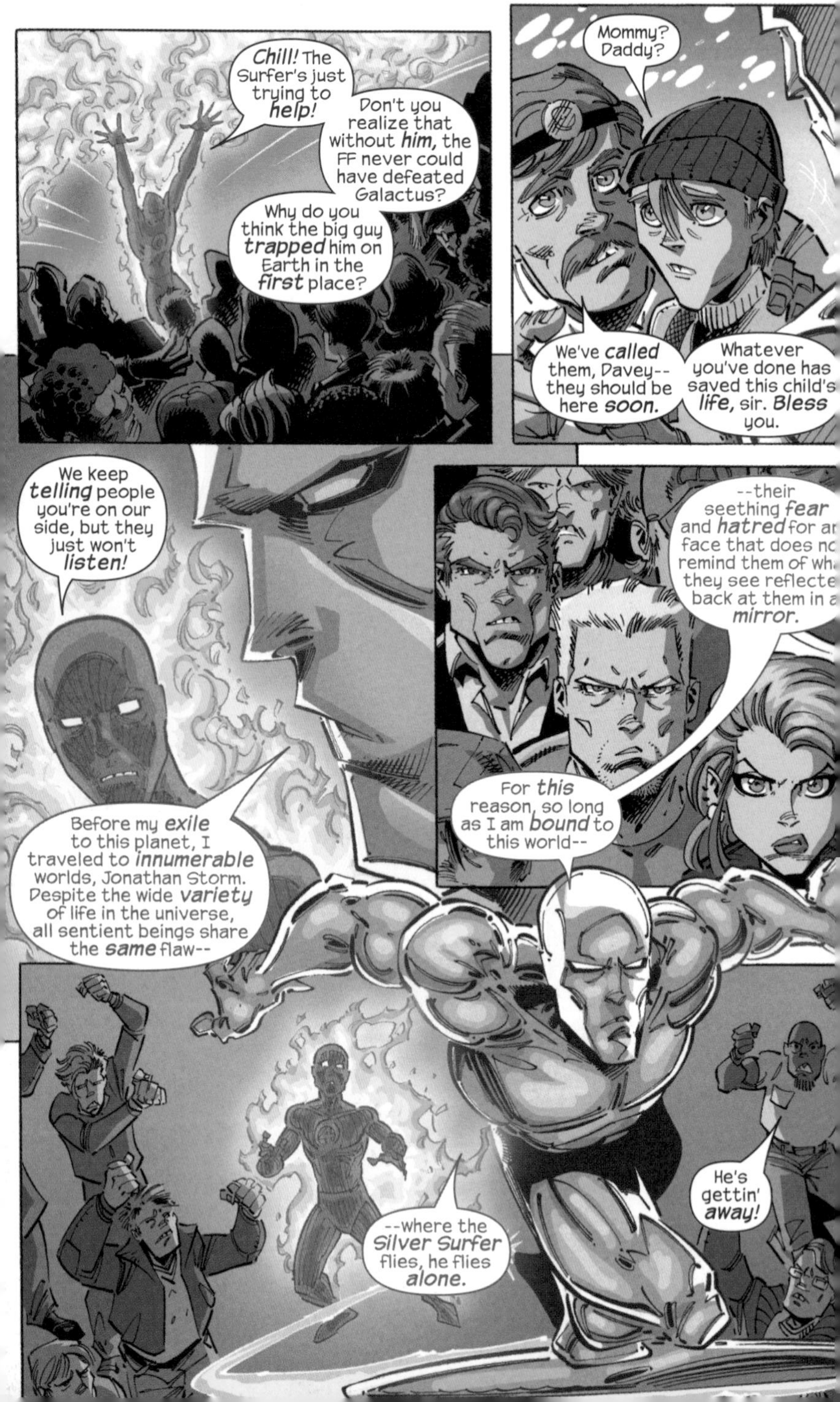

Chill! The Surfer's just trying to help!
Don't you realize that without him, the FF never could have defeated Galactus?
Why do you think the big guy trapped him on Earth in the first place?
Mommy? Daddy?
We've called them, Davey-- they should be here soon.
Whatever you've done has saved this child's life, sir. Bless you.
We keep telling people you're on our side, but they just won't listen!
Before my exile to this planet, I traveled to innumerable worlds, Jonathan Storm. Despite the wide variety of life in the universe, all sentient beings share the same flaw--
--their seething fear and hatred for a face that does no remind them of wh they see reflecte back at them in a mirror.
For this reason, so long as I am bound to this world--
--where the Silver Surfer flies, he flies alone.
He's gettin' away!

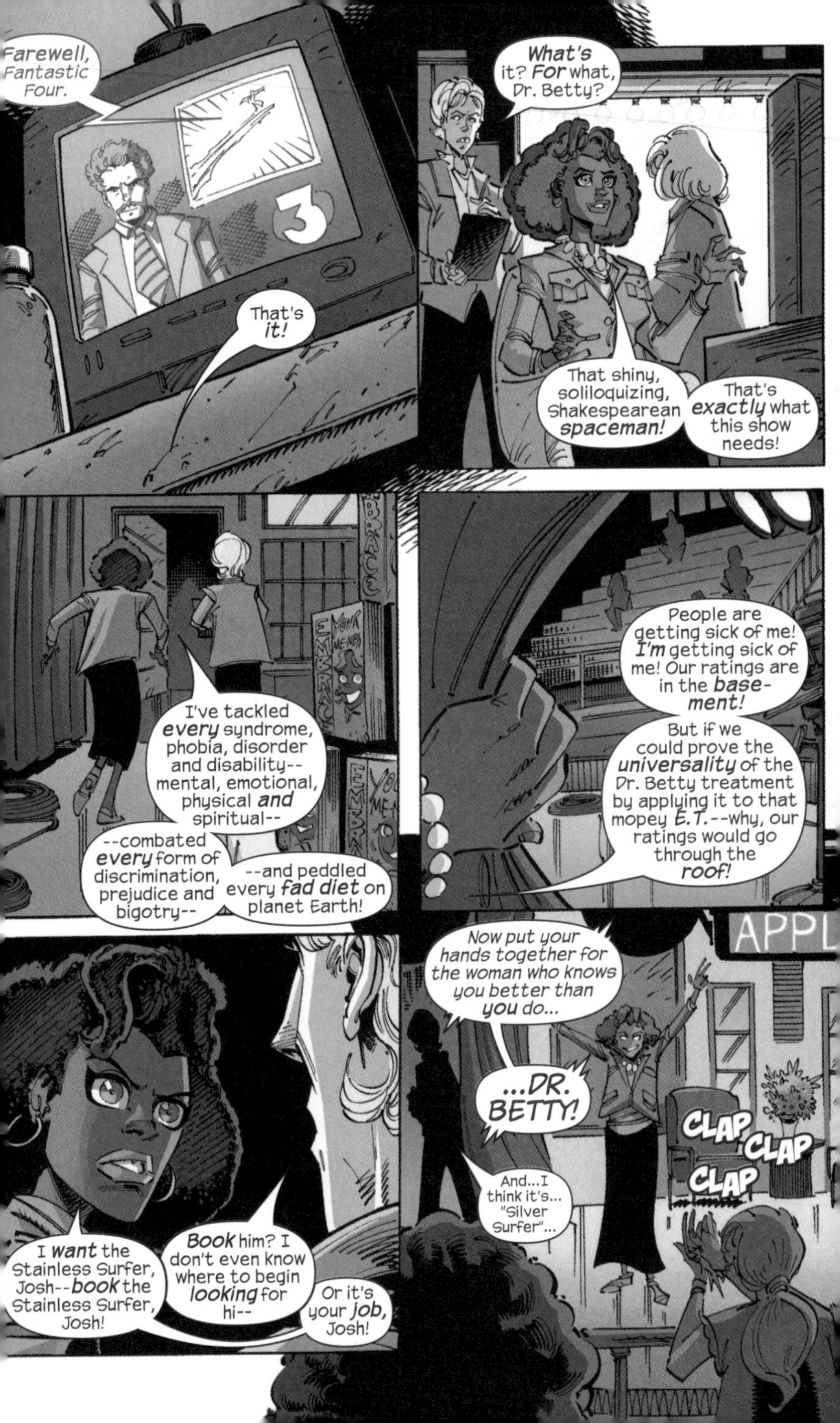
Farewell, Fantastic Four.
That's *it!*
3
What's it? *For* what, Dr. Betty?
That shiny, soliloquizing, Shakespearean *spaceman!*
That's *exactly* what this show needs!
I've tackled *every* syndrome, phobia, disorder and disability--mental, emotional, physical *and* spiritual--
--combated *every* form of discrimination, prejudice and bigotry--
--and peddled every *fad diet* on planet Earth!
EMBRACE YOUR ME-NESS
People are getting sick of me! *I'm* getting sick of me! Our ratings are in the *basement!*
But if we could prove the *universality* of the Dr. Betty treatment by applying it to that mopey *E.T.*--why, our ratings would go through the *roof!*
I *want* the Stainless Surfer, Josh--*book* the Stainless Surfer, Josh!
Book him? I don't even know where to begin *looking* for hi--
Or it's your *job,* Josh!
APPL
Now put your hands together for the woman who knows you better than *you* do...
...DR. BETTY!
And...I think it's... "Silver Surfer"...
CLAP CLAP CLAP

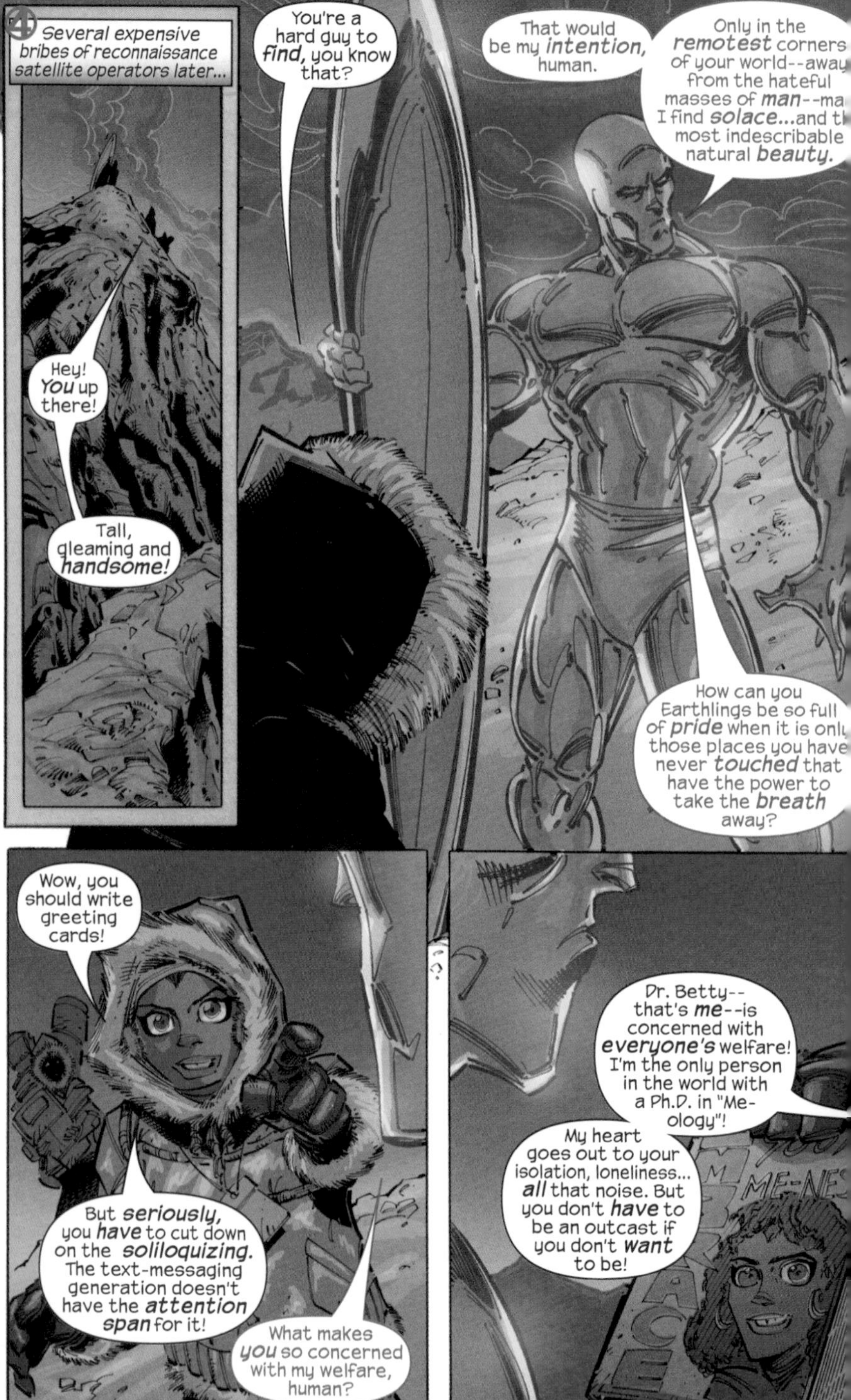

Several expensive bribes of reconnaissance satellite operators later...
Hey! *You* up there!
Tall, gleaming and *handsome!*
You're a hard guy to *find,* you know that?
That would be my *intention,* human.
Only in the *remotest* corners of your world--away from the hateful masses of *man*--ma I find *solace...*and th most indescribable natural *beauty.*
How can you Earthlings be so full of *pride* when it is only those places you have never *touched* that have the power to take the *breath* away?
Wow, you should write greeting cards!
But *seriously,* you *have* to cut down on the *soliloquizing.* The text-messaging generation doesn't have the *attention span* for it!
What makes *you* so concerned with my welfare, human?
Dr. Betty--that's *me*--is concerned with *everyone's* welfare! I'm the only person in the world with a Ph.D. in "Me-ology"!
My heart goes out to your isolation, loneliness... *all* that noise. But you don't *have* to be an outcast if you don't *want* to be!

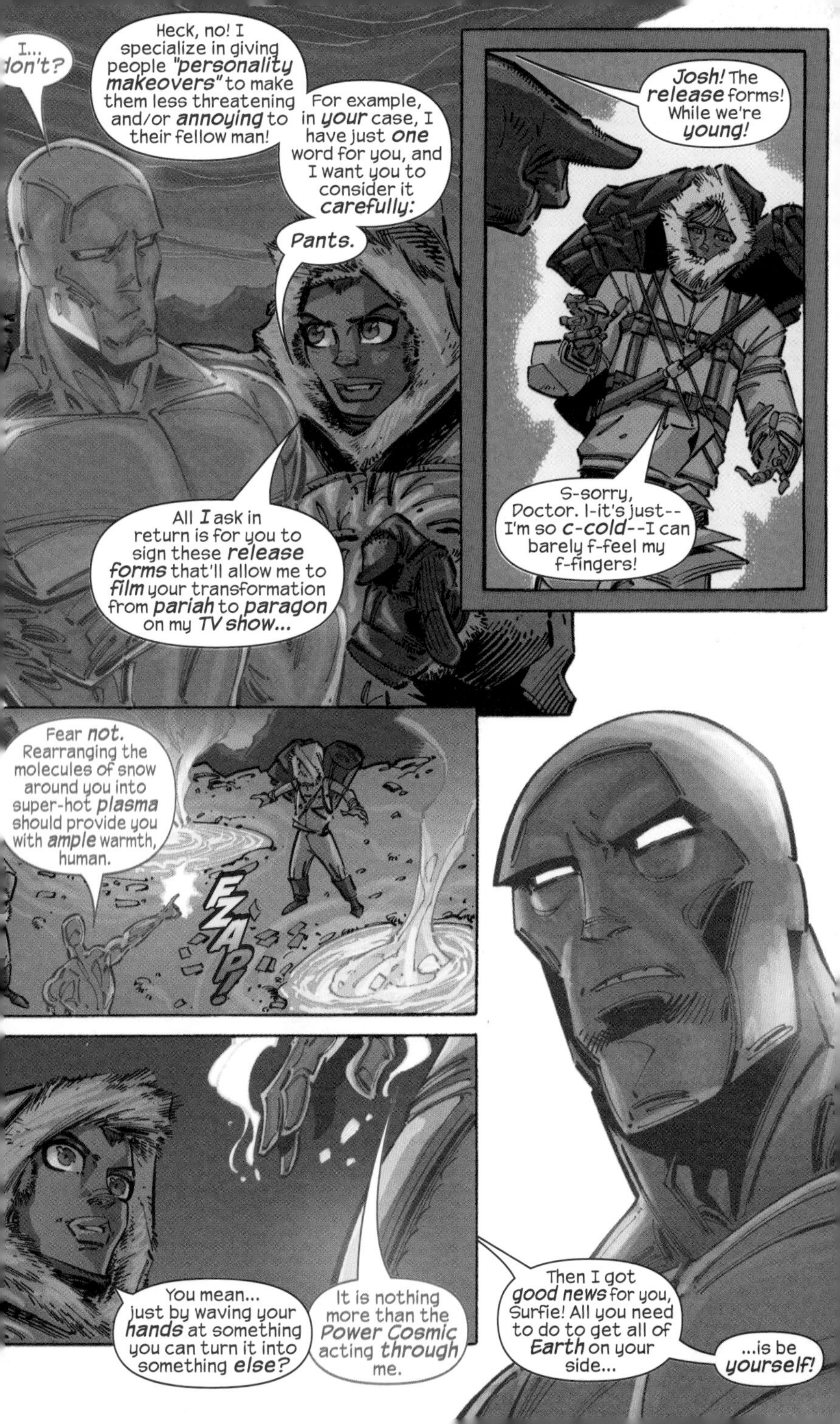

I... don't?
Heck, no! I specialize in giving people "personality makeovers" to make them less threatening and/or annoying to their fellow man!
For example, in your case, I have just one word for you, and I want you to consider it carefully:
Pants.
All I ask in return is for you to sign these release forms that'll allow me to film your transformation from pariah to paragon on my TV show...
Josh! The release forms! While we're young!
S-sorry, Doctor. I-it's just-- I'm so c-cold--I can barely f-feel my f-fingers!
Fear not. Rearranging the molecules of snow around you into super-hot plasma should provide you with ample warmth, human.
FZAP!
You mean... just by waving your hands at something you can turn it into something else?
It is nothing more than the Power Cosmic acting through me.
Then I got good news for you, Surfie! All you need to do to get all of Earth on your side...
...is be yourself!

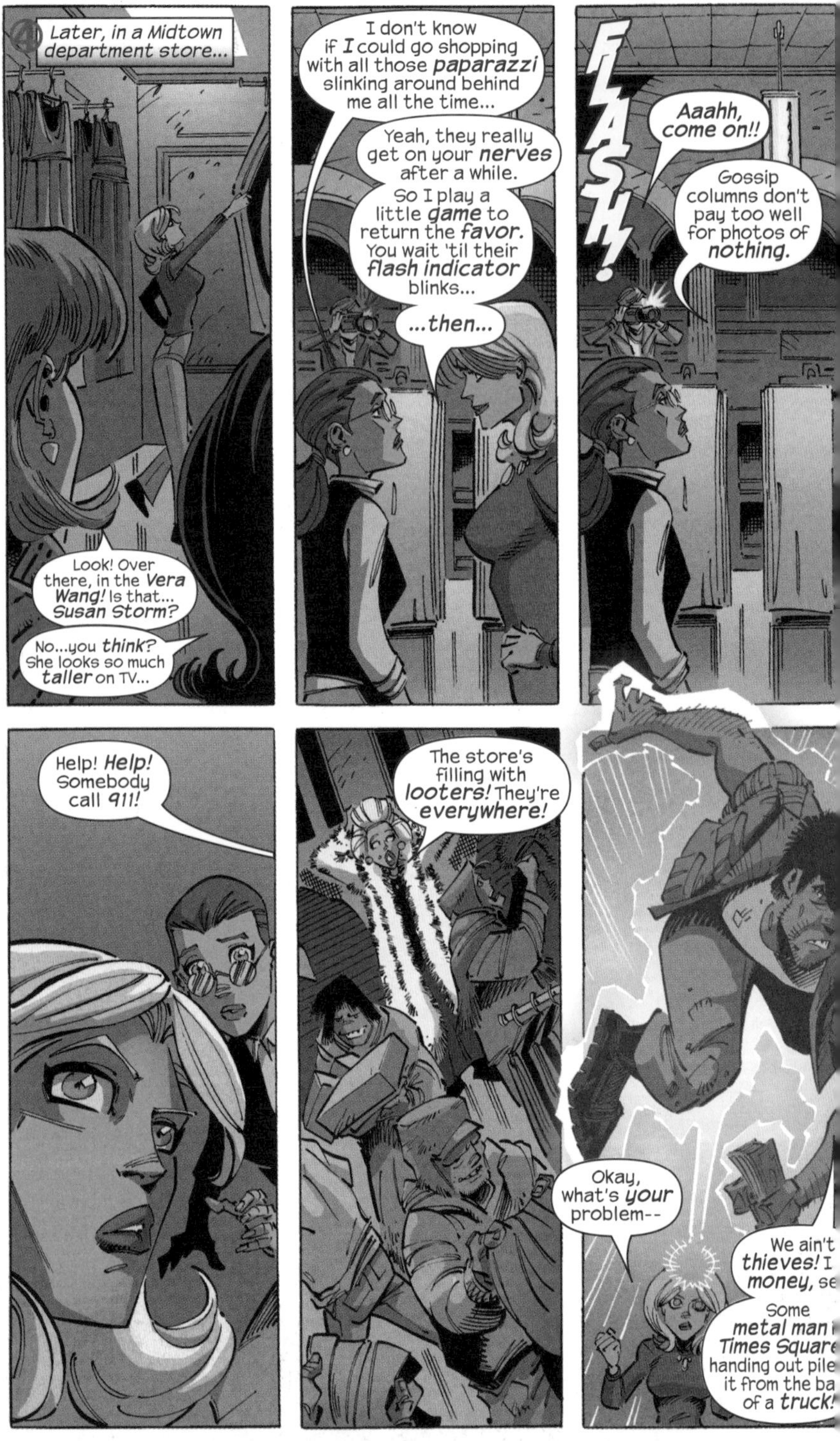

Later, in a Midtown department store...
Look! Over there, in the Vera Wang! Is that... Susan Storm?
No...you think? She looks so much taller on TV...
I don't know if I could go shopping with all those paparazzi slinking around behind me all the time...
Yeah, they really get on your nerves after a while.
So I play a little game to return the favor. You wait 'til their flash indicator blinks...
...then...
FLASH!
Aaahh, come on!!
Gossip columns don't pay too well for photos of nothing.
Help! Help! Somebody call 911!
The store's filling with looters! They're everywhere!
Okay, what's your problem--
We ain't
thieves! I
money, se
Some
metal man
Times Square
handing out pile
it from the ba
of a truck!

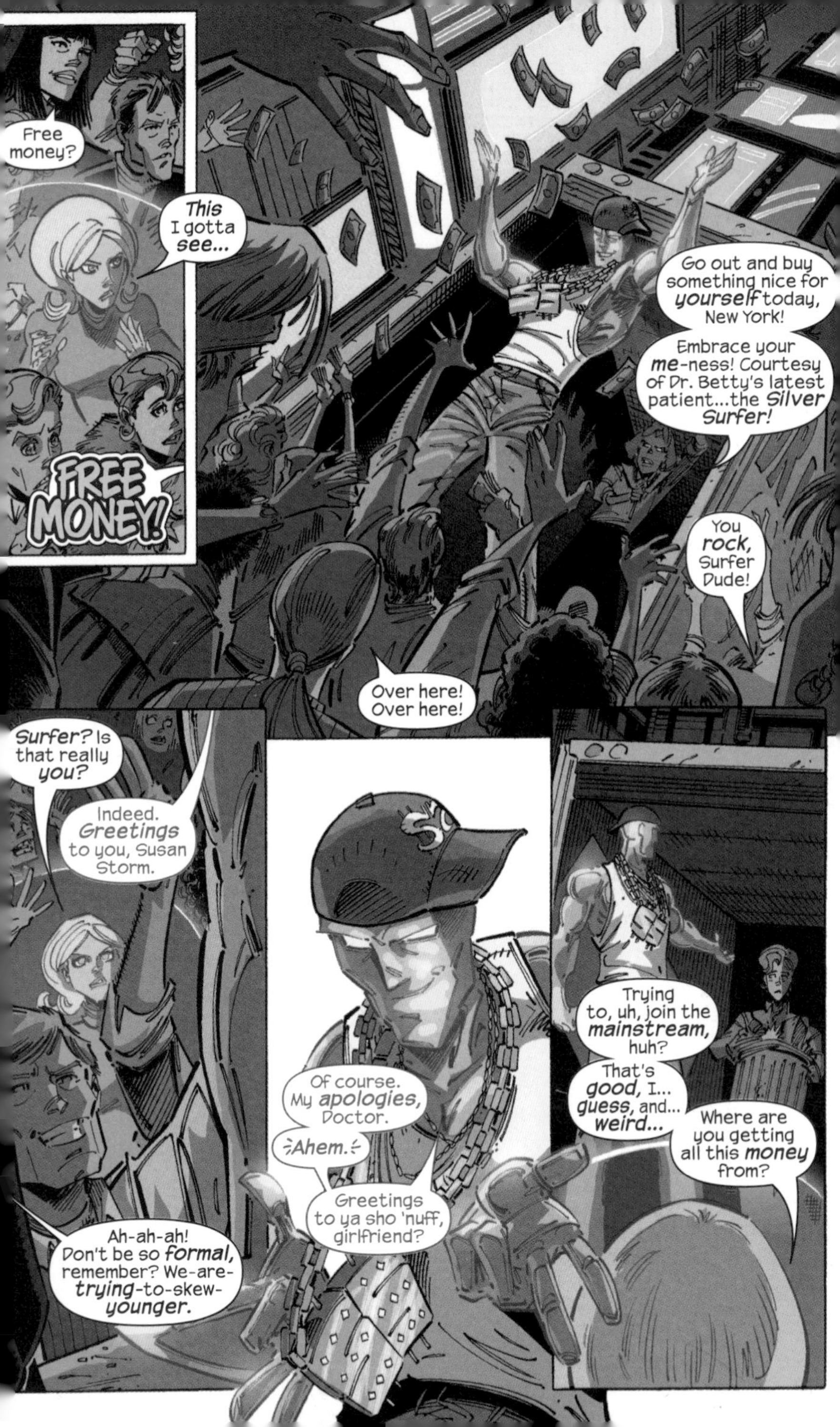
Free money?
This I gotta see...
FREE MONEY!
Go out and buy something nice for yourself today, New York!
Embrace your me-ness! Courtesy of Dr. Betty's latest patient...the Silver Surfer!
You rock, Surfer Dude!
Over here! Over here!
Surfer? Is that really you?
Indeed. Greetings to you, Susan Storm.
Ah-ah-ah! Don't be so formal, remember? We-are-trying-to-skew-younger.
Of course. My apologies, Doctor.
Ahem.
Greetings to ya sho 'nuff, girlfriend?
Trying to, uh, join the mainstream, huh?
That's good, I... guess, and... weird...
Where are you getting all this money from?

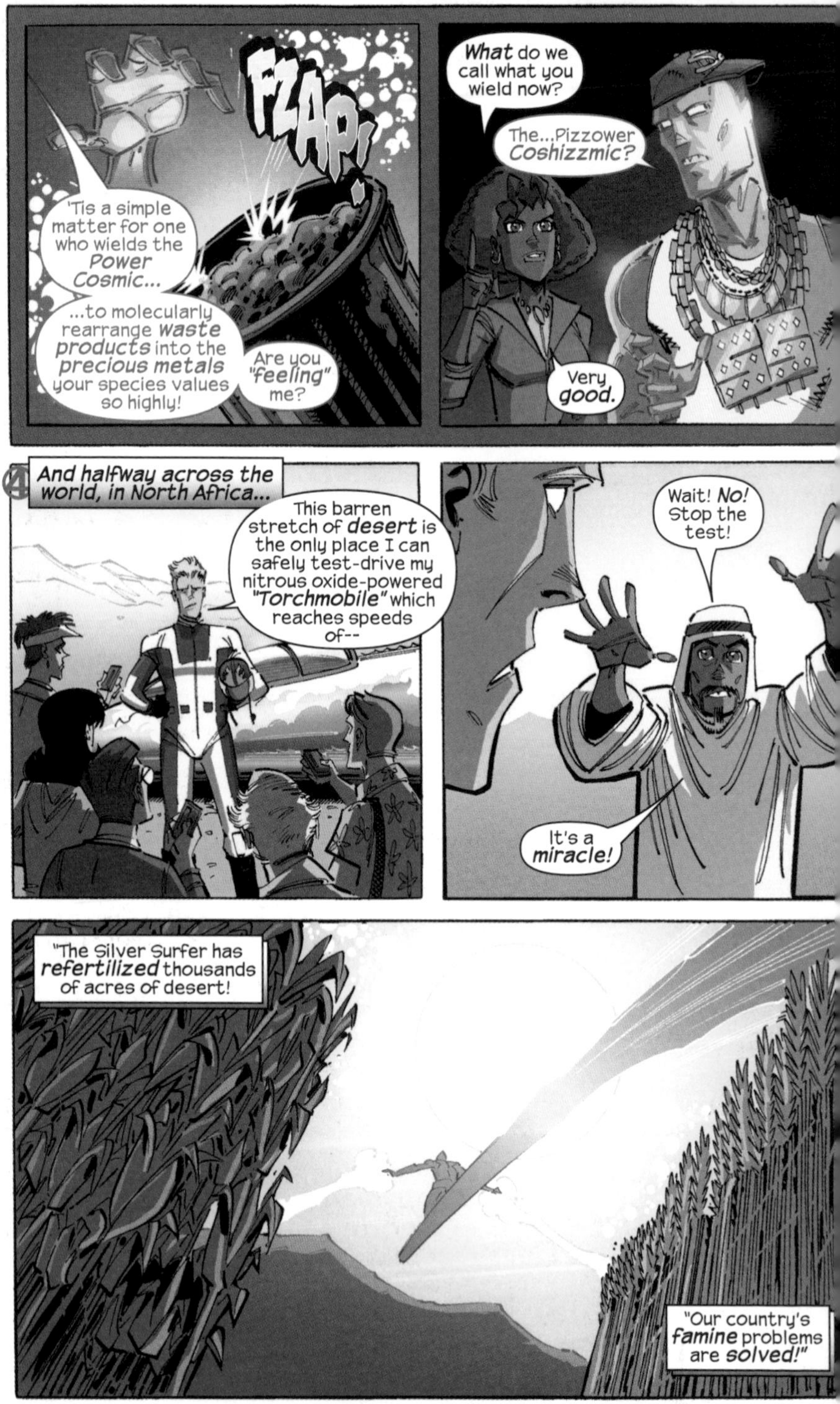
FZAP!
'Tis a simple matter for one who wields the Power Cosmic...
...to molecularly rearrange waste products into the precious metals your species values so highly!
Are you "feeling" me?
What do we call what you wield now?
The...Pizzower Coshizzmic?
Very good.
And halfway across the world, in North Africa...
This barren stretch of desert is the only place I can safely test-drive my nitrous oxide-powered "Torchmobile" which reaches speeds of--
Wait! No! Stop the test!
It's a miracle!
"The Silver Surfer has refertilized thousands of acres of desert!
"Our country's famine problems are solved!"

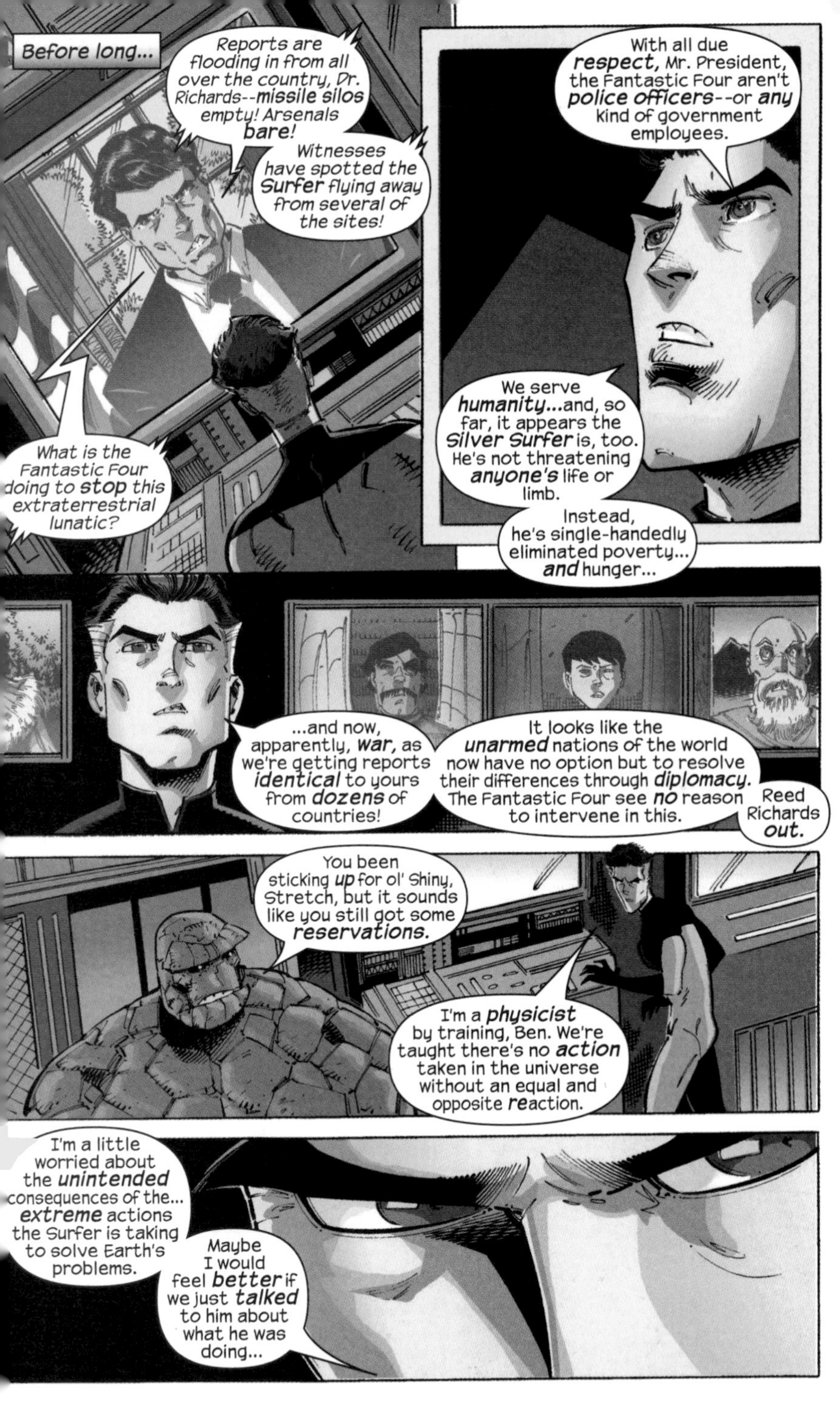
Before long...
Reports are flooding in from all over the country, Dr. Richards--missile silos empty! Arsenals bare!
Witnesses have spotted the Surfer flying away from several of the sites!
What is the Fantastic Four doing to stop this extraterrestrial lunatic?
With all due respect, Mr. President, the Fantastic Four aren't police officers--or any kind of government employees.
We serve humanity...and, so far, it appears the Silver Surfer is, too. He's not threatening anyone's life or limb.
Instead, he's single-handedly eliminated poverty... and hunger...
...and now, apparently, war, as we're getting reports identical to yours from dozens of countries!
It looks like the unarmed nations of the world now have no option but to resolve their differences through diplomacy. The Fantastic Four see no reason to intervene in this.
Reed Richards out.
You been sticking up for ol' Shiny, Stretch, but it sounds like you still got some reservations.
I'm a physicist by training, Ben. We're taught there's no action taken in the universe without an equal and opposite reaction.
I'm a little worried about the unintended consequences of the... extreme actions the Surfer is taking to solve Earth's problems.
Maybe I would feel better if we just talked to him about what he was doing...

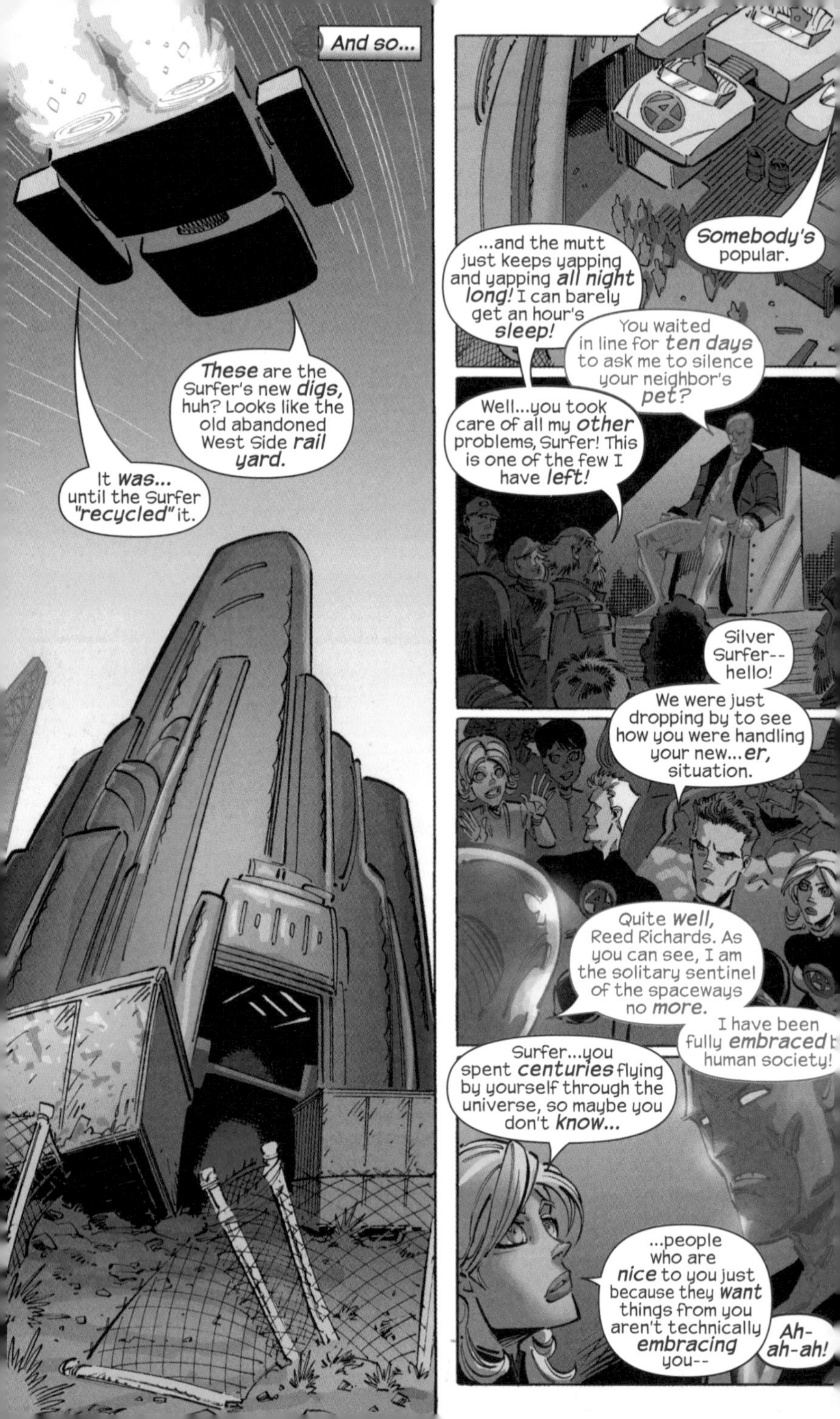
And so...
These are the Surfer's new digs, huh? Looks like the old abandoned West Side rail yard.
It was... until the Surfer "recycled" it.
Somebody's popular.
...and the mutt just keeps yapping and yapping all night long! I can barely get an hour's sleep!
You waited in line for ten days to ask me to silence your neighbor's pet?
Well...you took care of all my other problems, Surfer! This is one of the few I have left!
Silver Surfer-- hello!
We were just dropping by to see how you were handling your new...er, situation.
Quite well, Reed Richards. As you can see, I am the solitary sentinel of the spaceways no more.
I have been fully embraced by human society!
Surfer...you spent centuries flying by yourself through the universe, so maybe you don't know...
...people who are nice to you just because they want things from you aren't technically embracing you--
Ah-ah-ah!

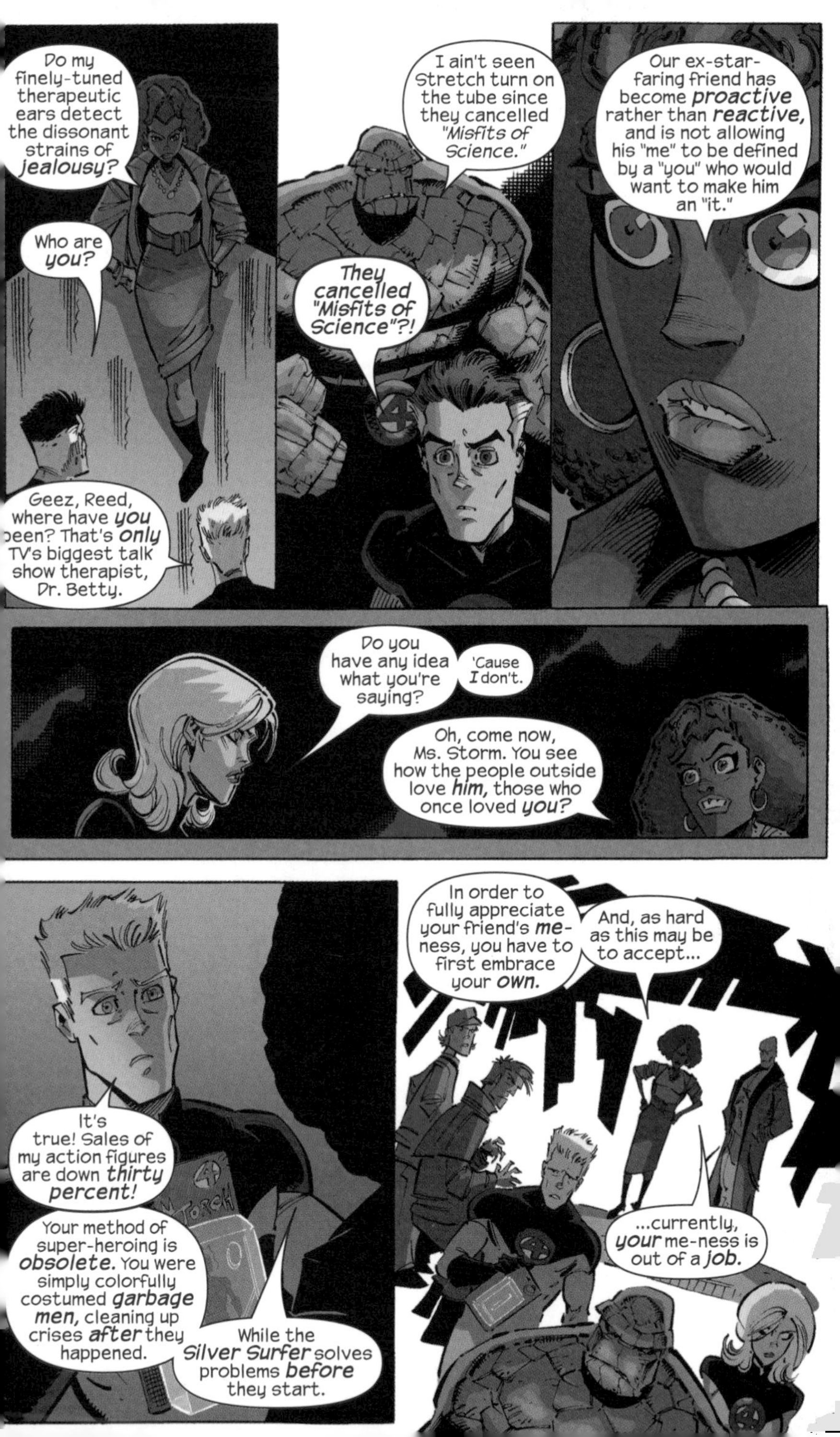
Do my finely-tuned therapeutic ears detect the dissonant strains of jealousy?
Who are you?
Geez, Reed, where have you been? That's only TV's biggest talk show therapist, Dr. Betty.
I ain't seen Stretch turn on the tube since they cancelled "Misfits of Science."
They cancelled "Misfits of Science"?!
Our ex-star-faring friend has become proactive rather than reactive, and is not allowing his "me" to be defined by a "you" who would want to make him an "it."
Do you have any idea what you're saying?
'Cause I don't.
Oh, come now, Ms. Storm. You see how the people outside love him, those who once loved you?
It's true! Sales of my action figures are down thirty percent!
Your method of super-heroing is obsolete. You were simply colorfully costumed garbage men, cleaning up crises after they happened.
While the Silver Surfer solves problems before they start.
In order to fully appreciate your friend's me-ness, you have to first embrace your own.
And, as hard as this may be to accept...
...currently, your me-ness is out of a job.

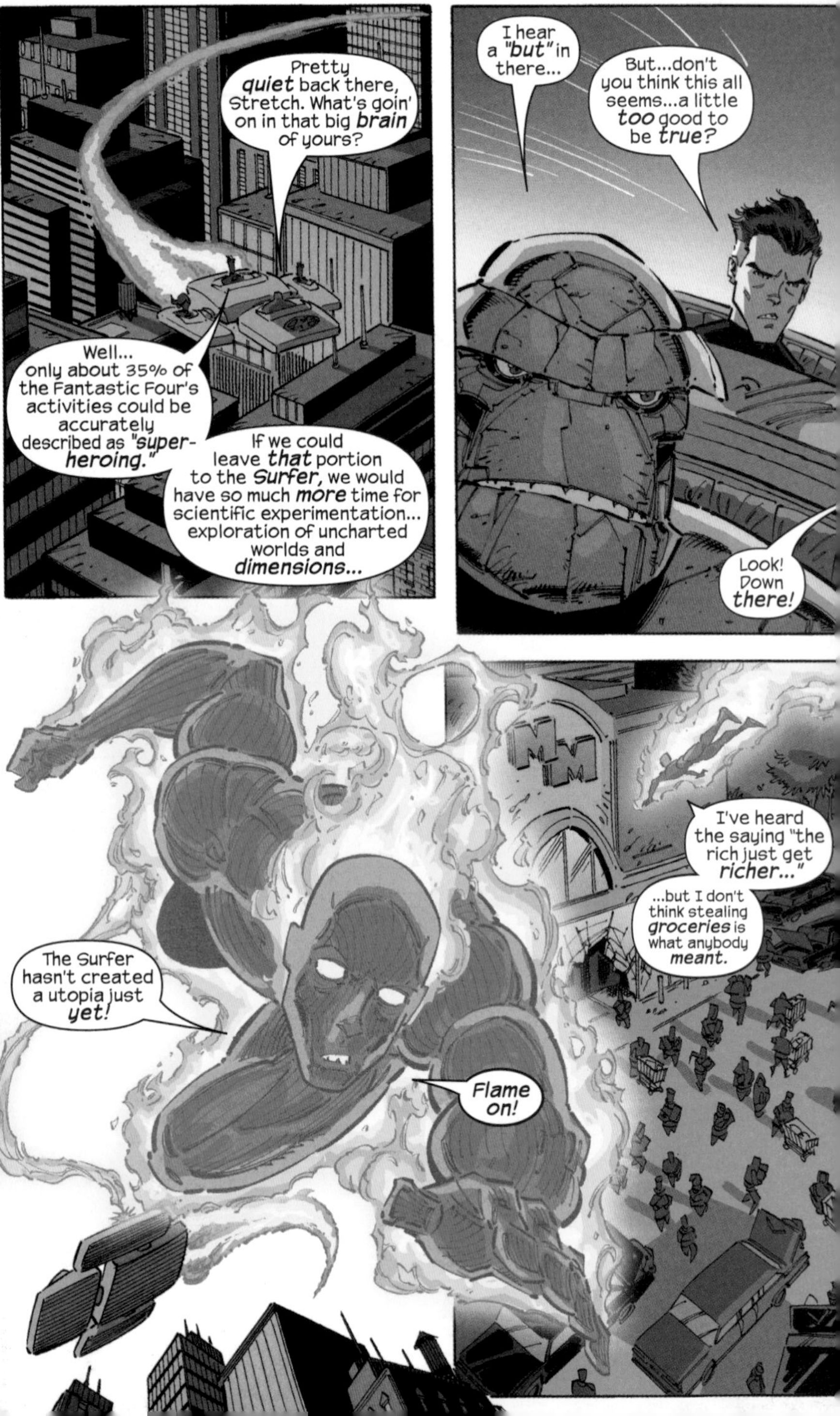
Pretty quiet back there, Stretch. What's goin' on in that big brain of yours?
Well... only about 35% of the Fantastic Four's activities could be accurately described as "super-heroing."
If we could leave that portion to the Surfer, we would have so much more time for scientific experimentation... exploration of uncharted worlds and dimensions...
I hear a "but" in there...
But...don't you think this all seems...a little too good to be true?
Look! Down there!
The Surfer hasn't created a utopia just yet!
Flame on!
I've heard the saying "the rich just get richer..."
...but I don't think stealing groceries is what anybody meant.

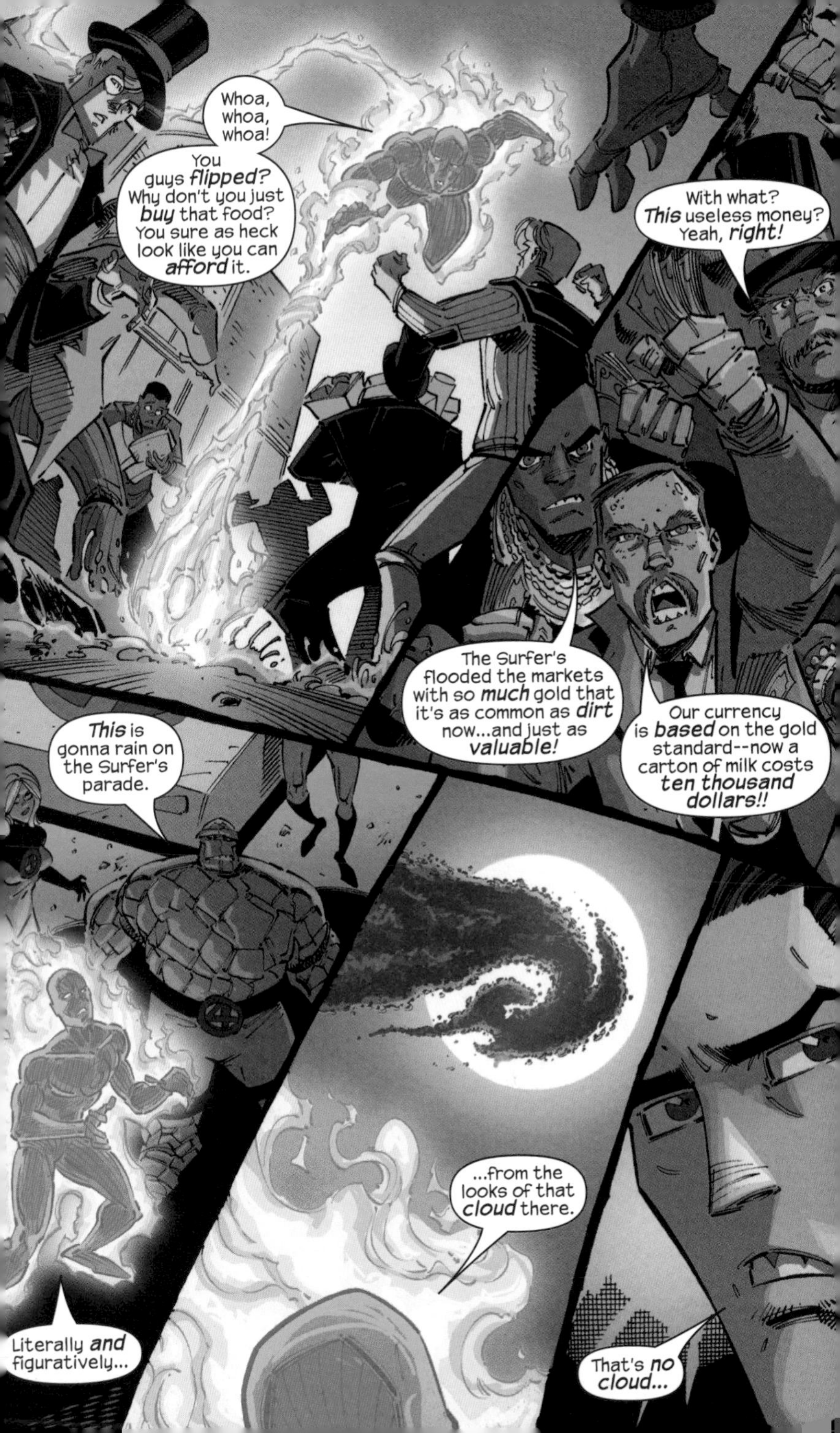
Whoa, whoa, whoa!
You guys *flipped*? Why don't you just *buy* that food? You sure as heck look like you can *afford* it.
With what? *This* useless money? Yeah, *right!*
The Surfer's flooded the markets with so *much* gold that it's as common as *dirt* now...and just as *valuable!*
Our currency is *based* on the gold standard--now a carton of milk costs *ten thousand dollars!!*
This is gonna rain on the Surfer's parade.
Literally *and* figuratively...
...from the looks of that *cloud* there.
That's *no cloud...*

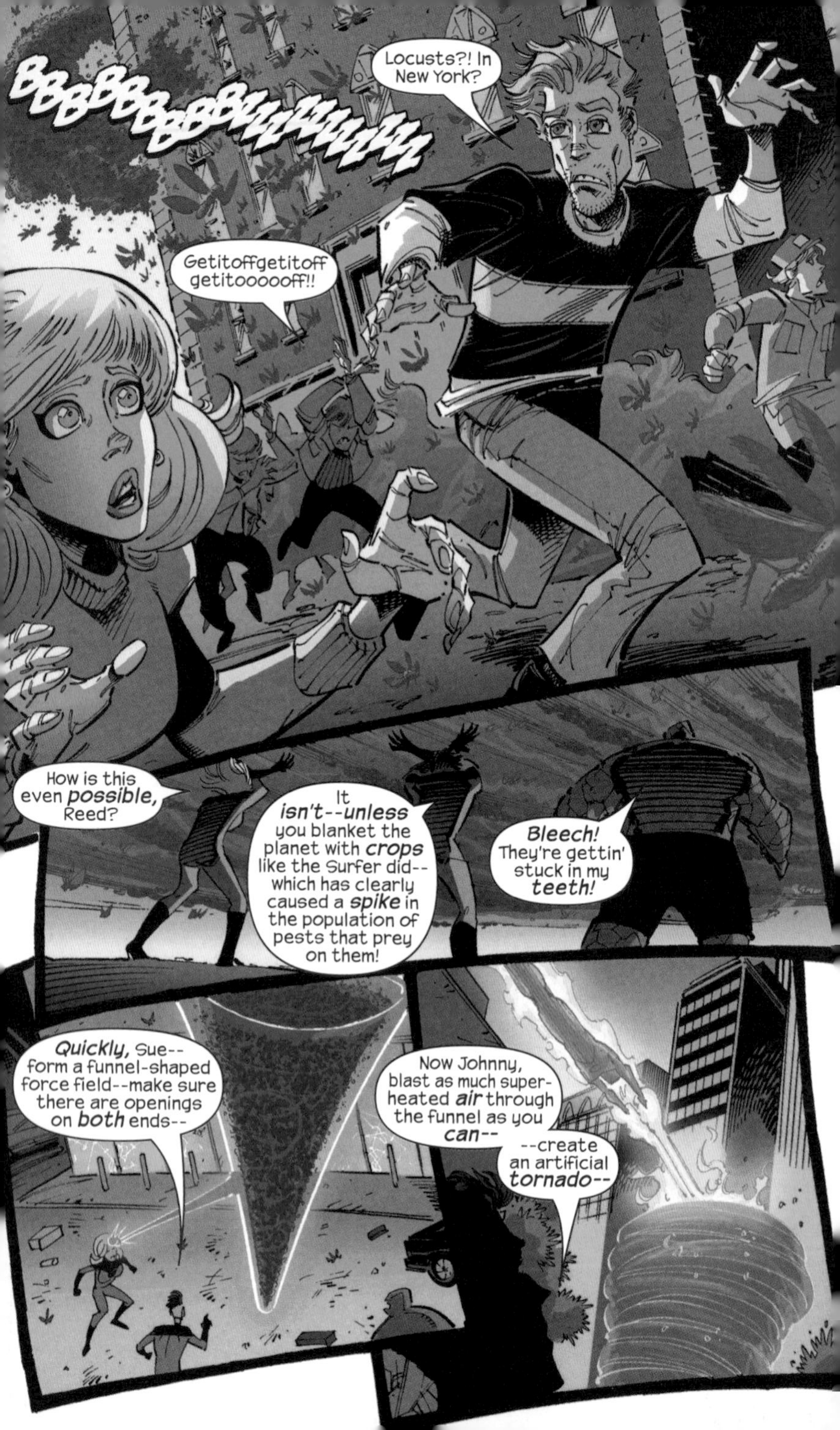
BBBBBBBBBBZZZZZZZZZZZ
Locusts?! In New York?
Getitoffgetitoff getitoooooff!!
How is this even *possible*, Reed?
It *isn't--unless* you blanket the planet with *crops* like the Surfer did--which has clearly caused a *spike* in the population of pests that prey on them!
Bleech! They're gettin' stuck in my *teeth!*
Quickly, Sue--form a funnel-shaped force field--make sure there are openings on *both* ends--
Now Johnny, blast as much super-heated *air* through the funnel as you *can--*
--create an artificial *tornado--*

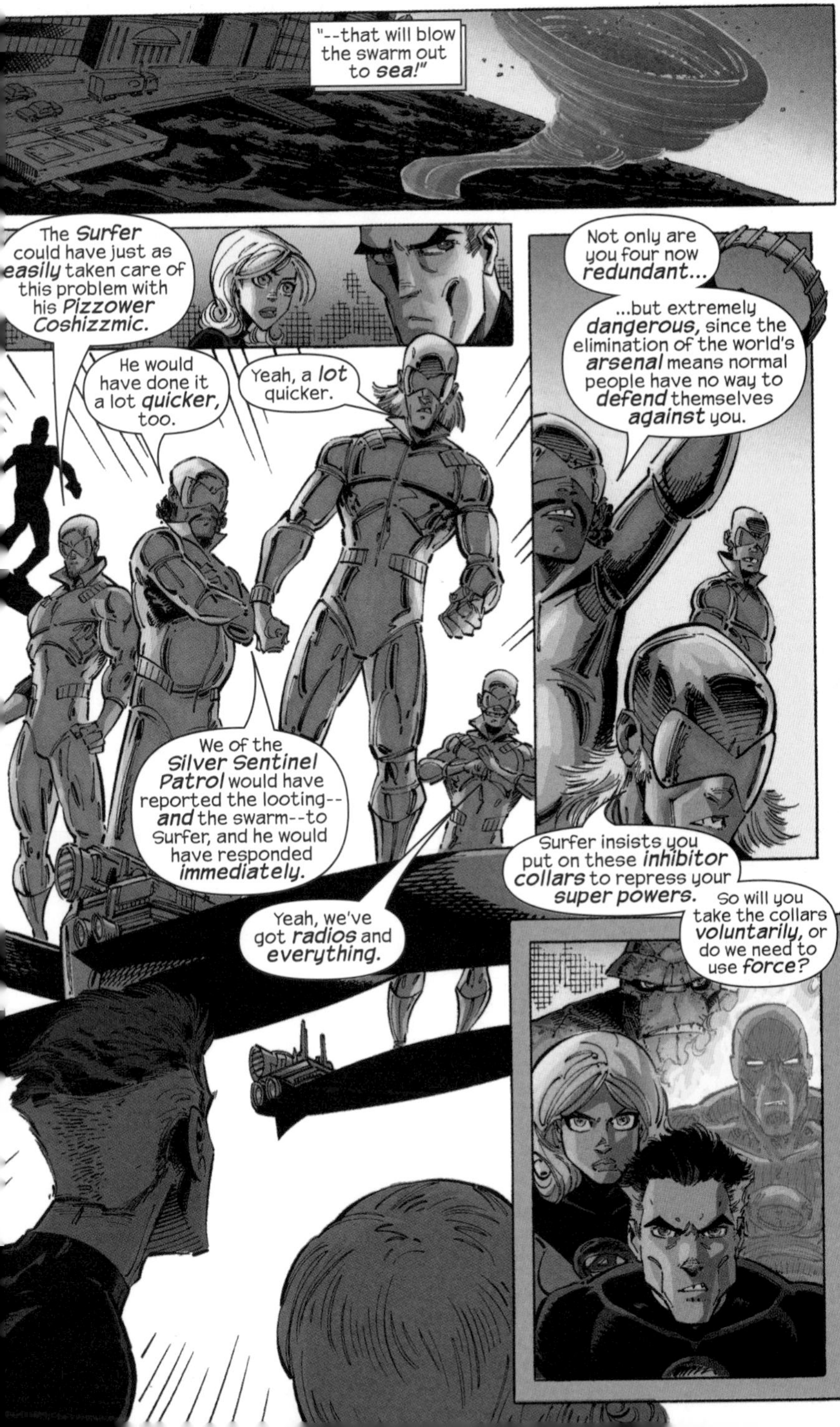
"--that will blow the swarm out to sea!"
The Surfer could have just as easily taken care of this problem with his Pizzower Coshizzmic.
He would have done it a lot quicker, too.
Yeah, a lot quicker.
Not only are you four now redundant...
...but extremely dangerous, since the elimination of the world's arsenal means normal people have no way to defend themselves against you.
We of the Silver Sentinel Patrol would have reported the looting--and the swarm--to Surfer, and he would have responded immediately.
Yeah, we've got radios and everything.
Surfer insists you put on these inhibitor collars to repress your super powers.
So will you take the collars voluntarily, or do we need to use force?

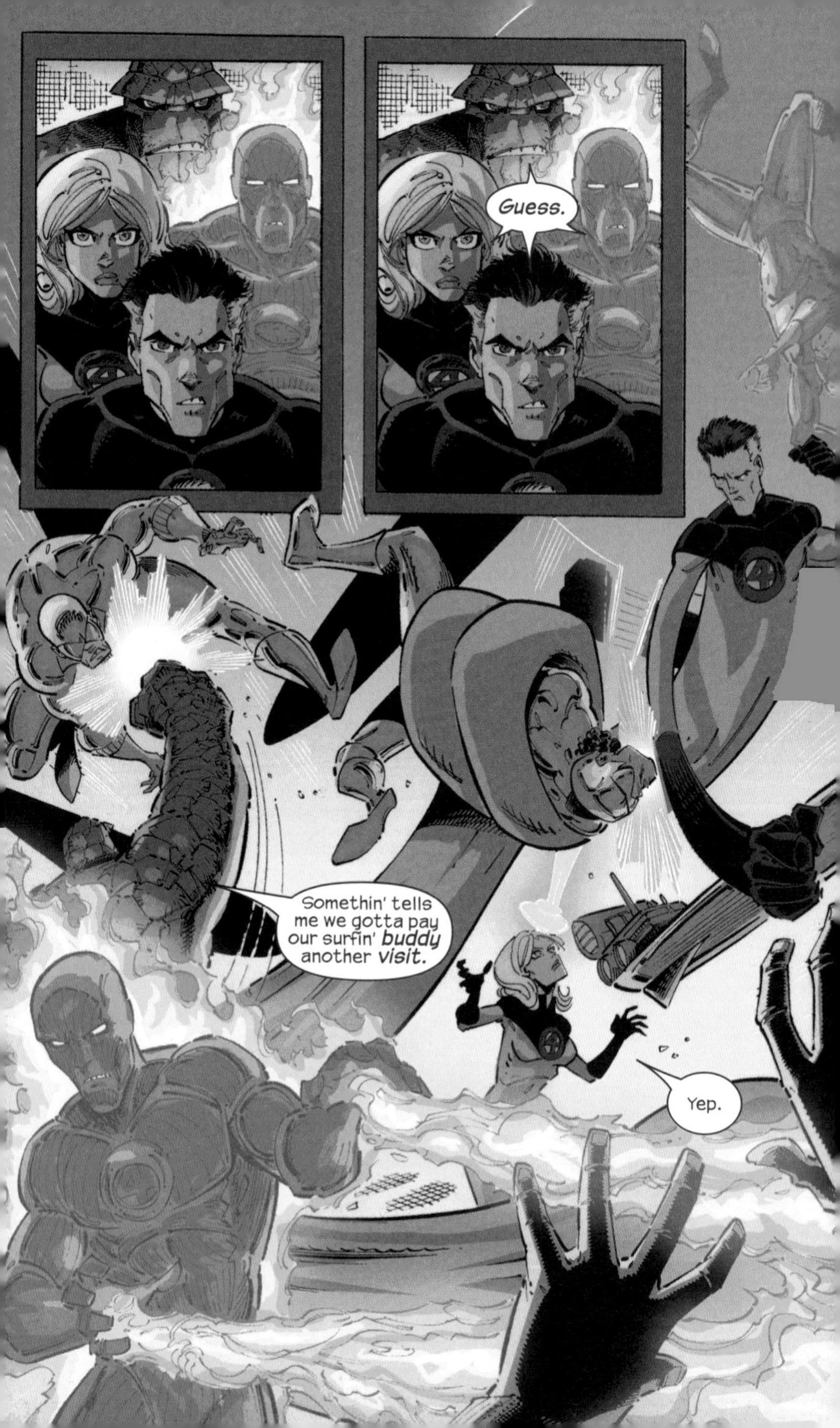
Guess.
Somethin' tells me we gotta pay our surfin' *buddy* another *visit.*
Yep.

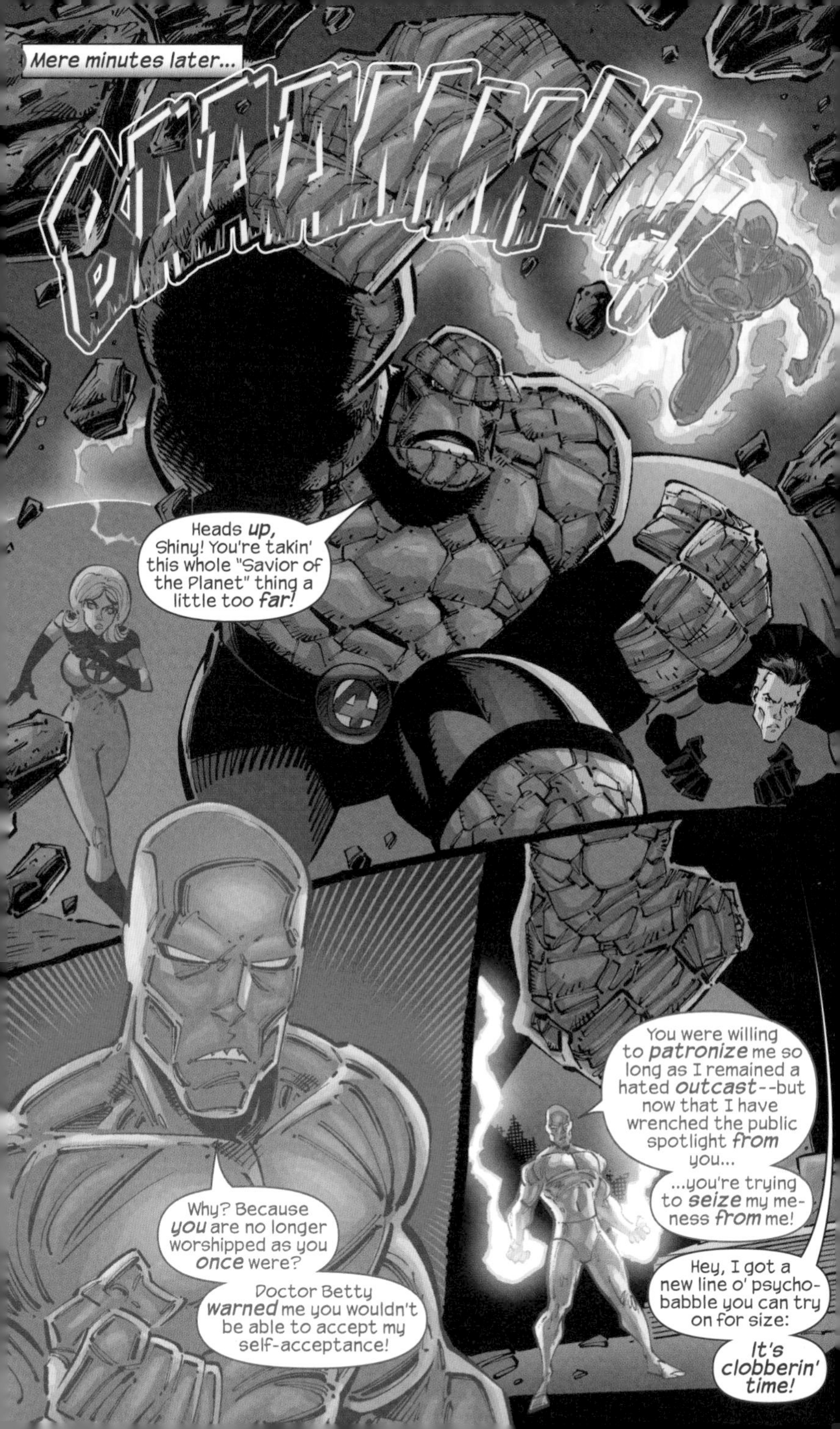
Mere minutes later...
Heads up, Shiny! You're takin' this whole "Savior of the Planet" thing a little too far!
Why? Because you are no longer worshipped as you once were?
Doctor Betty warned me you wouldn't be able to accept my self-acceptance!
You were willing to patronize me so long as I remained a hated outcast--but now that I have wrenched the public spotlight from you...
...you're trying to seize my me-ness from me!
Hey, I got a new line o' psycho-babble you can try on for size:
It's clobberin' time!

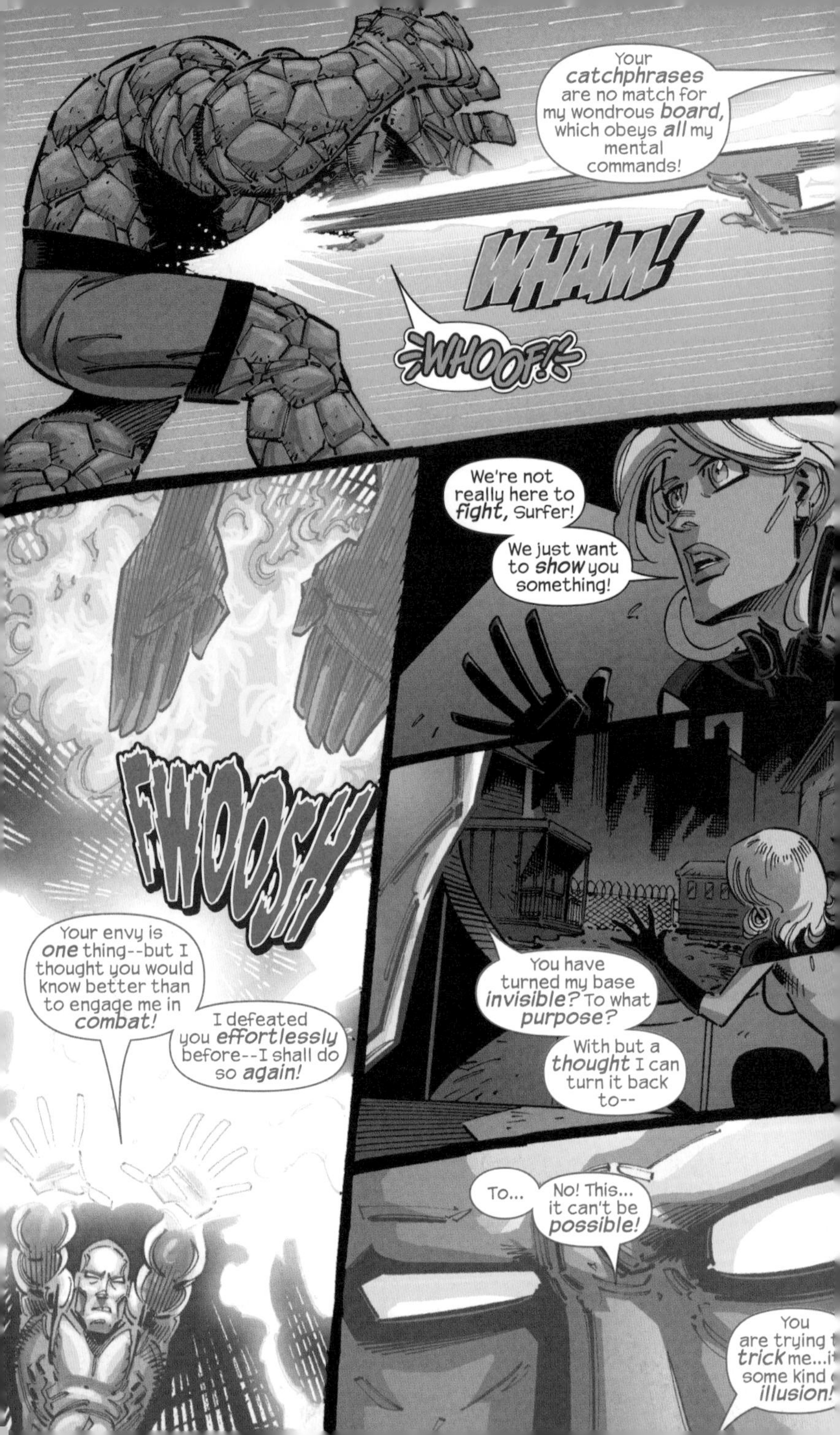
Your catchphrases are no match for my wondrous board, which obeys all my mental commands!
WHAM!
WHOOF!
We're not really here to fight, Surfer!
We just want to show you something!
FWOOSH
Your envy is one thing--but I thought you would know better than to engage me in combat!
I defeated you effortlessly before--I shall do so again!
You have turned my base invisible? To what purpose?
With but a thought I can turn it back to--
To...
No! This... it can't be possible!
You are trying t
trick me...i
some kind
illusion!

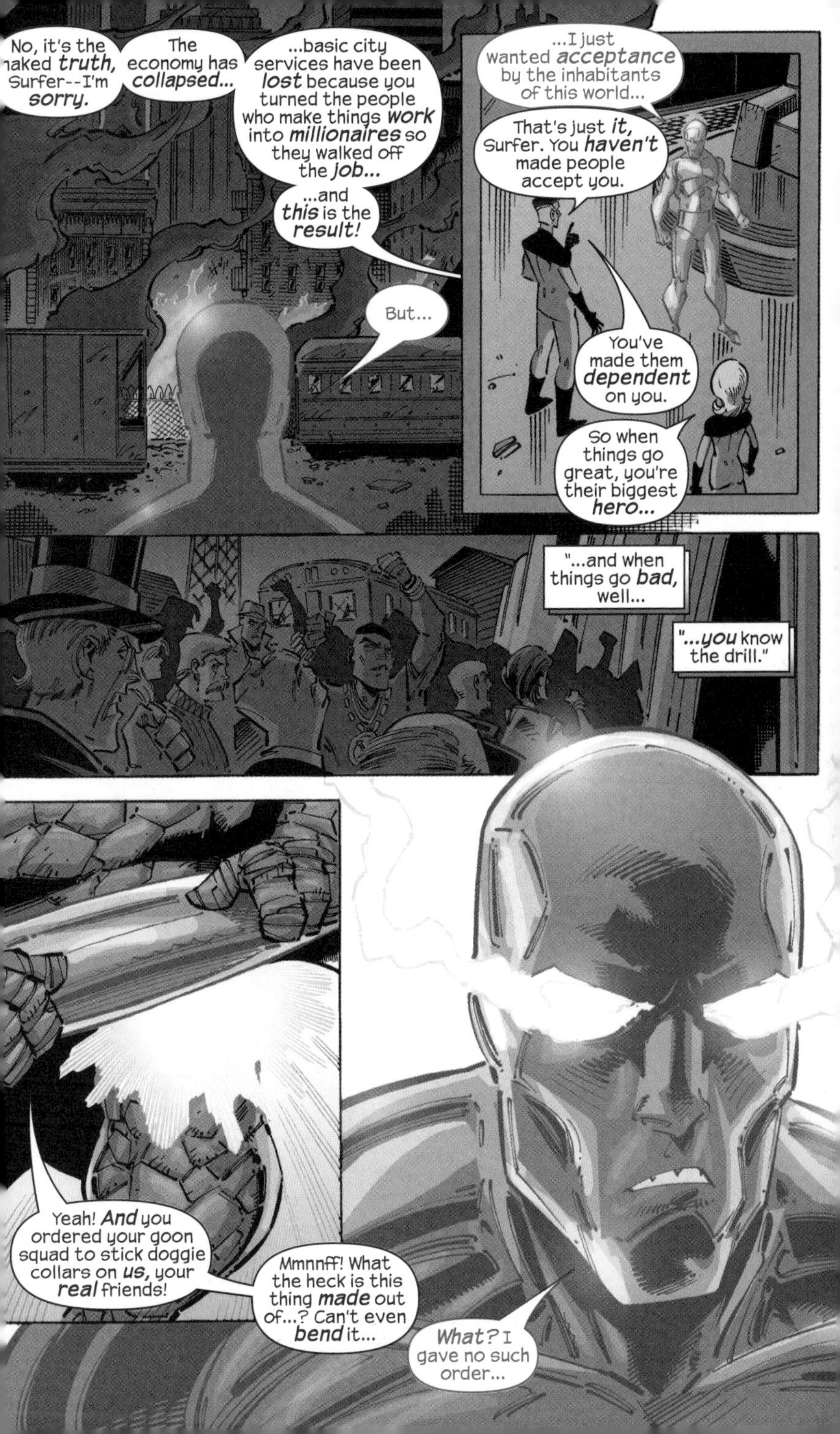
No, it's the naked truth, Surfer--I'm sorry.
The economy has collapsed...
...basic city services have been lost because you turned the people who make things work into millionaires so they walked off the job...
...and this is the result!
But...
...I just wanted acceptance by the inhabitants of this world...
That's just it, Surfer. You haven't made people accept you.
You've made them dependent on you.
So when things go great, you're their biggest hero...
"...and when things go bad, well...
"...you know the drill."
Yeah! And you ordered your goon squad to stick doggie collars on us, your real friends!
Mmnnff! What the heck is this thing made out of...? Can't even bend it...
What? I gave no such order...

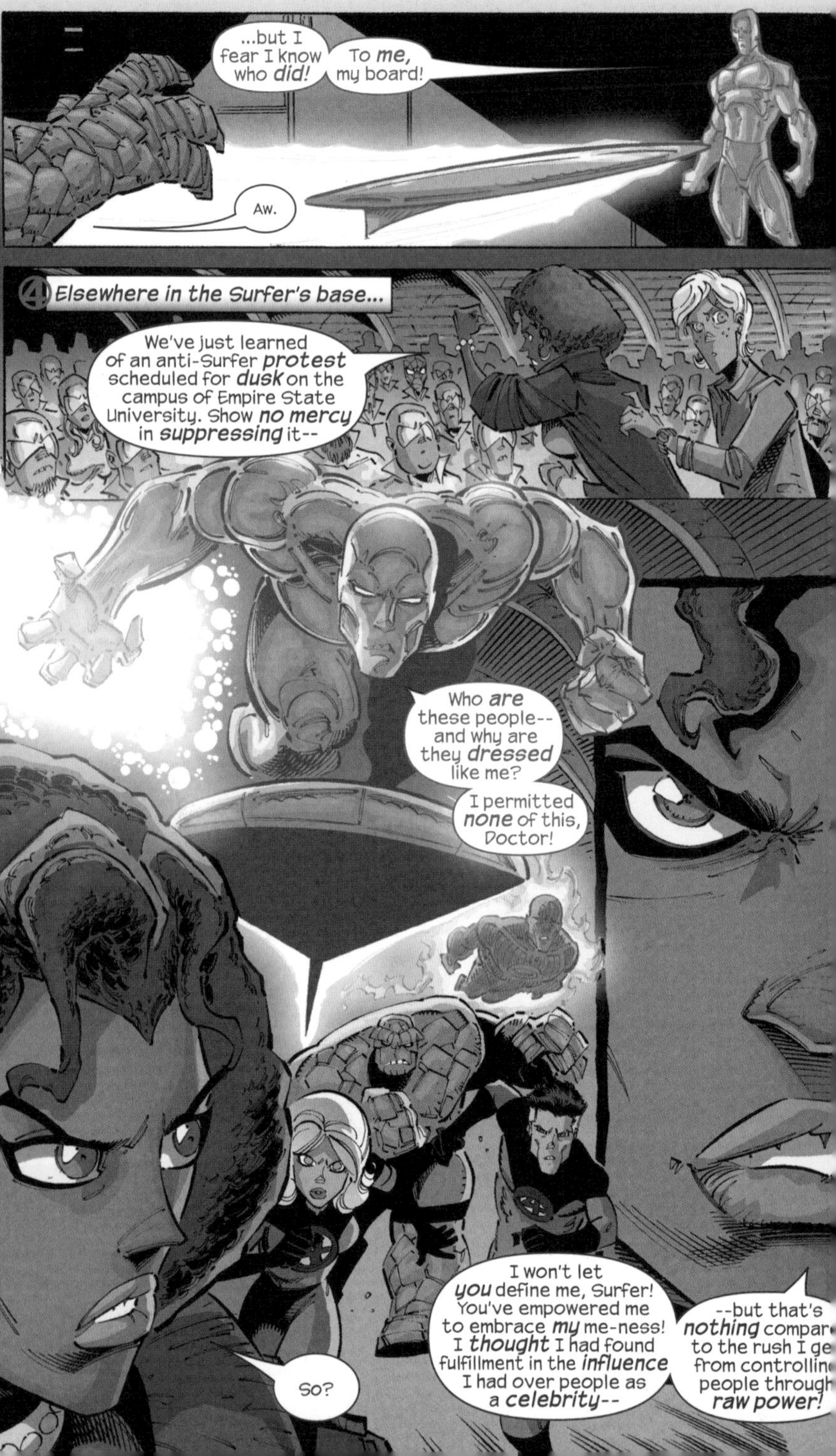
...but I fear I know who *did!*
To *me,* my board!
Aw.
Elsewhere in the Surfer's base...
We've just learned of an anti-Surfer *protest* scheduled for *dusk* on the campus of Empire State University. Show *no mercy* in *suppressing* it--
Who *are* these people-- and why are they *dressed* like me?
I permitted *none* of this, Doctor!
So?
I won't let *you* define me, Surfer! You've empowered me to embrace *my* me-ness! I *thought* I had found fulfillment in the *influence* I had over people as a *celebrity*--
--but that's *nothing* compare to the rush I ge from controllin people through *raw power!*

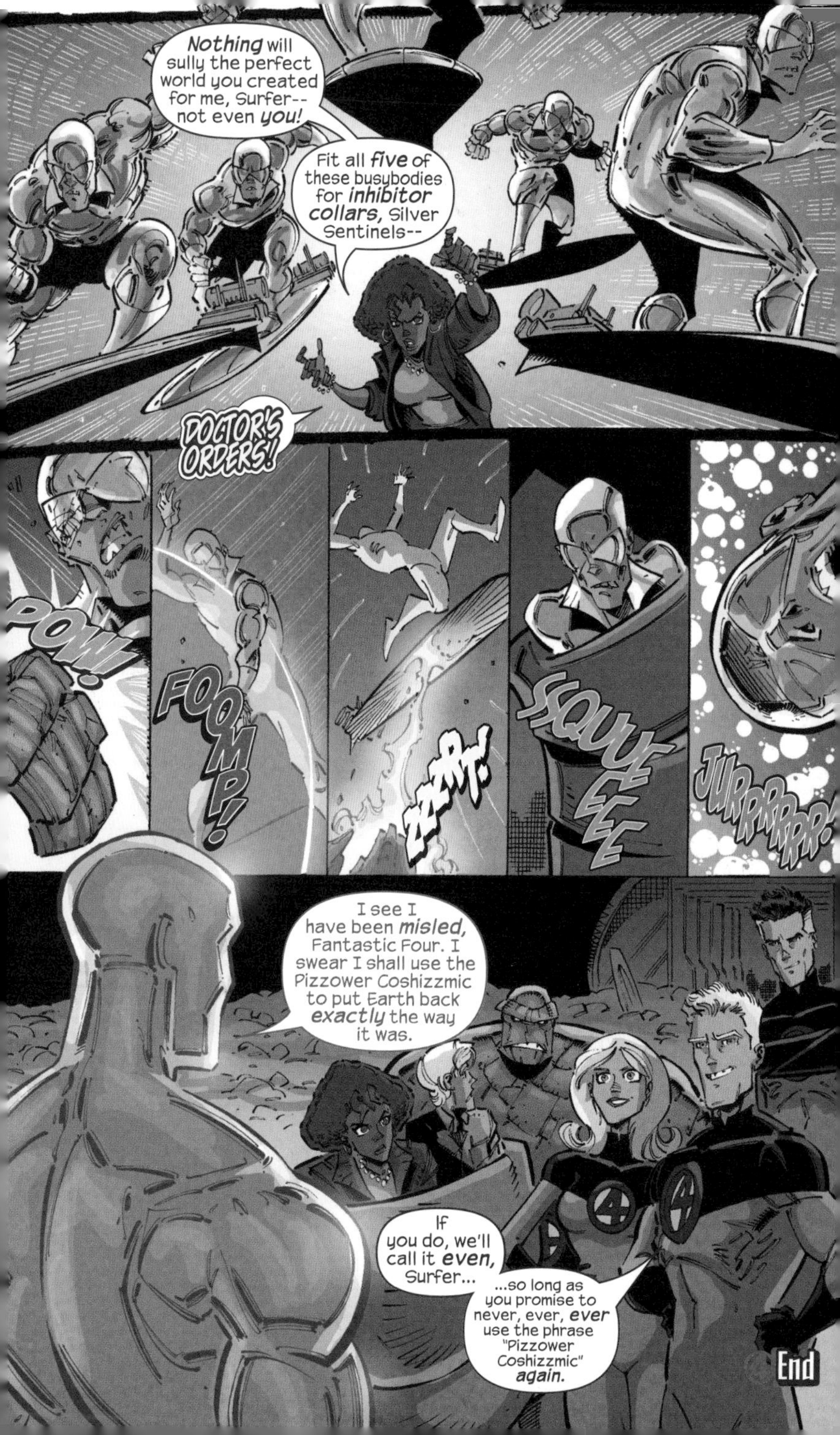
Nothing will sully the perfect world you created for me, Surfer-- not even you!
Fit all five of these busybodies for inhibitor collars, Silver Sentinels--
DOCTOR'S ORDERS!
POW!
FOOMP!
ZZZRT!
SSQUUEEEE
JURRRRRR!
I see I have been misled, Fantastic Four. I swear I shall use the Pizzower Coshizzmic to put Earth back exactly the way it was.
If you do, we'll call it even, Surfer...
...so long as you promise to never, ever, ever use the phrase "Pizzower Coshizzmic" again.
End